THE HAR
BOYS®

UNDERCOVER BROTHERS™

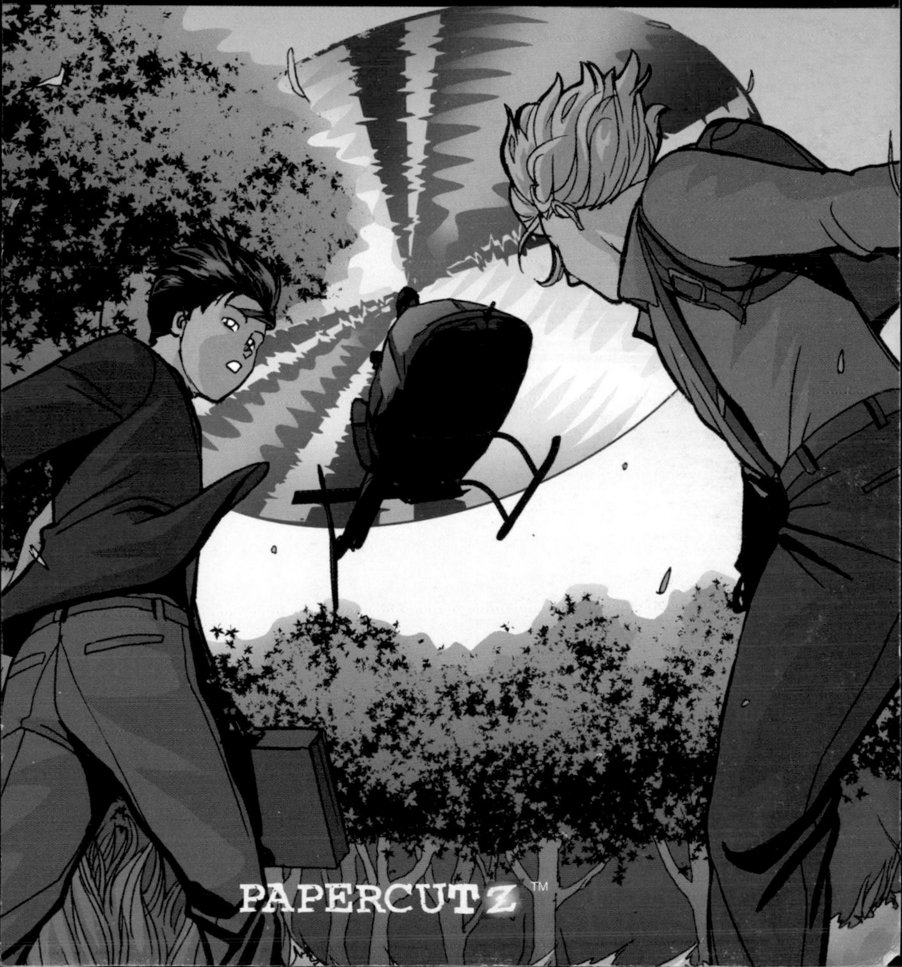

PAPERCUTZ™

THE HARDY BOYS GRAPHIC NOVELS FROM PAPERCUTZ

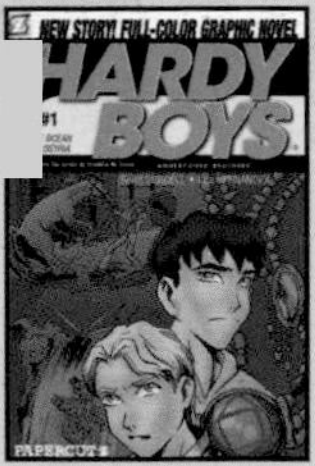
NEW STORY! FULL-COLOR GRAPHIC NOVEL
HARDY BOYS
#1
PAPERCUTZ

#1 "The Ocean of Osyria"

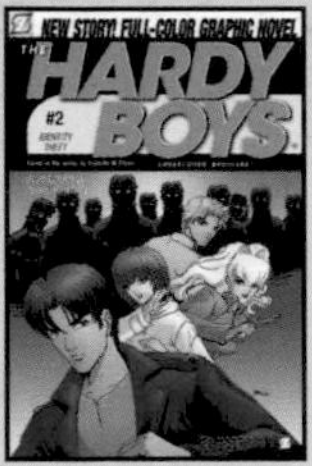
NEW STORY! FULL-COLOR GRAPHIC NOVEL
THE HARDY BOYS
#2

#2 "Identity Theft"

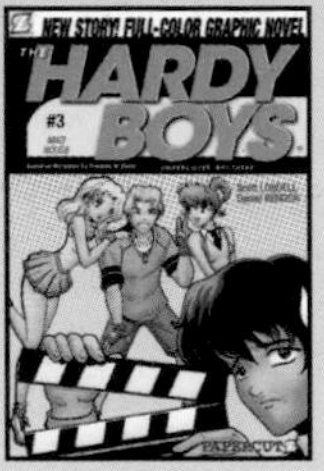
NEW STORY! FULL-COLOR GRAPHIC NOVEL
HARDY BOYS
#3
PAPERCUTZ

#3 "Mad House"

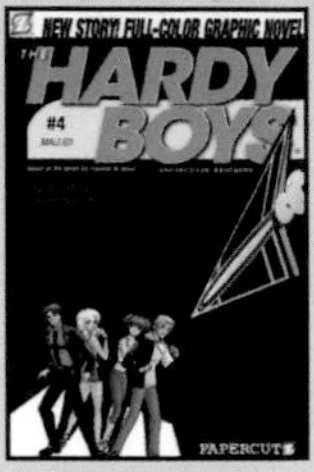
NEW STORY! FULL-COLOR GRAPHIC NOVEL
THE HARDY BOYS
#4
PAPERCUTZ

#4 "Malled"

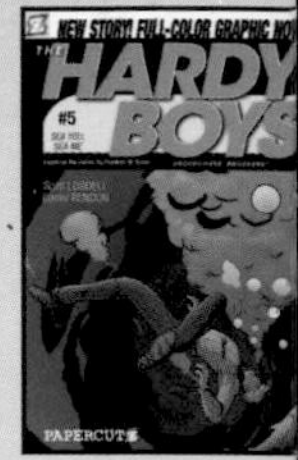
NEW STORY! FULL-COLOR GRAPHIC NOVEL
HARDY BOYS
#5
PAPERCUTZ

#5 "Sea You, Sea Me!"

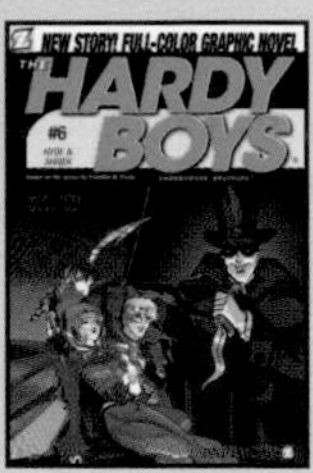
NEW STORY! FULL-COLOR GRAPHIC NOVEL
THE HARDY BOYS
#6

#6 "Hyde & Shriek"

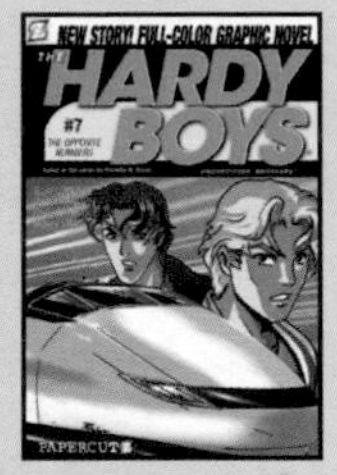
NEW STORY! FULL-COLOR GRAPHIC NOVEL
THE HARDY BOYS
#7
PAPERCUTZ

#7 "The Opposite Numbers"

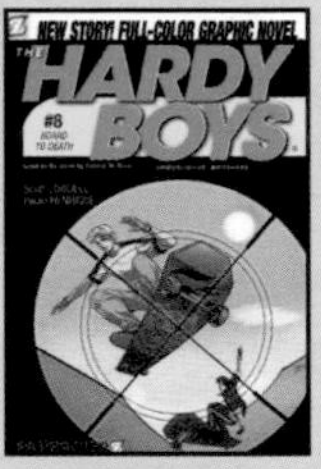
NEW STORY! FULL-COLOR GRAPHIC NOVEL
THE HARDY BOYS
#8

#8 "Board To Death"

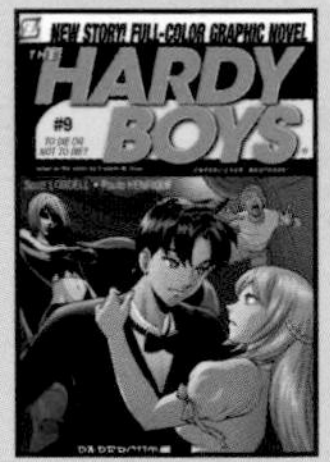
NEW STORY! FULL-COLOR GRAPHIC NOVEL
THE HARDY BOYS
#9

#9 "To Die Or Not To Die?"

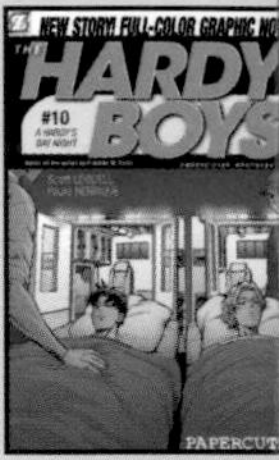
NEW STORY! FULL-COLOR GRAPHIC NOVEL
THE HARDY BOYS
#10
PAPERCUTZ

#10 "A Hardy Day's Night"

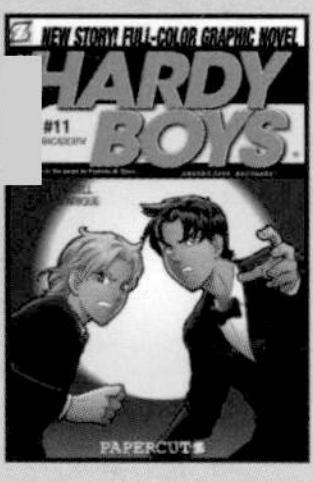
NEW STORY! FULL-COLOR GRAPHIC NOVEL
HARDY BOYS
#11
PAPERCUTZ

#11 "Abracadeath"

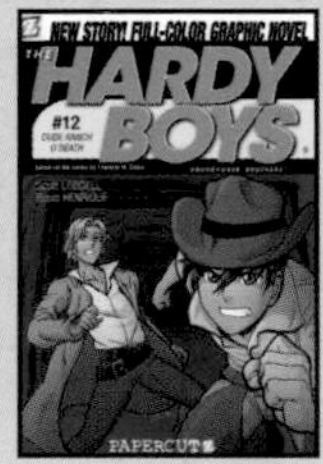
NEW STORY! FULL-COLOR GRAPHIC NOVEL
THE HARDY BOYS
#12
PAPERCUTZ

#12 "Dude Ranch O' Death!"

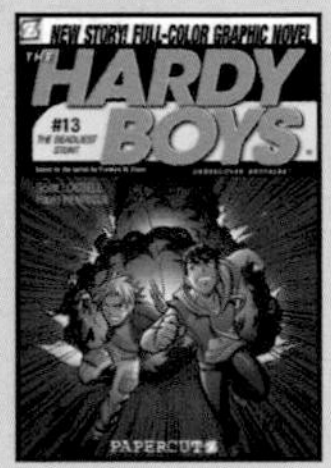
NEW STORY! FULL-COLOR GRAPHIC NOVEL
THE HARDY BOYS
#13
PAPERCUTZ

#13 "The Deadliest Stunt"

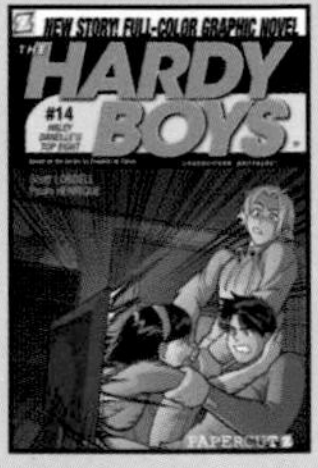
NEW STORY! FULL-COLOR GRAPHIC NOVEL
THE HARDY BOYS
#14
PAPERCUTZ

#14 "Haley Danelle's Top Eight!"

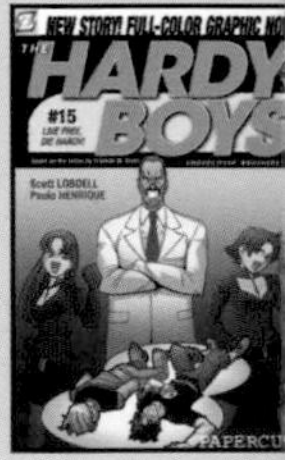
NEW STORY! FULL-COLOR GRAPHIC NOVEL
THE HARDY BOYS
#15

#15 "Live Free, Die Hardy!"

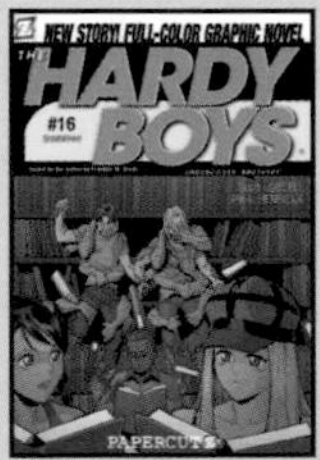
NEW STORY! FULL-COLOR GRAPHIC NOVEL
THE HARDY BOYS
#16
PAPERCUTZ

#16 "Shhhhhh!"

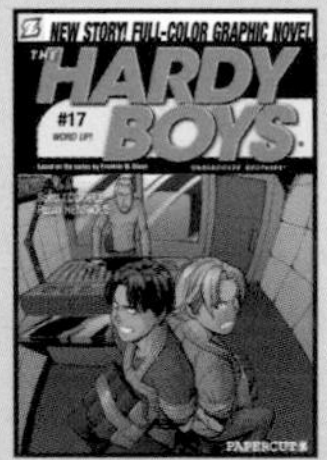
NEW STORY! FULL-COLOR GRAPHIC NOVEL
THE HARDY BOYS
#17
PAPERCUTZ

Coming Soon!
#17 "Word Up!"

$7.95 each in paperback, $12.95 each in hardcover.

Please add $4.00 for postage and handling for the first book, add $1.00 for each additional book. Please make check payable to NBM Publishing. Send to: **Papercutz, 40 Exchange Place Suite 1308, New York, NY 10005 • 1-800-886-1223 • www.papercutz.com**

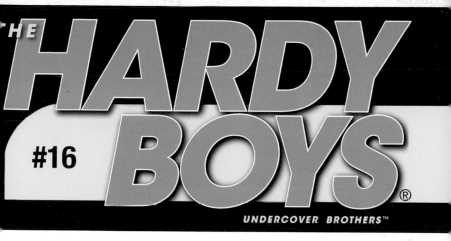

THE HARDY BOYS

#16

BOYS

UNDERCOVER BROTHERS™

Shhhhhh!

SCOTT LOBDELL • Writer
PAULO HENRIQUE MARCONDES • Artist

Based on the series by
FRANKLIN W. DIXON

New York

Shhhhhh!
SCOTT LOBDELL — Writer
PAULO HENRIQUE MARCONDES — Artist
MARK LERER — Letterer
LAURIE E. SMITH — Colorist
MIKHAELA REID & MASHEKA WOOD— Production
MICHAEL PETRANEK — Editorial Assistant
JIM SALICRUP
Editor-in-Chief

ISBN 13: 978-1-59707-138-3 paperback edition
ISBN 10: 1-59707-138-2 paperback edition
ISBN 13: 978-1-59707-139-0 hardcover edition
ISBN 10: 1-59707-139-0 hardcover edition

Published by arrangement with Aladdin Paperbacks,
an imprint of Simon & Schuster Children's Publishing Division.

Distributed by Macmillan.

Printed in China.

10 9 8 7 6 5 4 3 2 1

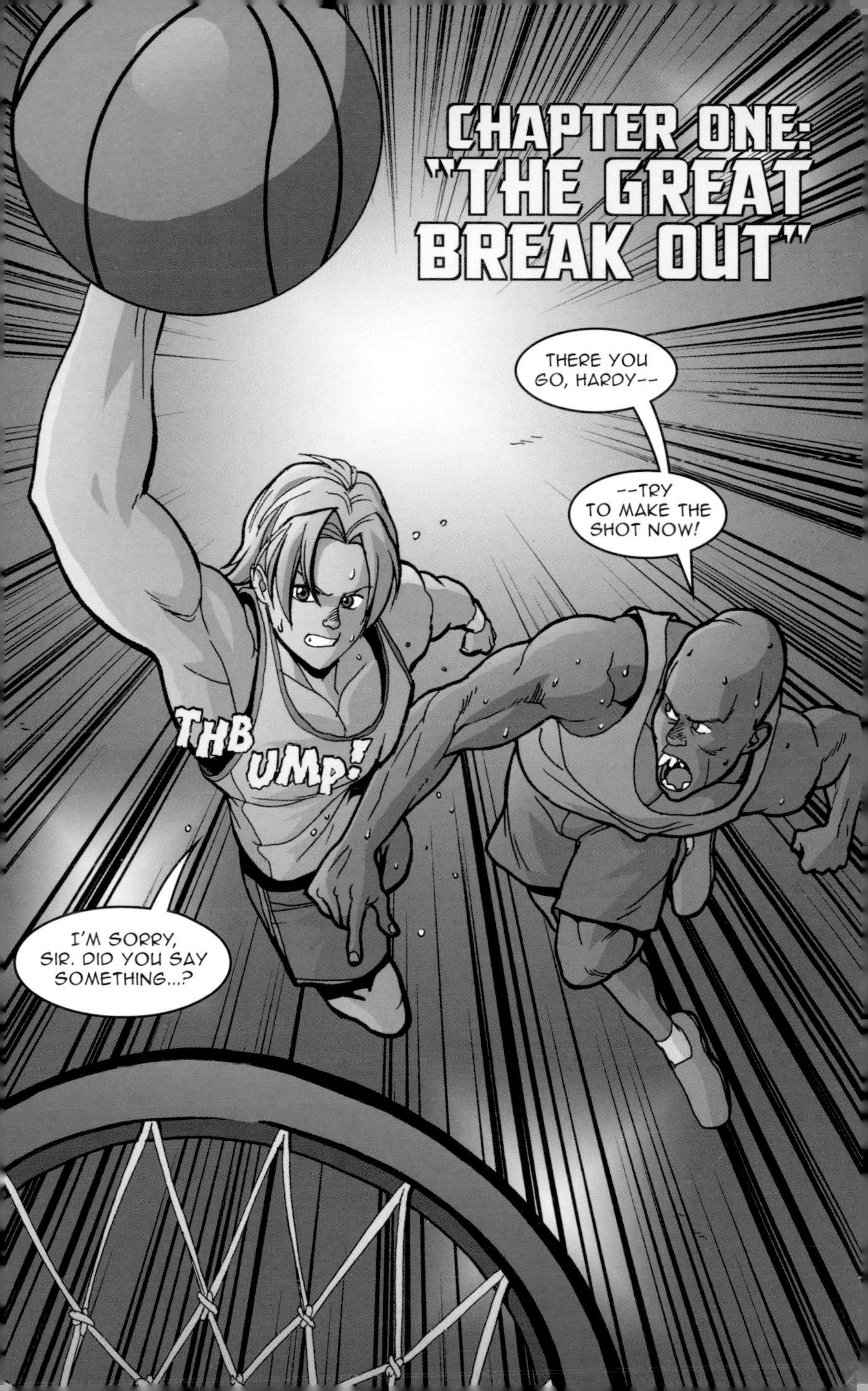
CHAPTER ONE:
"THE GREAT BREAK OUT"
THERE YOU GO, HARDY--
--TRY TO MAKE THE SHOT NOW!
THBUMP!
I'M SORRY, SIR. DID YOU SAY SOMETHING...?

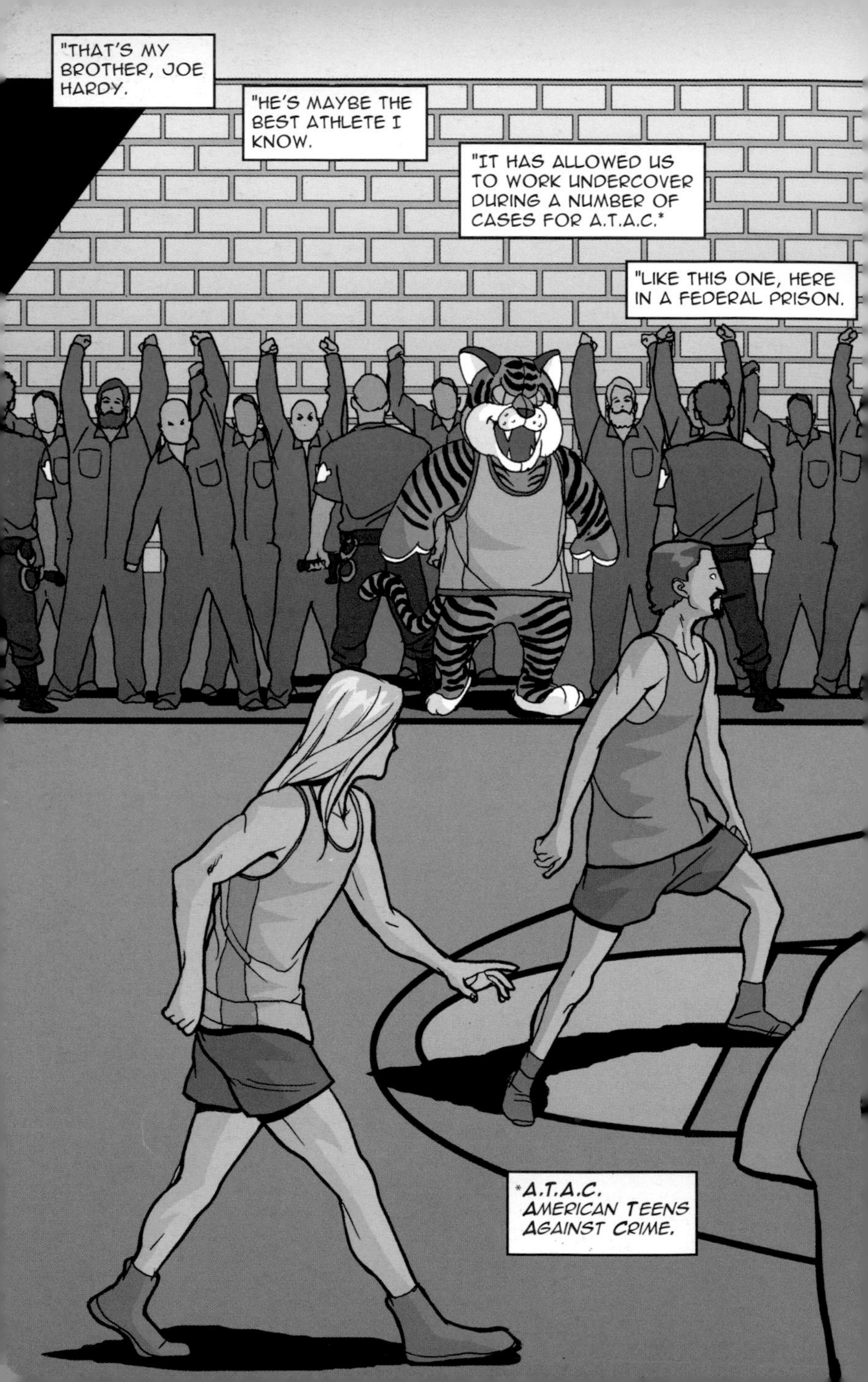
"THAT'S MY BROTHER, JOE HARDY.
"HE'S MAYBE THE BEST ATHLETE I KNOW.
"IT HAS ALLOWED US TO WORK UNDERCOVER DURING A NUMBER OF CASES FOR A.T.A.C.*
"LIKE THIS ONE, HERE IN A FEDERAL PRISON.
*A.T.A.C. AMERICAN TEENS AGAINST CRIME.

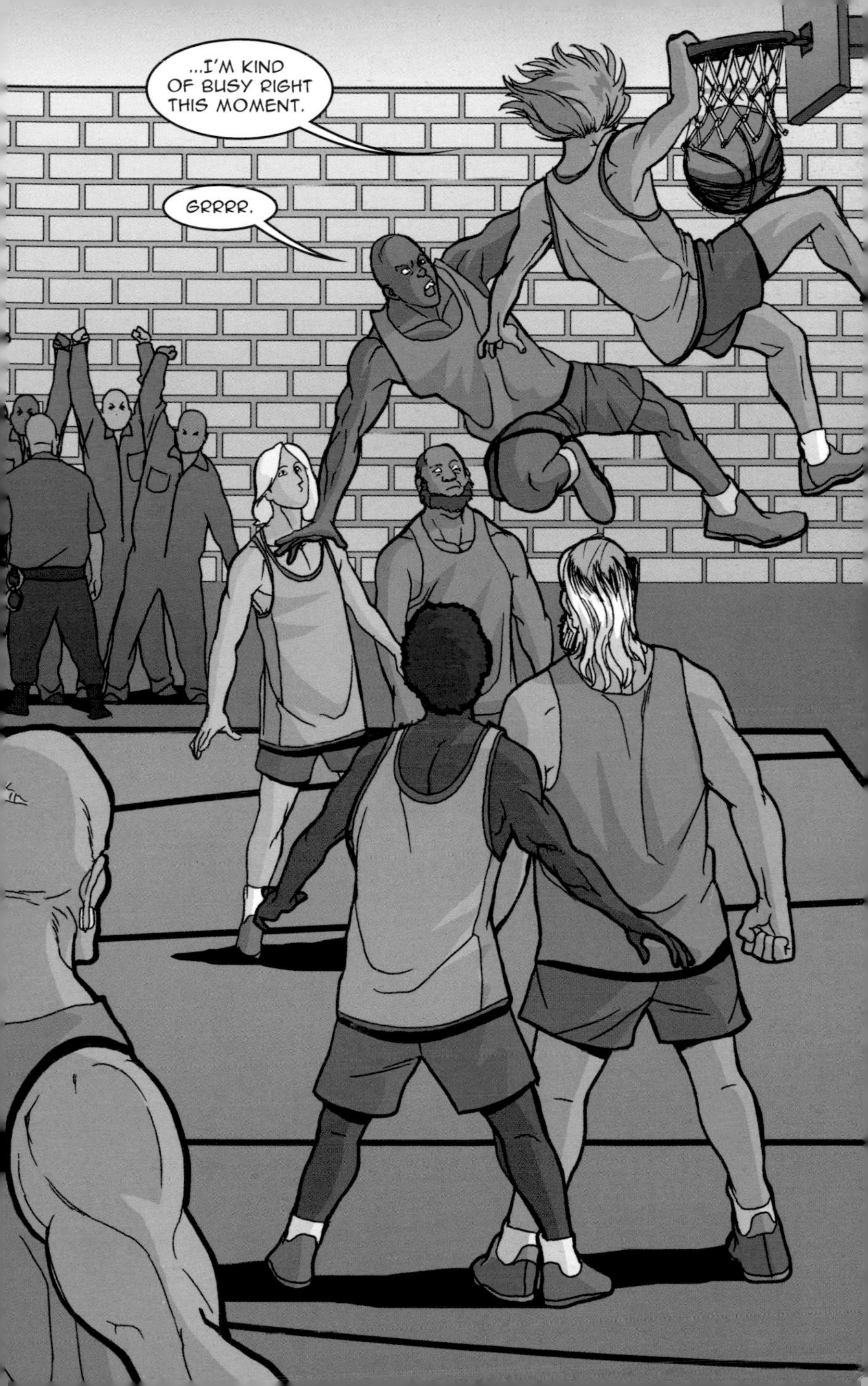
...I'M KIND OF BUSY RIGHT THIS MOMENT.
GRRRR.

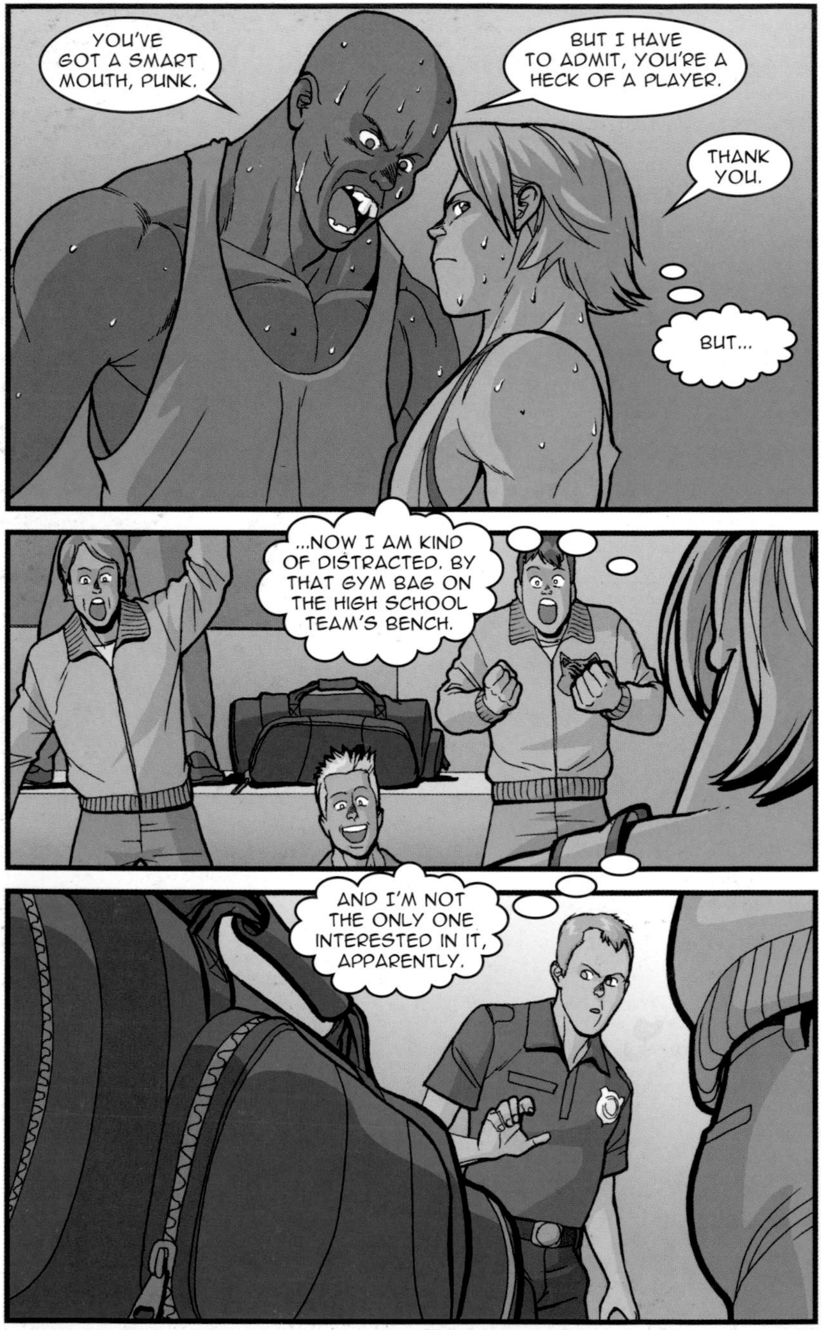
YOU'VE GOT A SMART MOUTH, PUNK.
BUT I HAVE TO ADMIT, YOU'RE A HECK OF A PLAYER.
THANK YOU.
BUT...
...NOW I AM KIND OF DISTRACTED. BY THAT GYM BAG ON THE HIGH SCHOOL TEAM'S BENCH.
AND I'M NOT THE ONLY ONE INTERESTED IN IT, APPARENTLY.

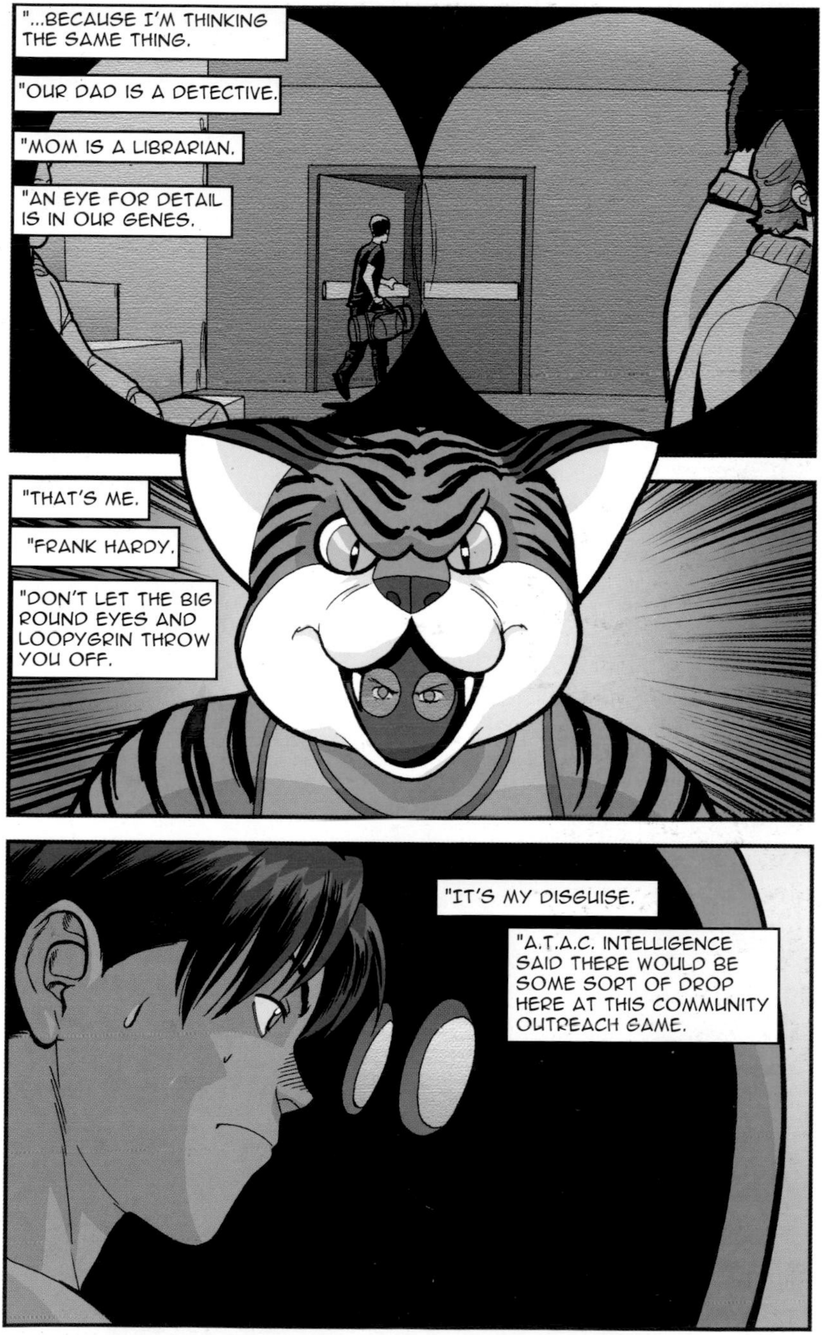
"...BECAUSE I'M THINKING THE SAME THING.
"OUR DAD IS A DETECTIVE.
"MOM IS A LIBRARIAN.
"AN EYE FOR DETAIL IS IN OUR GENES.
"THAT'S ME.
"FRANK HARDY.
"DON'T LET THE BIG ROUND EYES AND LOOPYGRIN THROW YOU OFF.
"IT'S MY DISGUISE.
"A.T.A.C. INTELLIGENCE SAID THERE WOULD BE SOME SORT OF DROP HERE AT THIS COMMUNITY OUTREACH GAME.

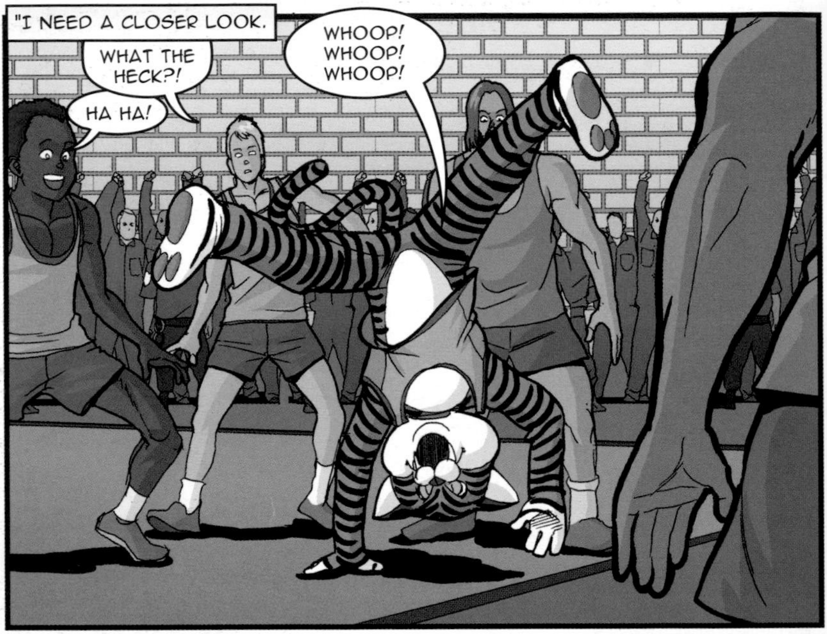
"I NEED A CLOSER LOOK.
WHAT THE HECK?!
HA HA!
WHOOP! WHOOP! WHOOP!

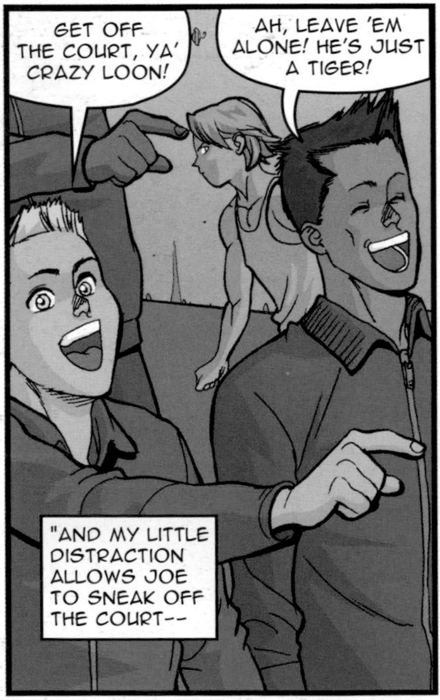
GET OFF THE COURT, YA' CRAZY LOON!
AH, LEAVE 'EM ALONE! HE'S JUST A TIGER!
"AND MY LITTLE DISTRACTION ALLOWS JOE TO SNEAK OFF THE COURT--

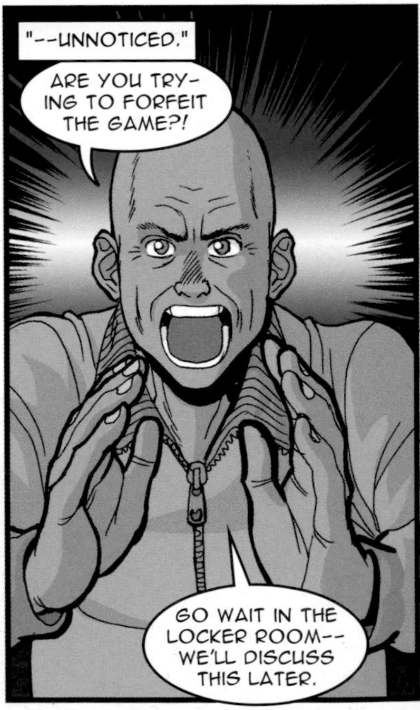
"--UNNOTICED."
ARE YOU TRY-ING TO FORFEIT THE GAME?!
GO WAIT IN THE LOCKER ROOM--WE'LL DISCUSS THIS LATER.

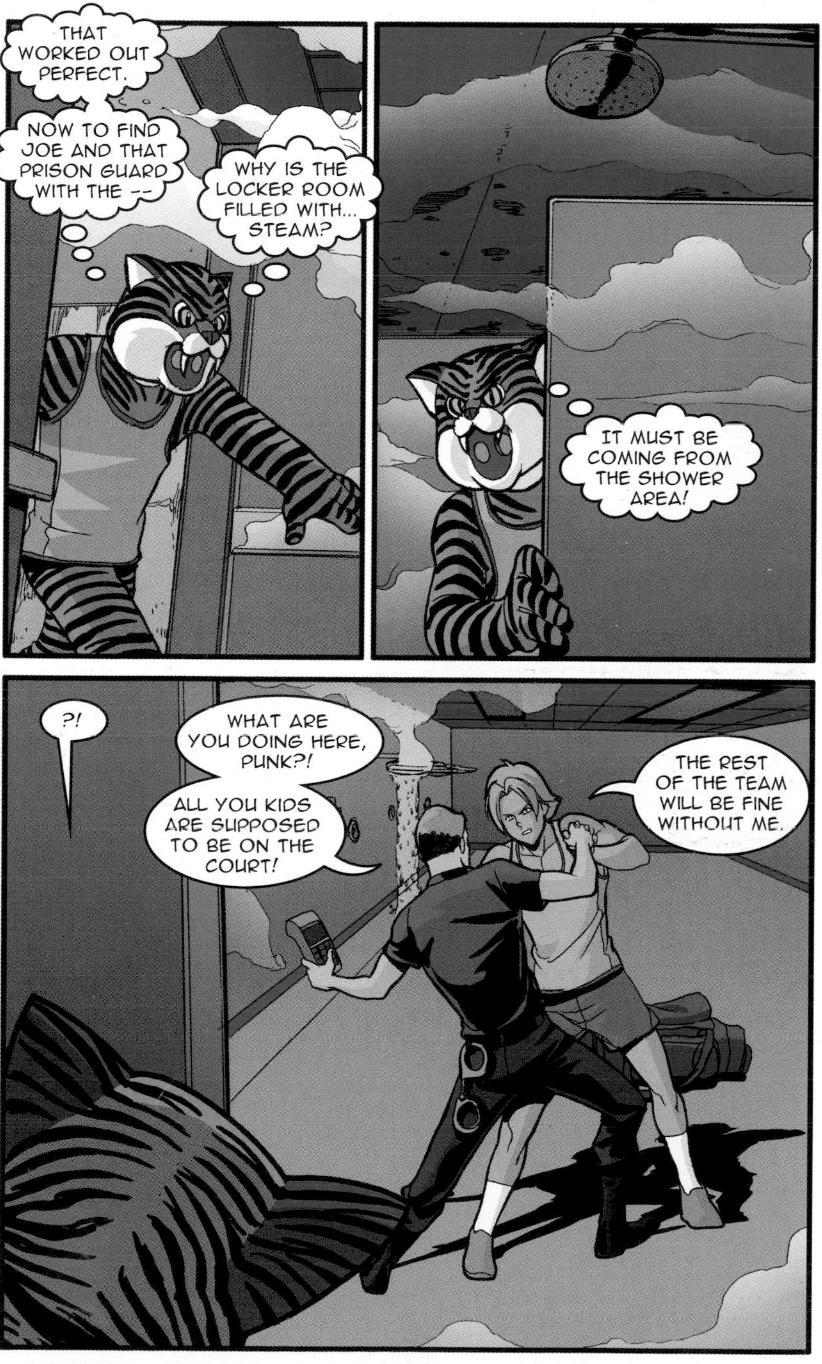
THAT WORKED OUT PERFECT.
NOW TO FIND JOE AND THAT PRISON GUARD WITH THE --
WHY IS THE LOCKER ROOM FILLED WITH... STEAM?
IT MUST BE COMING FROM THE SHOWER AREA!
?!
WHAT ARE YOU DOING HERE, PUNK?!
ALL YOU KIDS ARE SUPPOSED TO BE ON THE COURT!
THE REST OF THE TEAM WILL BE FINE WITHOUT ME.

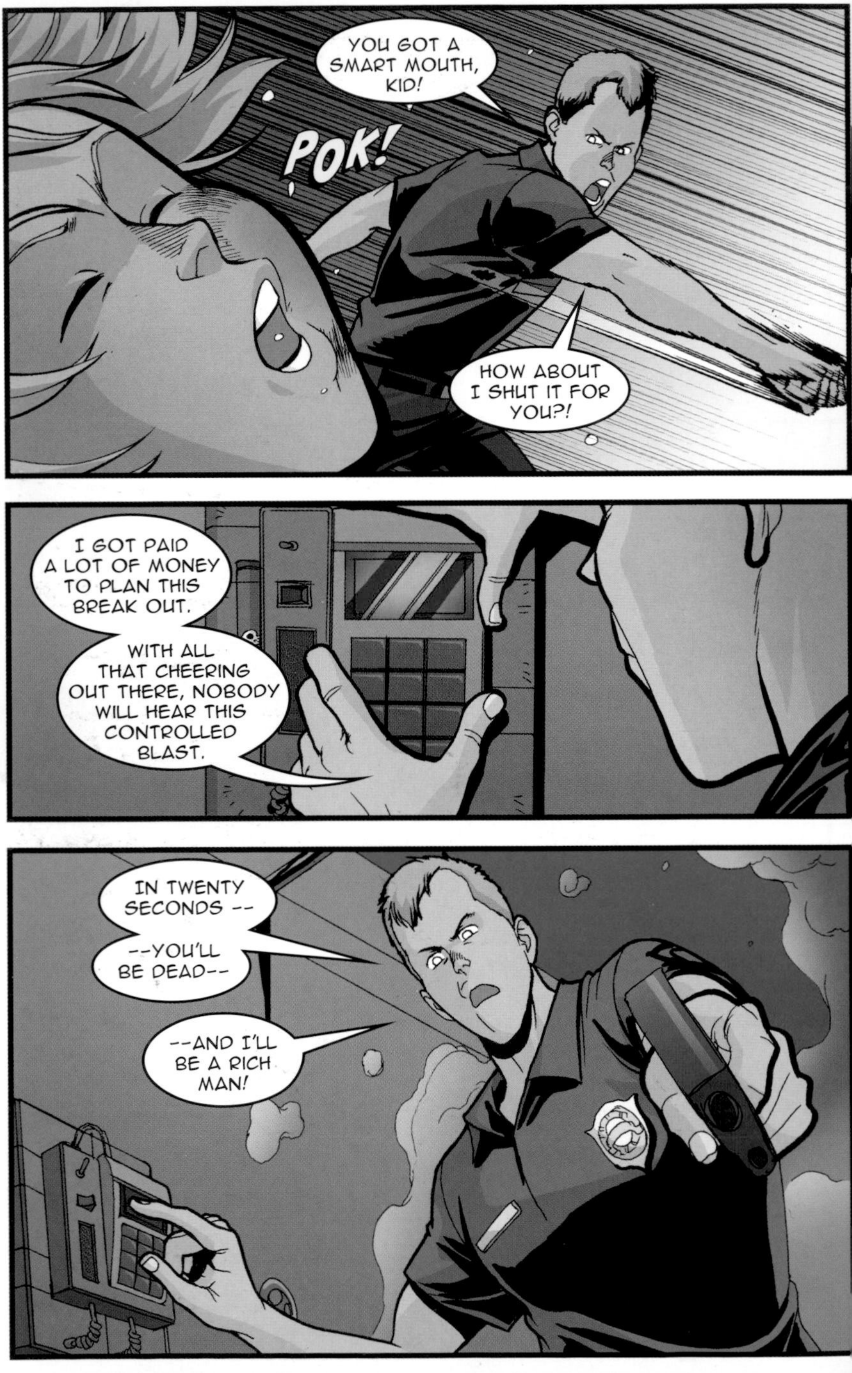
YOU GOT A SMART MOUTH, KID!
POK!
HOW ABOUT I SHUT IT FOR YOU?!
I GOT PAID A LOT OF MONEY TO PLAN THIS BREAK OUT.
WITH ALL THAT CHEERING OUT THERE, NOBODY WILL HEAR THIS CONTROLLED BLAST.
IN TWENTY SECONDS --
--YOU'LL BE DEAD--
--AND I'LL BE A RICH MAN!

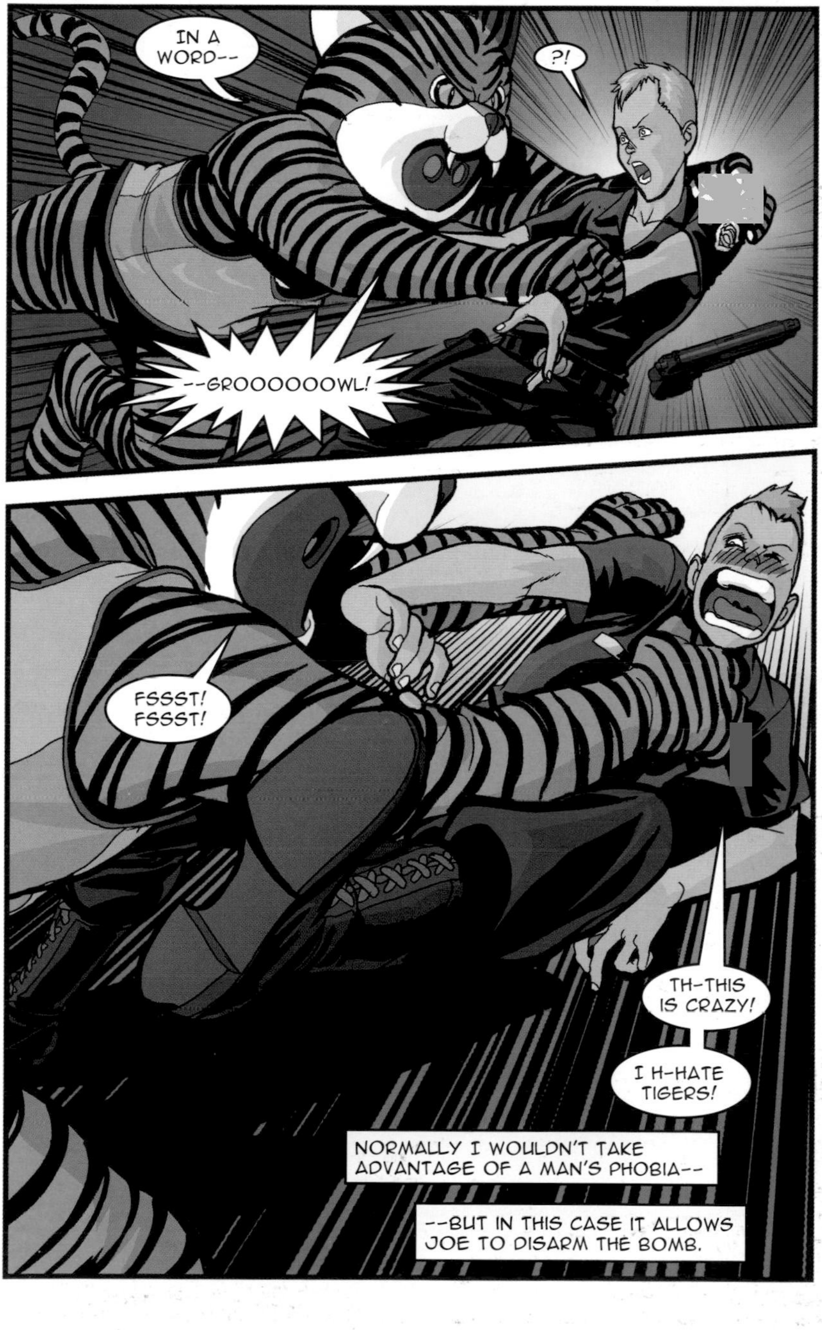
IN A WORD--
?!
--GROOOOOOWL!
FSSST! FSSST!
TH-THIS IS CRAZY!
I H-HATE TIGERS!
NORMALLY I WOULDN'T TAKE ADVANTAGE OF A MAN'S PHOBIA--
--BUT IN THIS CASE IT ALLOWS JOE TO DISARM THE BOMB.

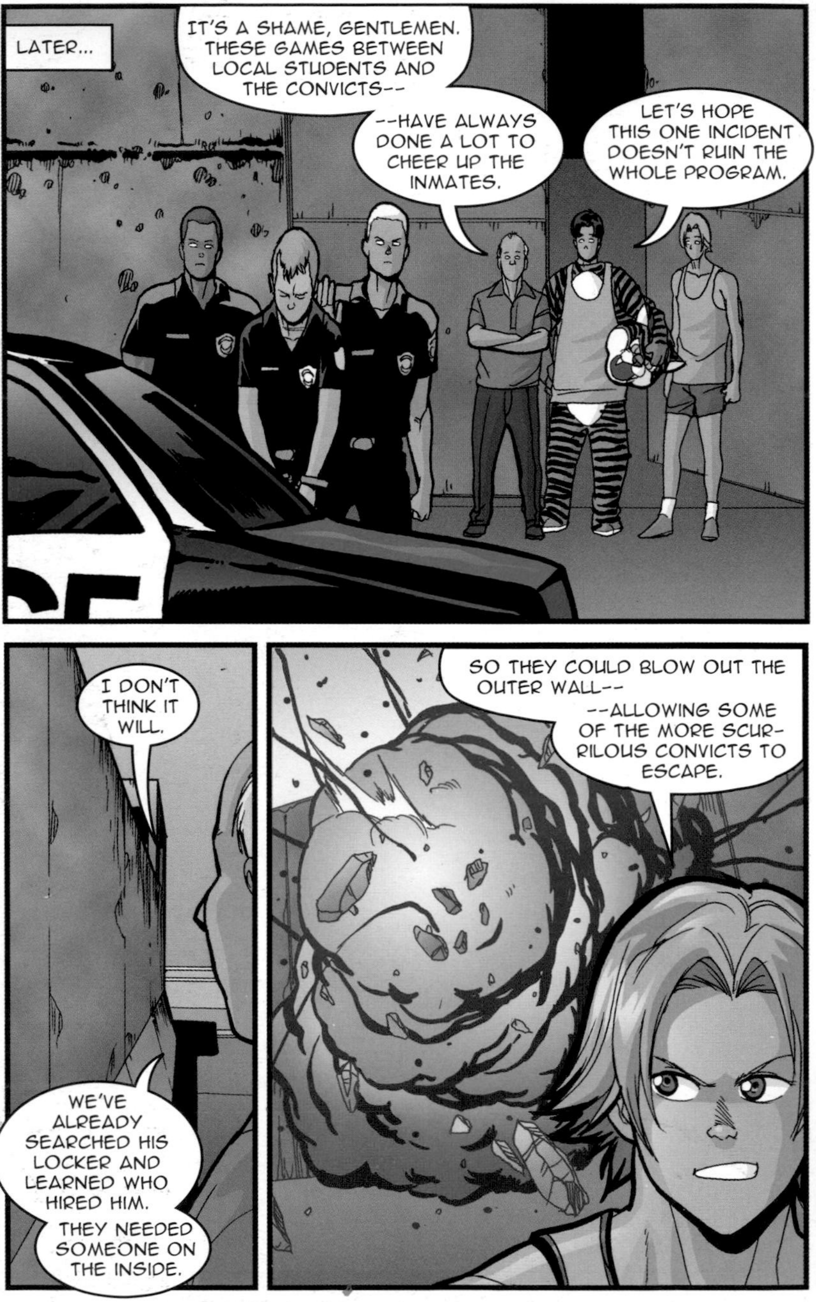
LATER...
IT'S A SHAME, GENTLEMEN. THESE GAMES BETWEEN LOCAL STUDENTS AND THE CONVICTS--
--HAVE ALWAYS DONE A LOT TO CHEER UP THE INMATES.
LET'S HOPE THIS ONE INCIDENT DOESN'T RUIN THE WHOLE PROGRAM.
I DON'T THINK IT WILL.
WE'VE ALREADY SEARCHED HIS LOCKER AND LEARNED WHO HIRED HIM.
THEY NEEDED SOMEONE ON THE INSIDE.
SO THEY COULD BLOW OUT THE OUTER WALL--
--ALLOWING SOME OF THE MORE SCURRILOUS CONVICTS TO ESCAPE.

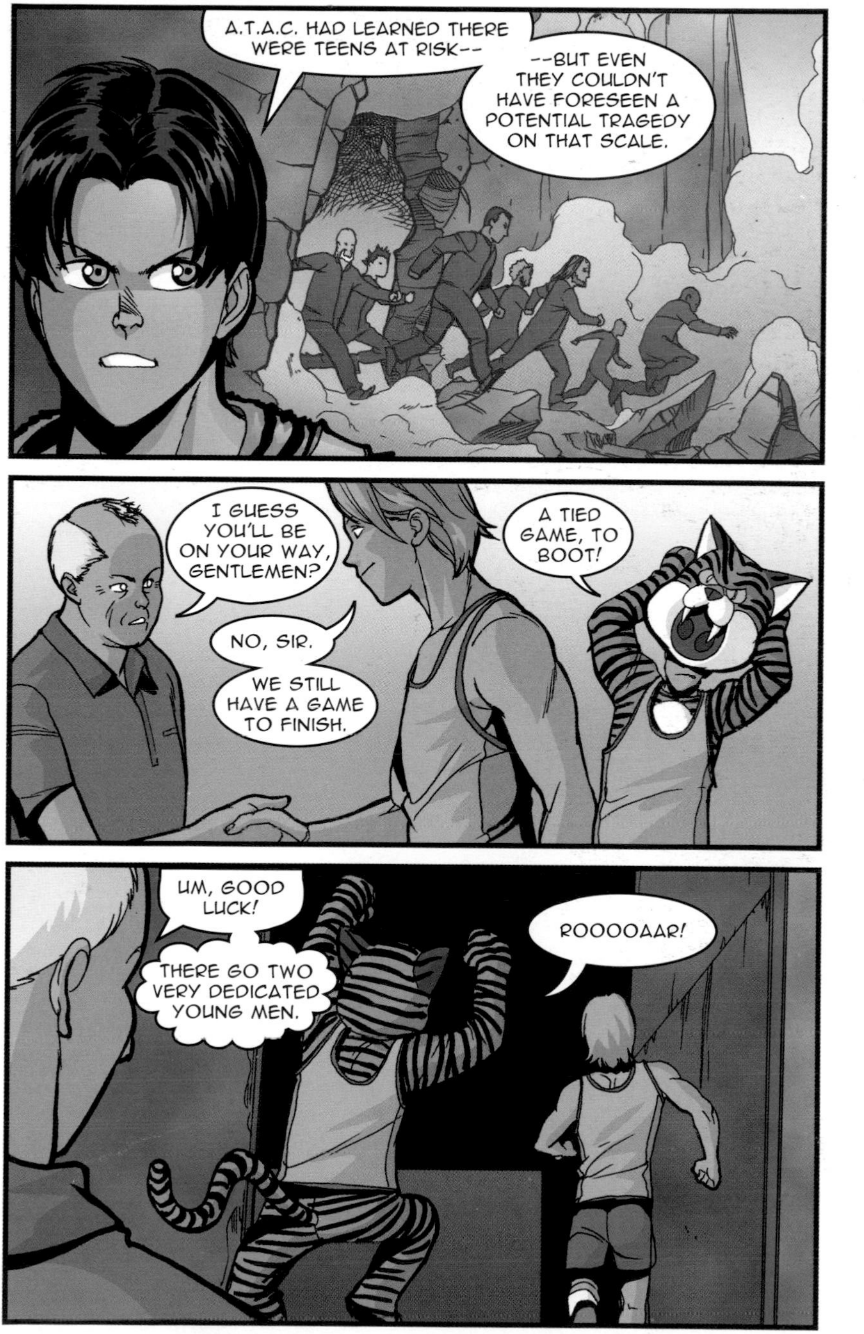
A.T.A.C. HAD LEARNED THERE WERE TEENS AT RISK--
--BUT EVEN THEY COULDN'T HAVE FORESEEN A POTENTIAL TRAGEDY ON THAT SCALE.
I GUESS YOU'LL BE ON YOUR WAY, GENTLEMEN?
NO, SIR.
WE STILL HAVE A GAME TO FINISH.
A TIED GAME, TO BOOT!
UM, GOOD LUCK!
THERE GO TWO VERY DEDICATED YOUNG MEN.
ROOOOAAR!

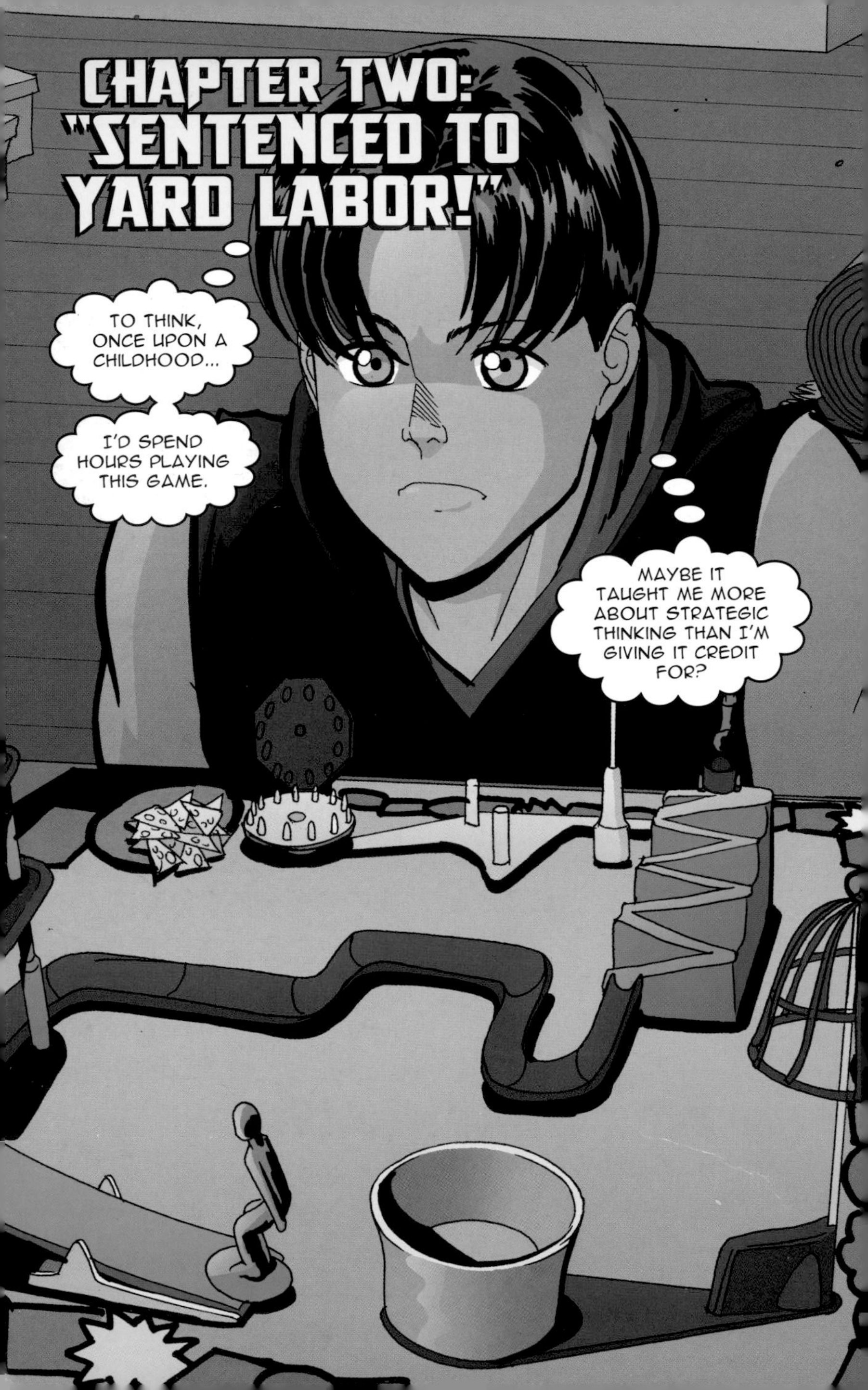
CHAPTER TWO: "SENTENCED TO YARD LABOR!"
TO THINK, ONCE UPON A CHILDHOOD...
I'D SPEND HOURS PLAYING THIS GAME.
MAYBE IT TAUGHT ME MORE ABOUT STRATEGIC THINKING THAN I'M GIVING IT CREDIT FOR?

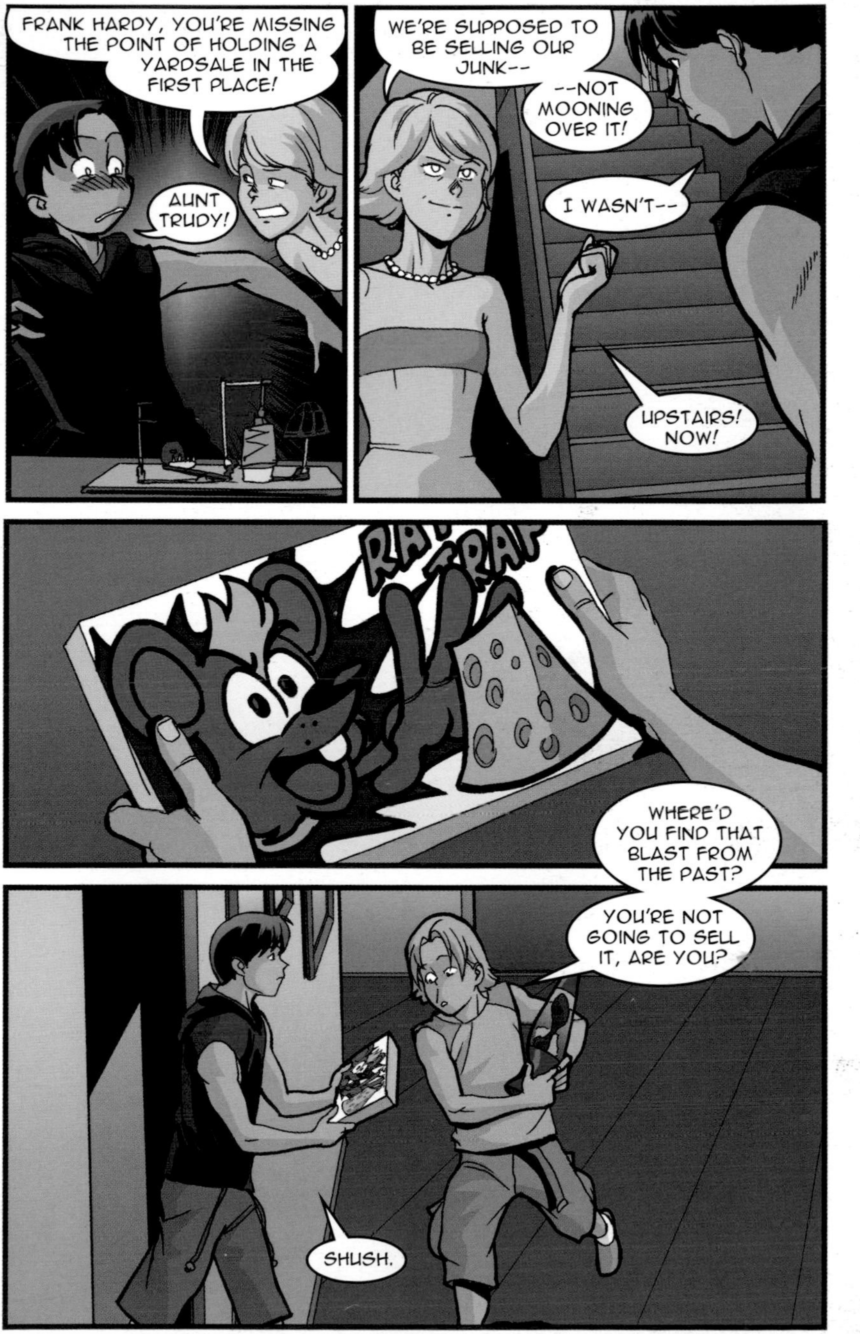
FRANK HARDY, YOU'RE MISSING THE POINT OF HOLDING A YARDSALE IN THE FIRST PLACE!
AUNT TRUDY!
WE'RE SUPPOSED TO BE SELLING OUR JUNK--
--NOT MOONING OVER IT!
I WASN'T--
UPSTAIRS! NOW!
RAT TRAP
WHERE'D YOU FIND THAT BLAST FROM THE PAST?
YOU'RE NOT GOING TO SELL IT, ARE YOU?
SHUSH.

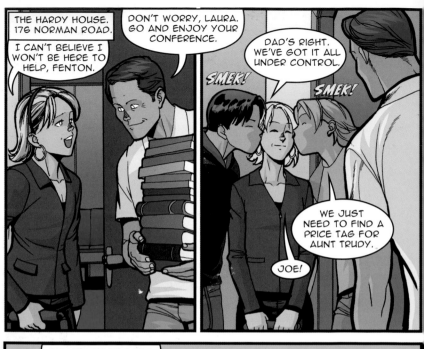

THE HARDY HOUSE. 176 NORMAN ROAD.

I CAN'T BELIEVE I WON'T BE HERE TO HELP, FENTON.

DON'T WORRY, LAURA. GO AND ENJOY YOUR CONFERENCE.

DAD'S RIGHT. WE'VE GOT IT ALL UNDER CONTROL.

SMEK!

SMEK!

WE JUST NEED TO FIND A PRICE TAG FOR AUNT TRUDY.

JOE!

I CAN'T BELIEVE I'VE BEEN CALLED AWAY. I SHOULD HAVE DECLINED.

AND DENY THE ASSOCIATION OF NATIONAL LIBRARIANS THEIR KEYNOTE SPEAKER? NEVER.

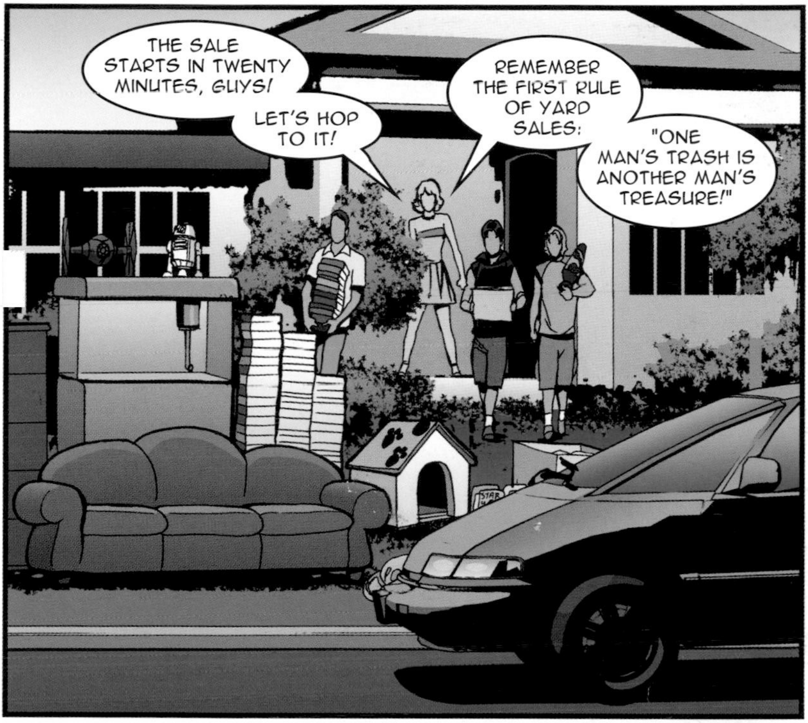
THE SALE STARTS IN TWENTY MINUTES, GUYS!
LET'S HOP TO IT!
REMEMBER THE FIRST RULE OF YARD SALES:
"ONE MAN'S TRASH IS ANOTHER MAN'S TREASURE!"

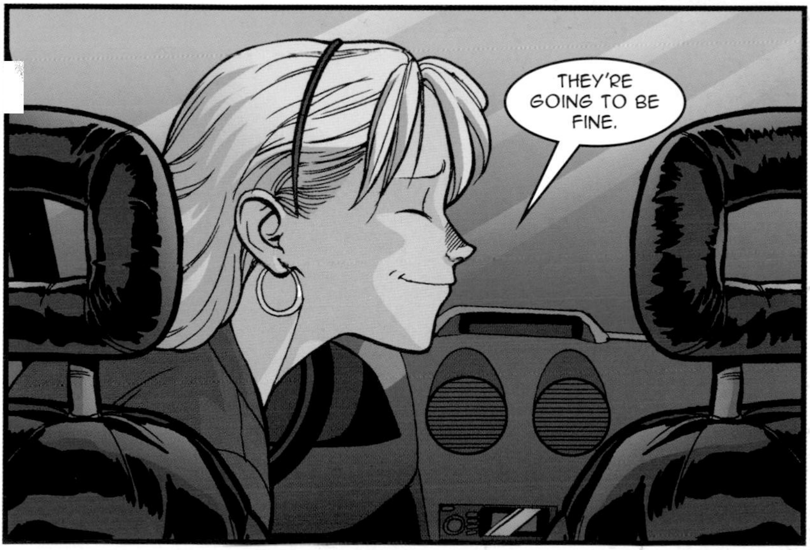
THEY'RE GOING TO BE FINE.

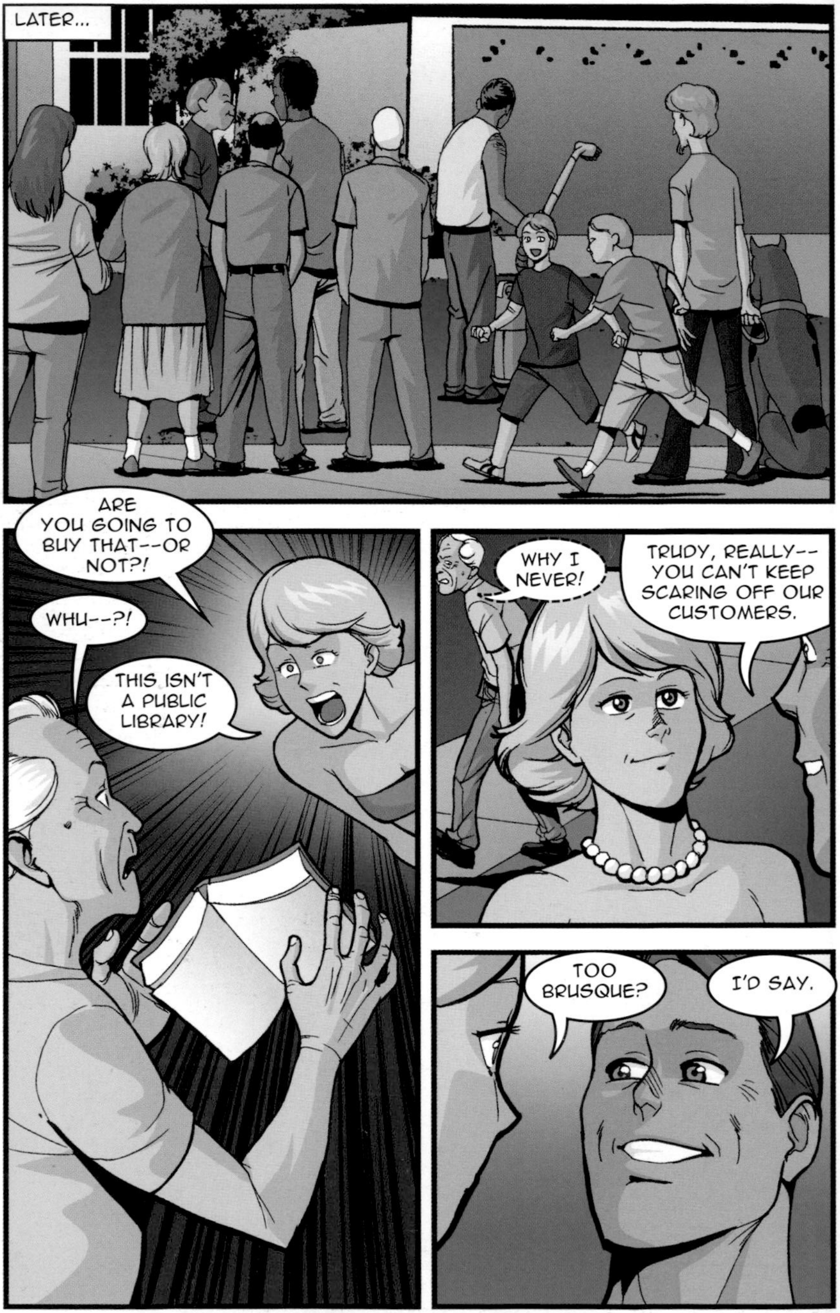

LATER...
ARE YOU GOING TO BUY THAT--OR NOT?!
WHU--?!
THIS ISN'T A PUBLIC LIBRARY!
WHY I NEVER!
TRUDY, REALLY--YOU CAN'T KEEP SCARING OFF OUR CUSTOMERS.
TOO BRUSQUE?
I'D SAY.

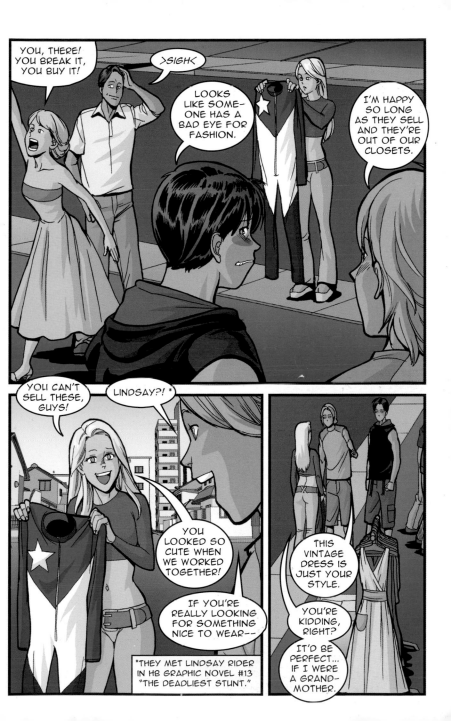

YOU, THERE! YOU BREAK IT, YOU BUY IT!

>SIGH<

LOOKS LIKE SOMEONE HAS A BAD EYE FOR FASHION.

I'M HAPPY SO LONG AS THEY SELL AND THEY'RE OUT OF OUR CLOSETS.

YOU CAN'T SELL THESE, GUYS!

LINDSAY?! *

YOU LOOKED SO CUTE WHEN WE WORKED TOGETHER!

IF YOU'RE REALLY LOOKING FOR SOMETHING NICE TO WEAR--

"THEY MET LINDSAY RIDER IN HB GRAPHIC NOVEL #13 "THE DEADLIEST STUNT."

THIS VINTAGE DRESS IS JUST YOUR STYLE.

YOU'RE KIDDING, RIGHT?

IT'D BE PERFECT... IF I WERE A GRANDMOTHER.

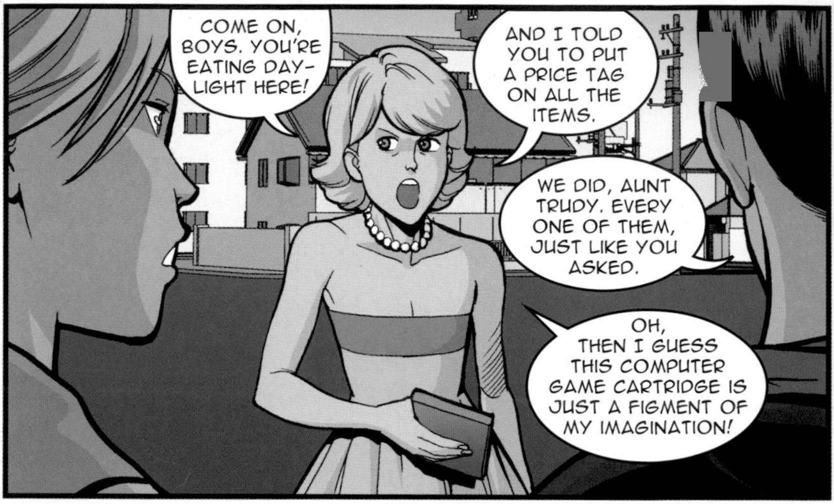
COME ON, BOYS. YOU'RE EATING DAY-LIGHT HERE!
AND I TOLD YOU TO PUT A PRICE TAG ON ALL THE ITEMS.
WE DID, AUNT TRUDY. EVERY ONE OF THEM, JUST LIKE YOU ASKED.
OH, THEN I GUESS THIS COMPUTER GAME CARTRIDGE IS JUST A FIGMENT OF MY IMAGINATION!

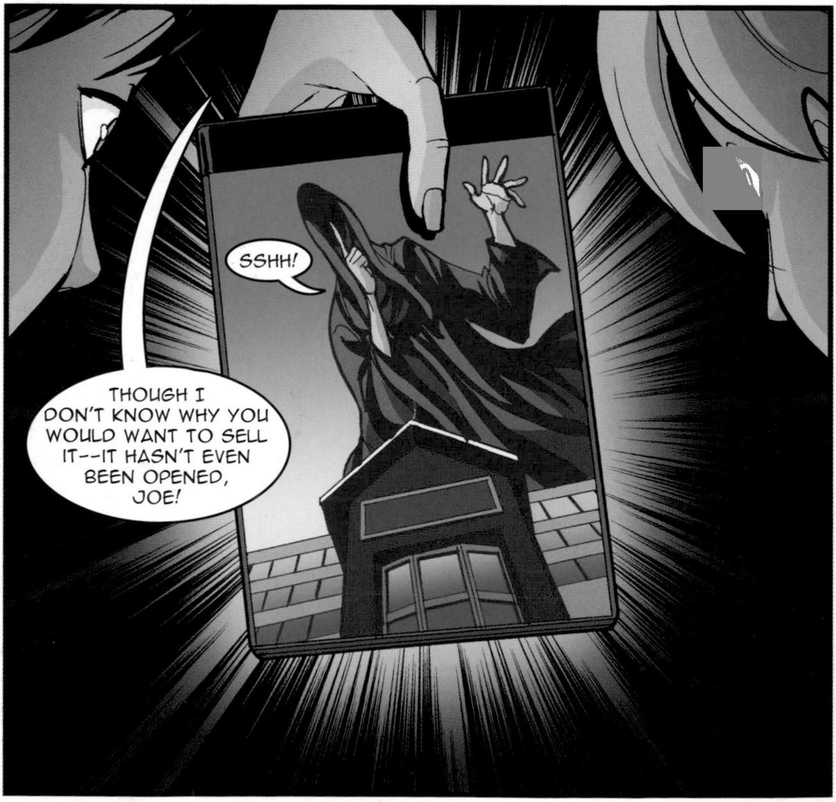
SSHH!
THOUGH I DON'T KNOW WHY YOU WOULD WANT TO SELL IT--IT HASN'T EVEN BEEN OPENED, JOE!

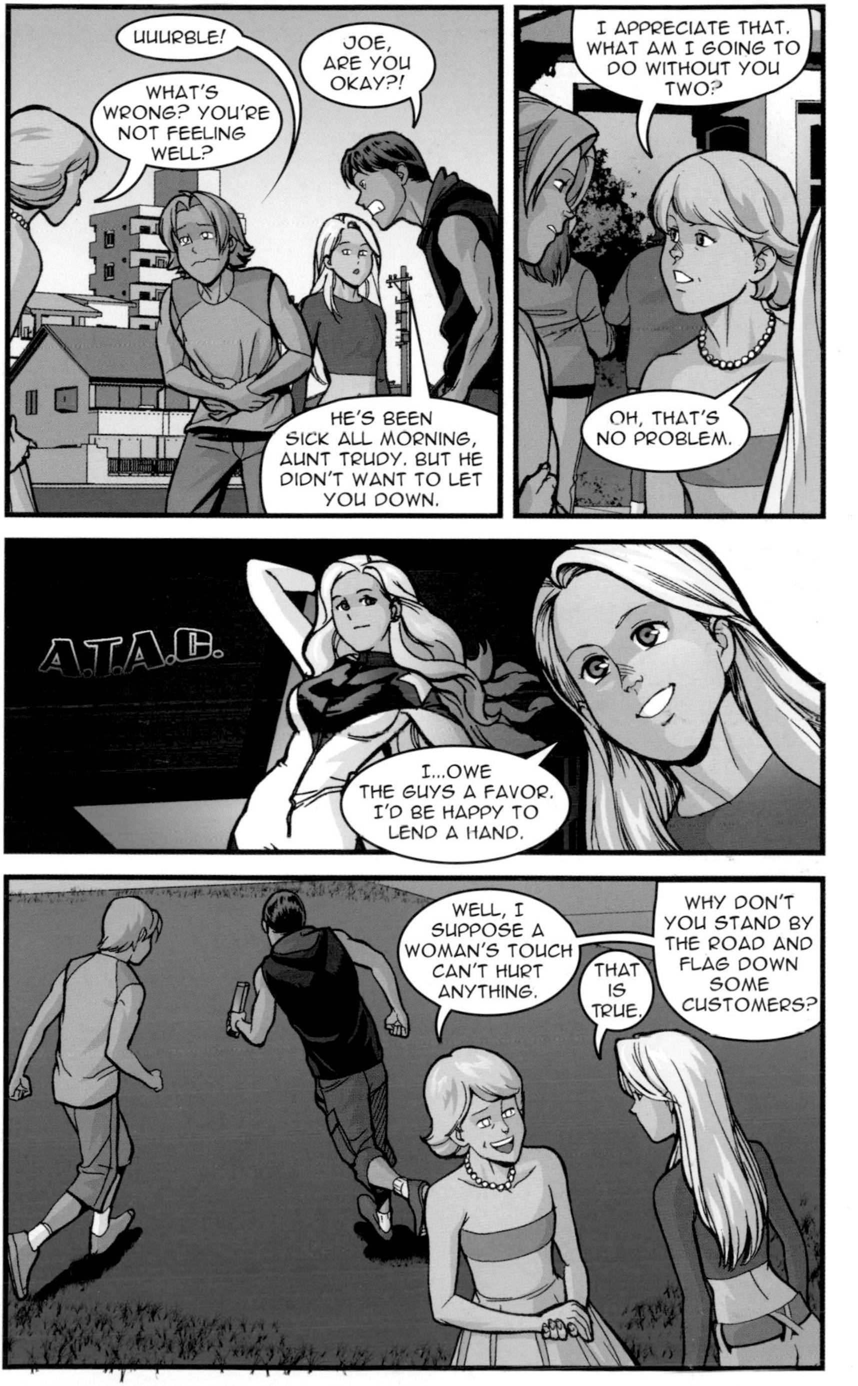
UUURBLE!
WHAT'S WRONG? YOU'RE NOT FEELING WELL?
JOE, ARE YOU OKAY?!
HE'S BEEN SICK ALL MORNING, AUNT TRUDY. BUT HE DIDN'T WANT TO LET YOU DOWN.
I APPRECIATE THAT. WHAT AM I GOING TO DO WITHOUT YOU TWO?
OH, THAT'S NO PROBLEM.
A.T.A.C.
I...OWE THE GUYS A FAVOR. I'D BE HAPPY TO LEND A HAND.
WELL, I SUPPOSE A WOMAN'S TOUCH CAN'T HURT ANYTHING.
WHY DON'T YOU STAND BY THE ROAD AND FLAG DOWN SOME CUSTOMERS?
THAT IS TRUE.

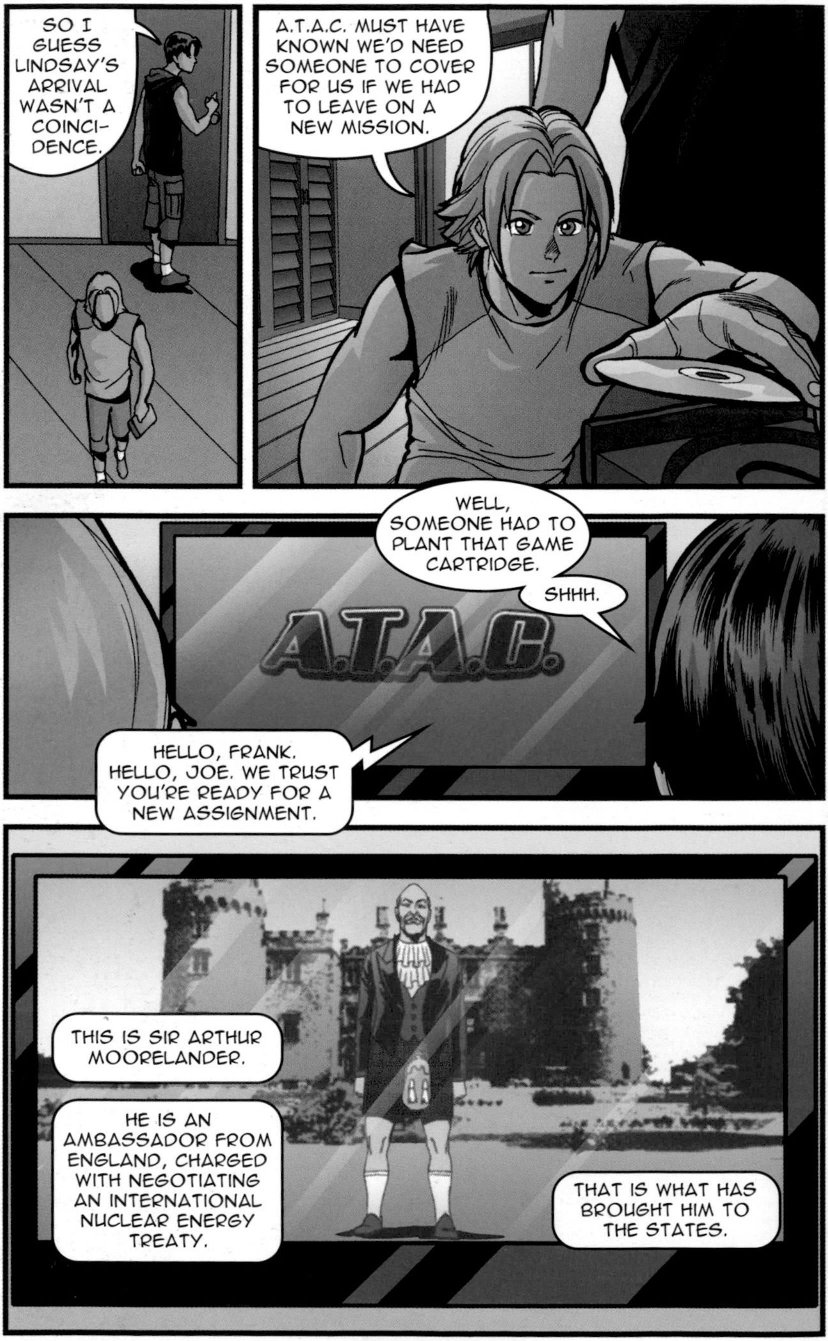
SO I GUESS LINDSAY'S ARRIVAL WASN'T A COINCI-DENCE.
A.T.A.C. MUST HAVE KNOWN WE'D NEED SOMEONE TO COVER FOR US IF WE HAD TO LEAVE ON A NEW MISSION.
WELL, SOMEONE HAD TO PLANT THAT GAME CARTRIDGE.
SHHH.
A.T.A.C.
HELLO, FRANK. HELLO, JOE. WE TRUST YOU'RE READY FOR A NEW ASSIGNMENT.
THIS IS SIR ARTHUR MOORELANDER.
HE IS AN AMBASSADOR FROM ENGLAND, CHARGED WITH NEGOTIATING AN INTERNATIONAL NUCLEAR ENERGY TREATY.
THAT IS WHAT HAS BROUGHT HIM TO THE STATES.

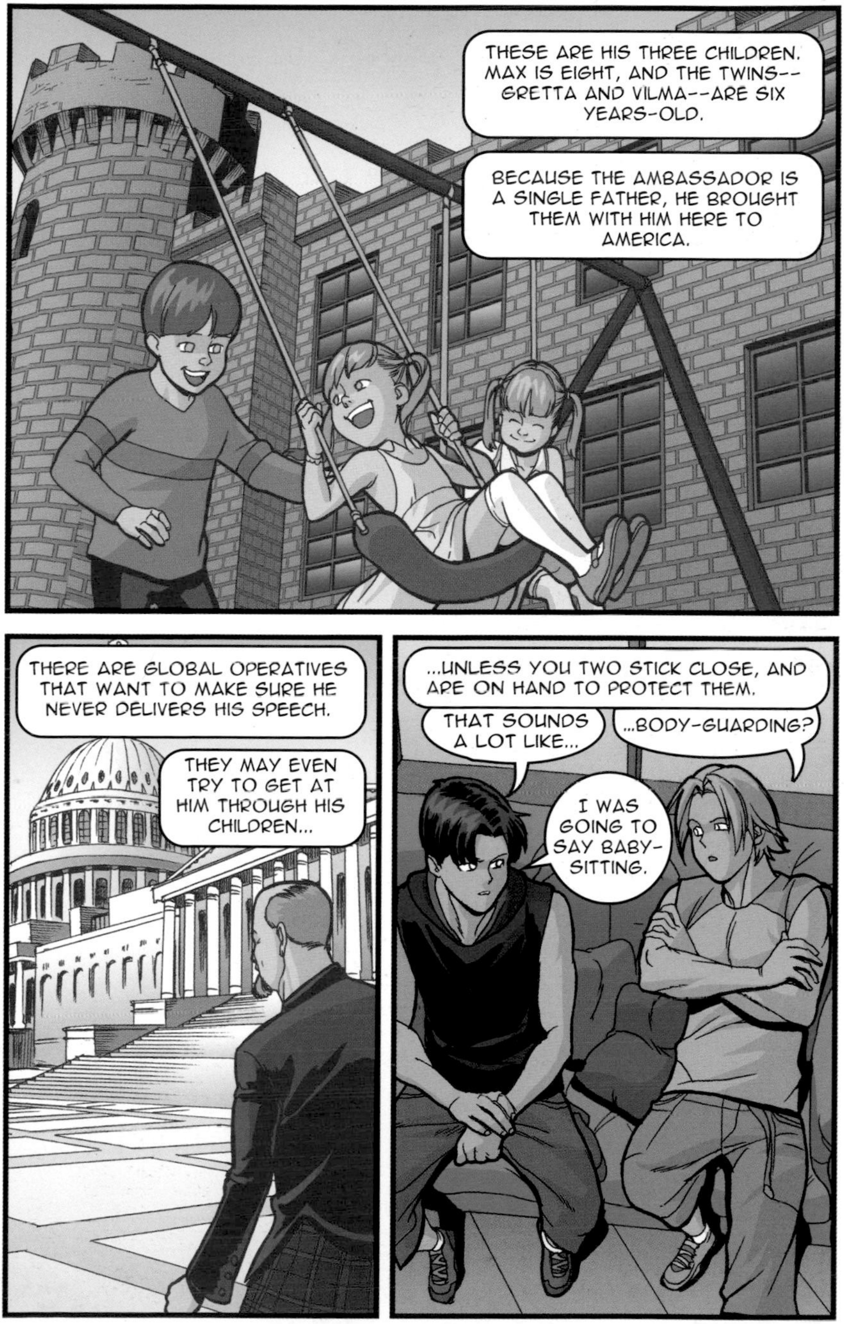
THESE ARE HIS THREE CHILDREN. MAX IS EIGHT, AND THE TWINS--GRETTA AND VILMA--ARE SIX YEARS-OLD.
BECAUSE THE AMBASSADOR IS A SINGLE FATHER, HE BROUGHT THEM WITH HIM HERE TO AMERICA.
THERE ARE GLOBAL OPERATIVES THAT WANT TO MAKE SURE HE NEVER DELIVERS HIS SPEECH.
THEY MAY EVEN TRY TO GET AT HIM THROUGH HIS CHILDREN...
...UNLESS YOU TWO STICK CLOSE, AND ARE ON HAND TO PROTECT THEM.
THAT SOUNDS A LOT LIKE...
...BODY-GUARDING?
I WAS GOING TO SAY BABY-SITTING.

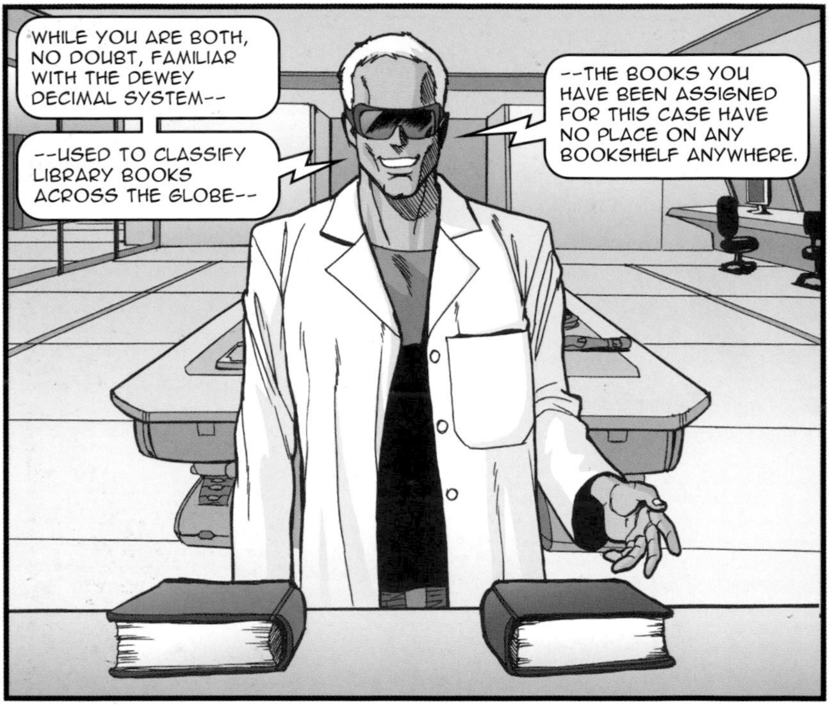
WHILE YOU ARE BOTH, NO DOUBT, FAMILIAR WITH THE DEWEY DECIMAL SYSTEM--
--USED TO CLASSIFY LIBRARY BOOKS ACROSS THE GLOBE--
--THE BOOKS YOU HAVE BEEN ASSIGNED FOR THIS CASE HAVE NO PLACE ON ANY BOOKSHELF ANYWHERE.

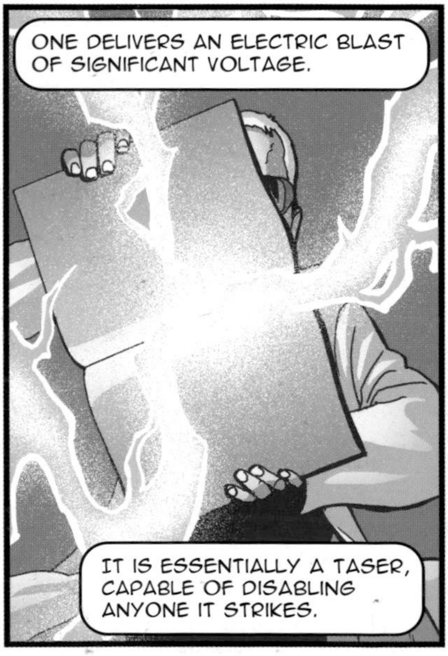
ONE DELIVERS AN ELECTRIC BLAST OF SIGNIFICANT VOLTAGE.
IT IS ESSENTIALLY A TASER, CAPABLE OF DISABLING ANYONE IT STRIKES.

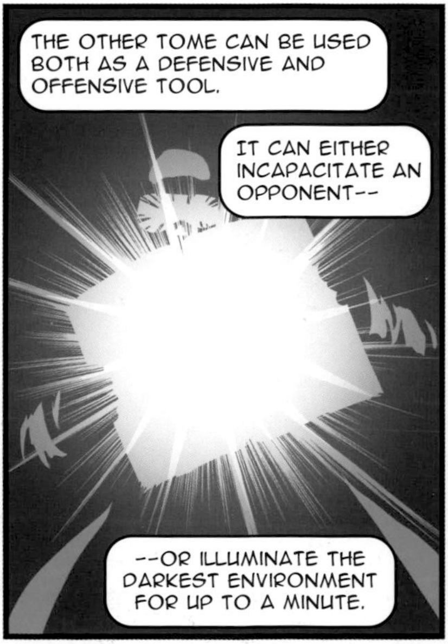
THE OTHER TOME CAN BE USED BOTH AS A DEFENSIVE AND OFFENSIVE TOOL.
IT CAN EITHER INCAPACITATE AN OPPONENT--
--OR ILLUMINATE THE DARKEST ENVIRONMENT FOR UP TO A MINUTE.

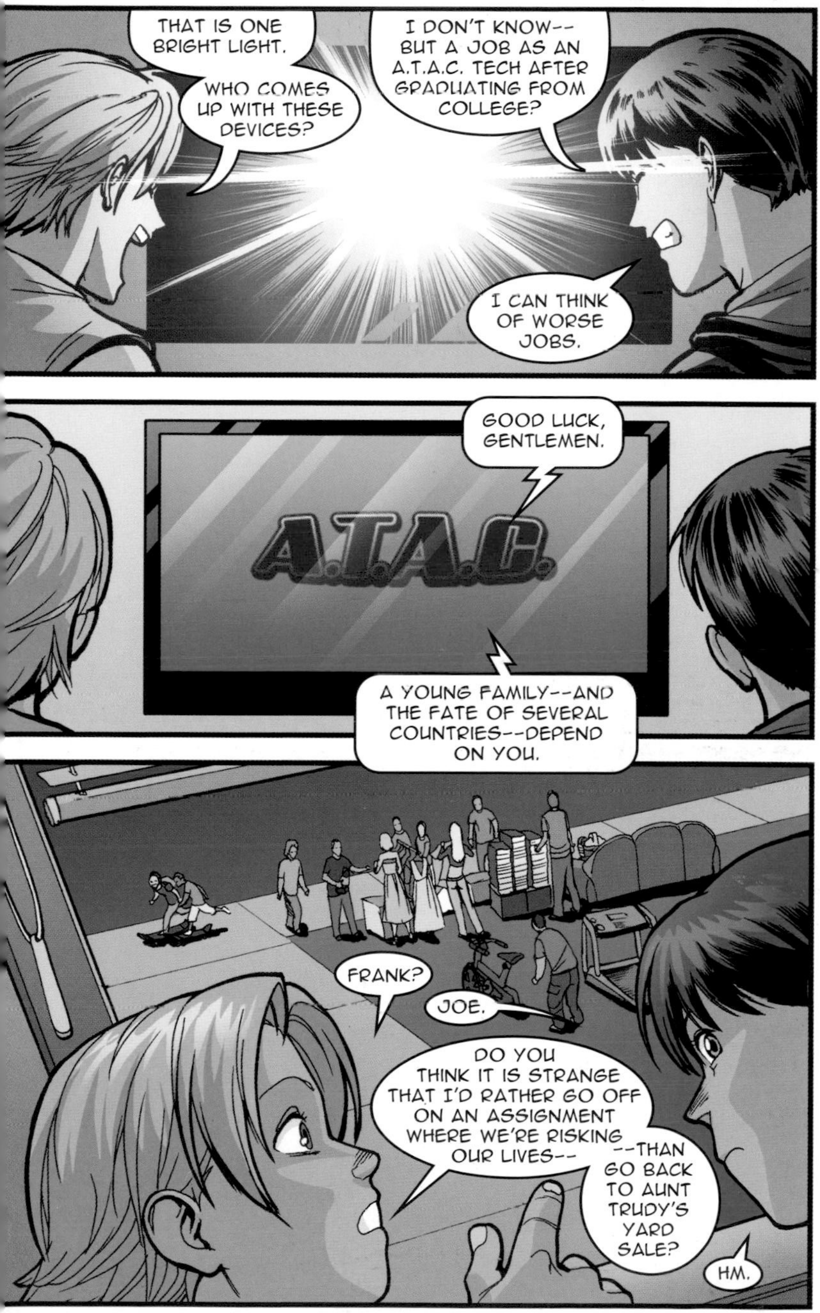
THAT IS ONE BRIGHT LIGHT.
WHO COMES UP WITH THESE DEVICES?
I DON'T KNOW-- BUT A JOB AS AN A.T.A.C. TECH AFTER GRADUATING FROM COLLEGE?
I CAN THINK OF WORSE JOBS.
GOOD LUCK, GENTLEMEN.
A.T.A.C.
A YOUNG FAMILY--AND THE FATE OF SEVERAL COUNTRIES--DEPEND ON YOU.
FRANK?
JOE.
DO YOU THINK IT IS STRANGE THAT I'D RATHER GO OFF ON AN ASSIGNMENT WHERE WE'RE RISKING OUR LIVES--
--THAN GO BACK TO AUNT TRUDY'S YARD SALE?
HM.

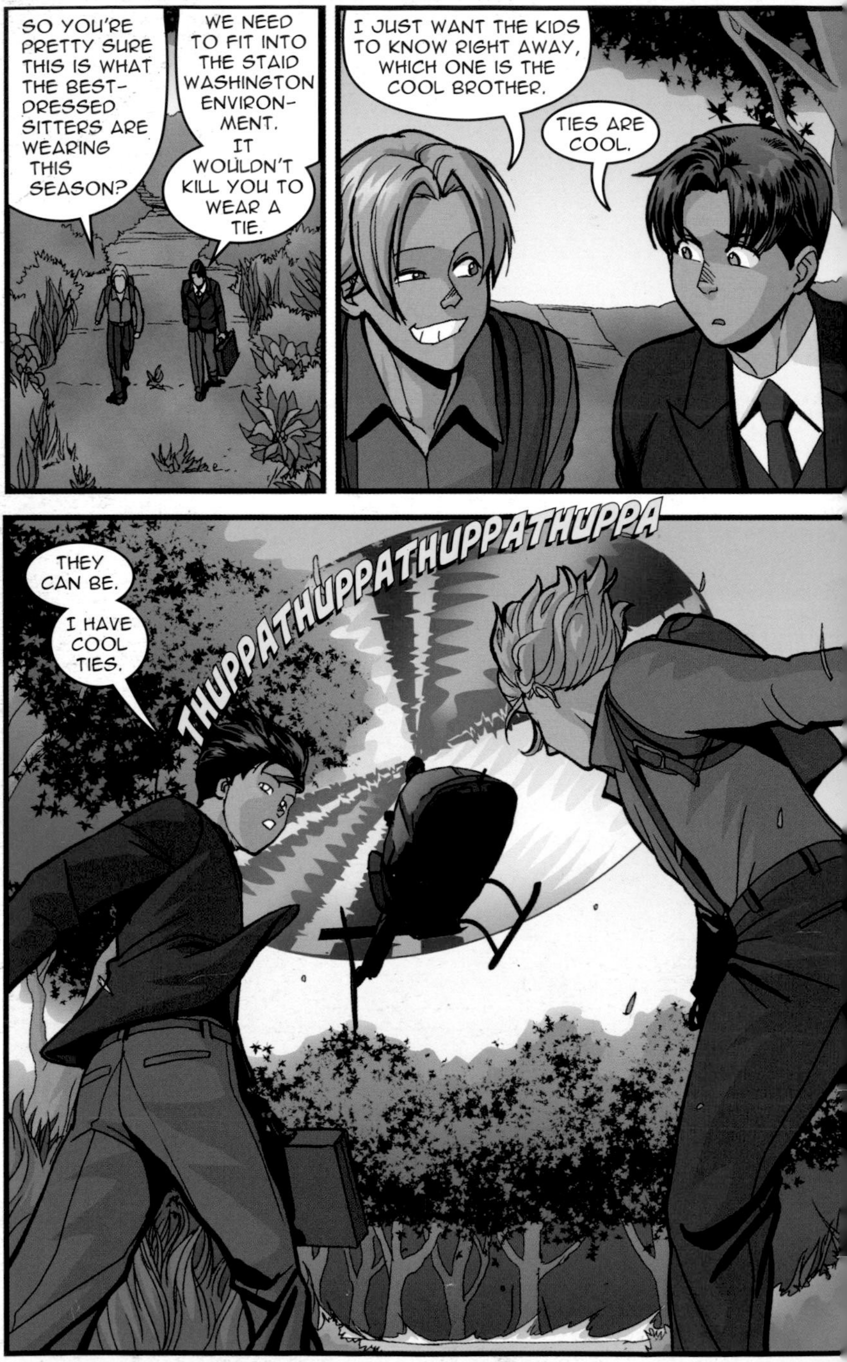
SO YOU'RE PRETTY SURE THIS IS WHAT THE BEST-DRESSED SITTERS ARE WEARING THIS SEASON?
WE NEED TO FIT INTO THE STAID WASHINGTON ENVIRONMENT.
IT WOULDN'T KILL YOU TO WEAR A TIE.
I JUST WANT THE KIDS TO KNOW RIGHT AWAY, WHICH ONE IS THE COOL BROTHER.
TIES ARE COOL.
THEY CAN BE.
I HAVE COOL TIES.
THUPPATHUPPATHUPPATHUPPA

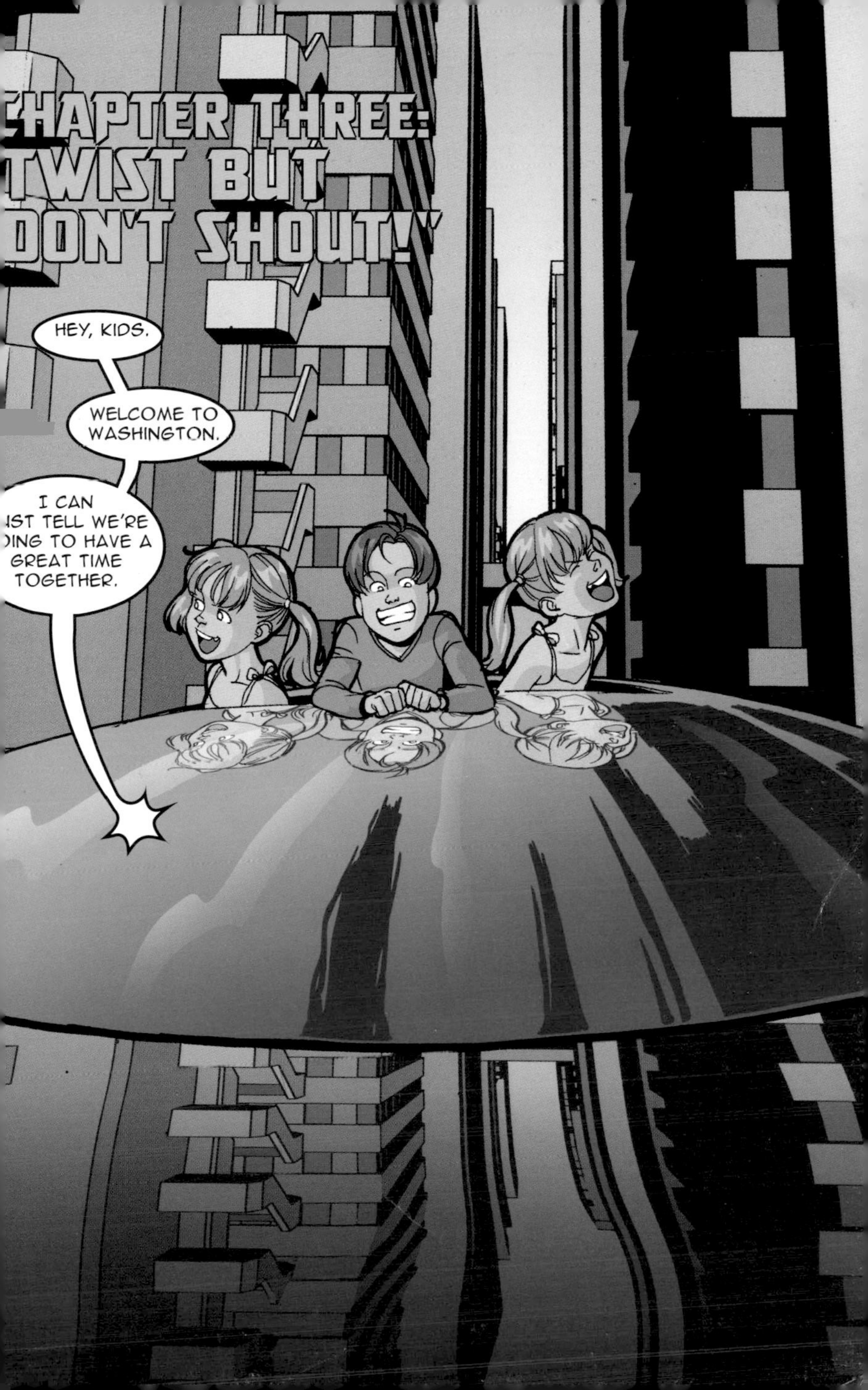
HAPTER THREE:
TWIST BUT
DON'T SHOUT!"
HEY, KIDS.
WELCOME TO WASHINGTON.
I CAN IST TELL WE'RE OING TO HAVE A GREAT TIME TOGETHER.

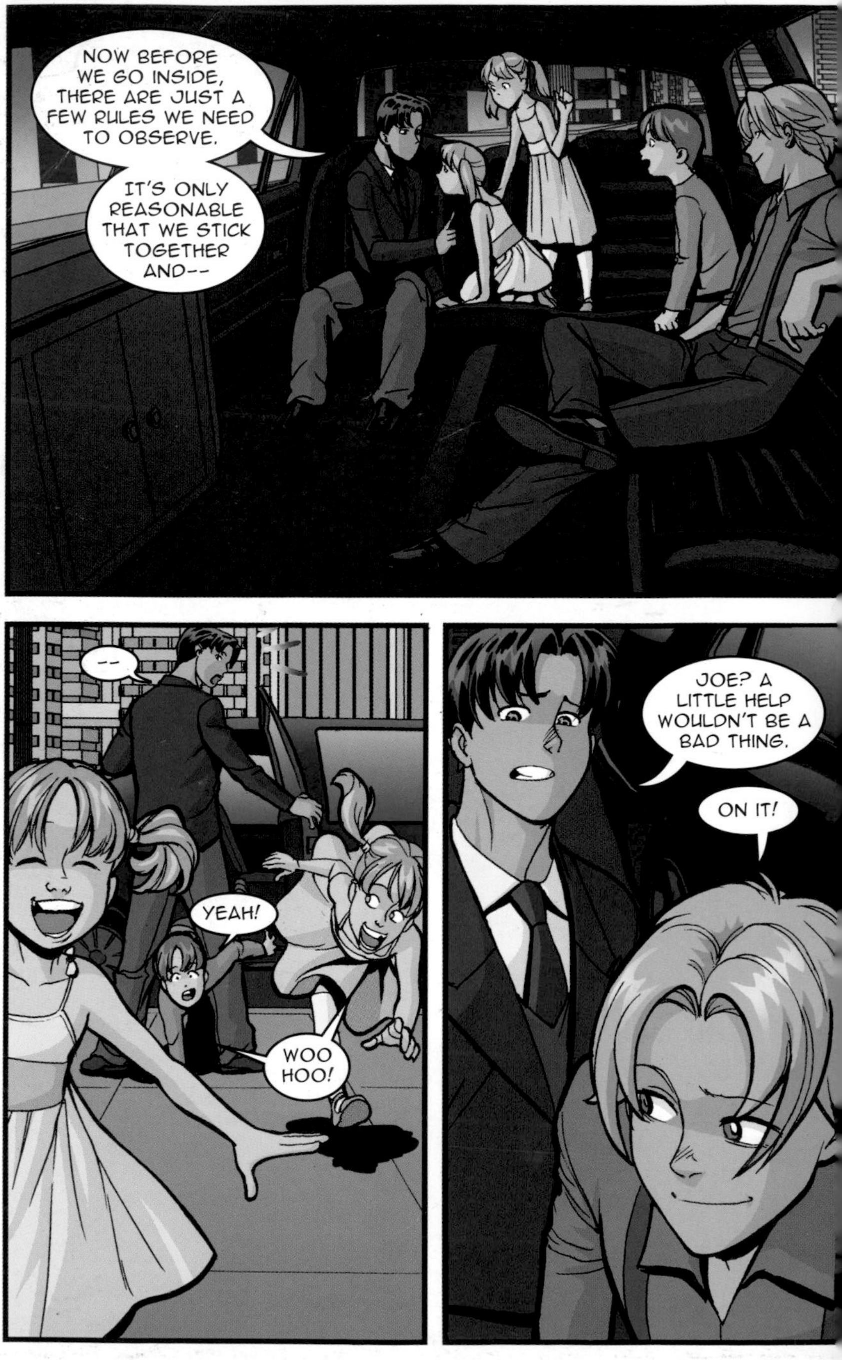
NOW BEFORE WE GO INSIDE, THERE ARE JUST A FEW RULES WE NEED TO OBSERVE.
IT'S ONLY REASONABLE THAT WE STICK TOGETHER AND--
--
YEAH!
WOO HOO!
JOE? A LITTLE HELP WOULDN'T BE A BAD THING.
ON IT!

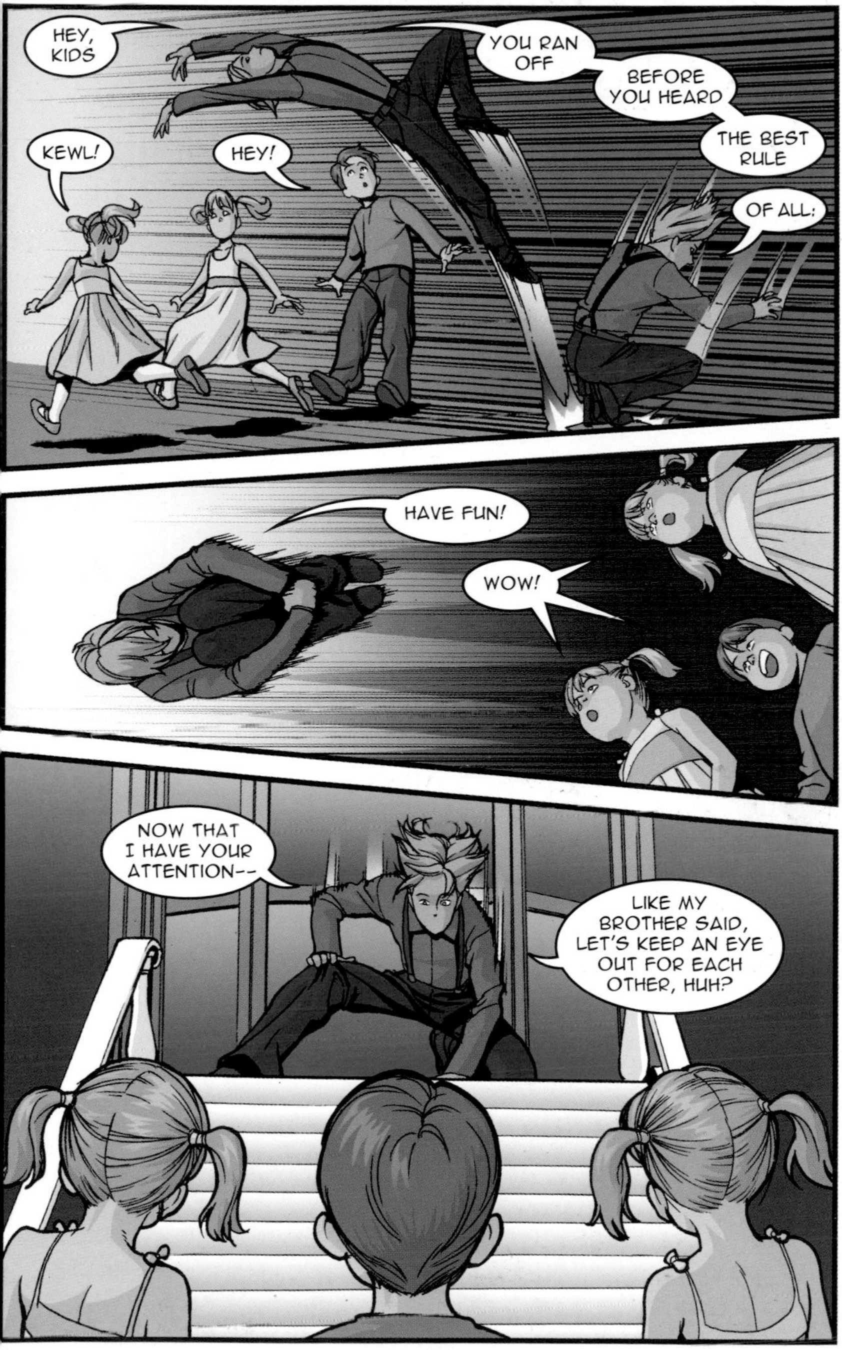
HEY, KIDS
YOU RAN OFF
BEFORE YOU HEARD
THE BEST RULE
OF ALL:
KEWL!
HEY!
HAVE FUN!
WOW!
NOW THAT I HAVE YOUR ATTENTION--
LIKE MY BROTHER SAID, LET'S KEEP AN EYE OUT FOR EACH OTHER, HUH?

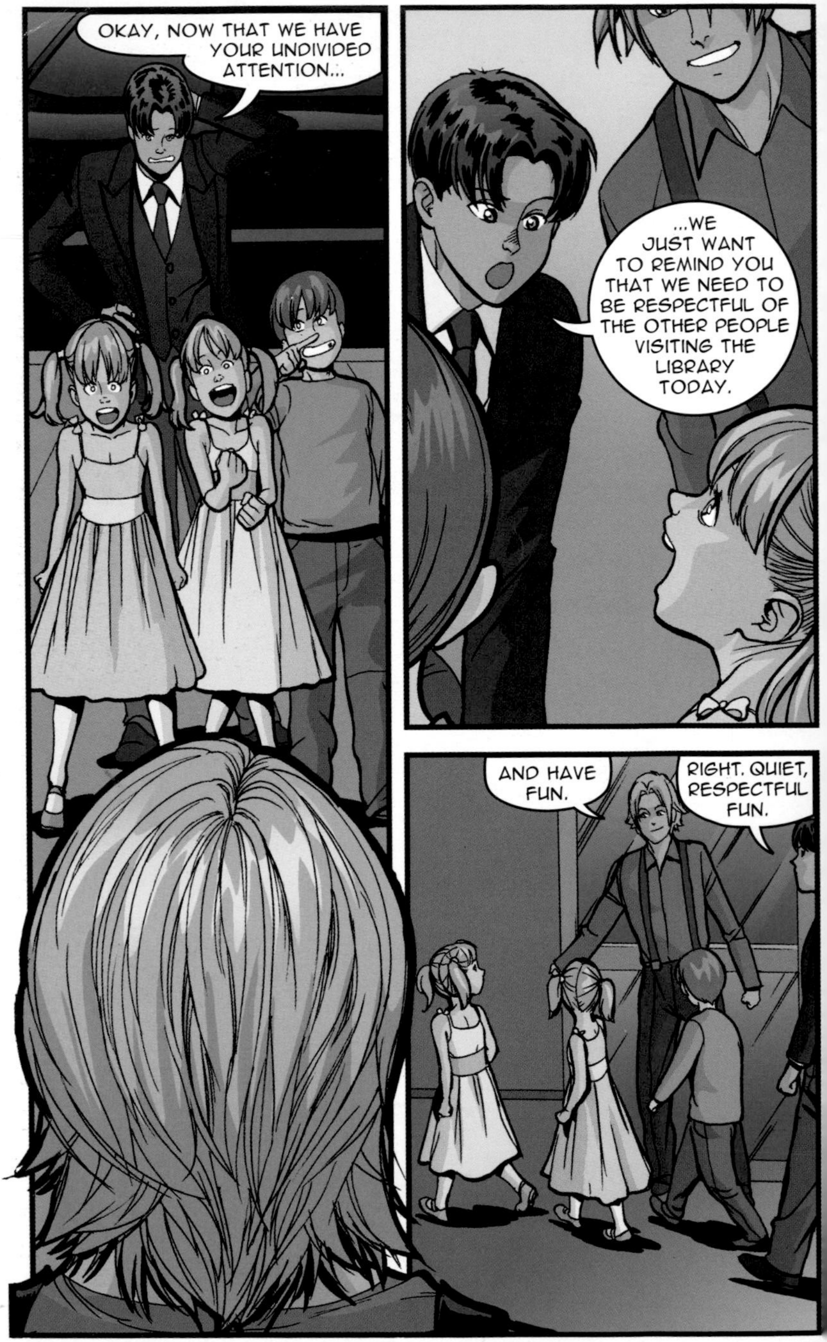
OKAY, NOW THAT WE HAVE YOUR UNDIVIDED ATTENTION...
...WE JUST WANT TO REMIND YOU THAT WE NEED TO BE RESPECTFUL OF THE OTHER PEOPLE VISITING THE LIBRARY TODAY.
AND HAVE FUN.
RIGHT. QUIET, RESPECTFUL FUN.

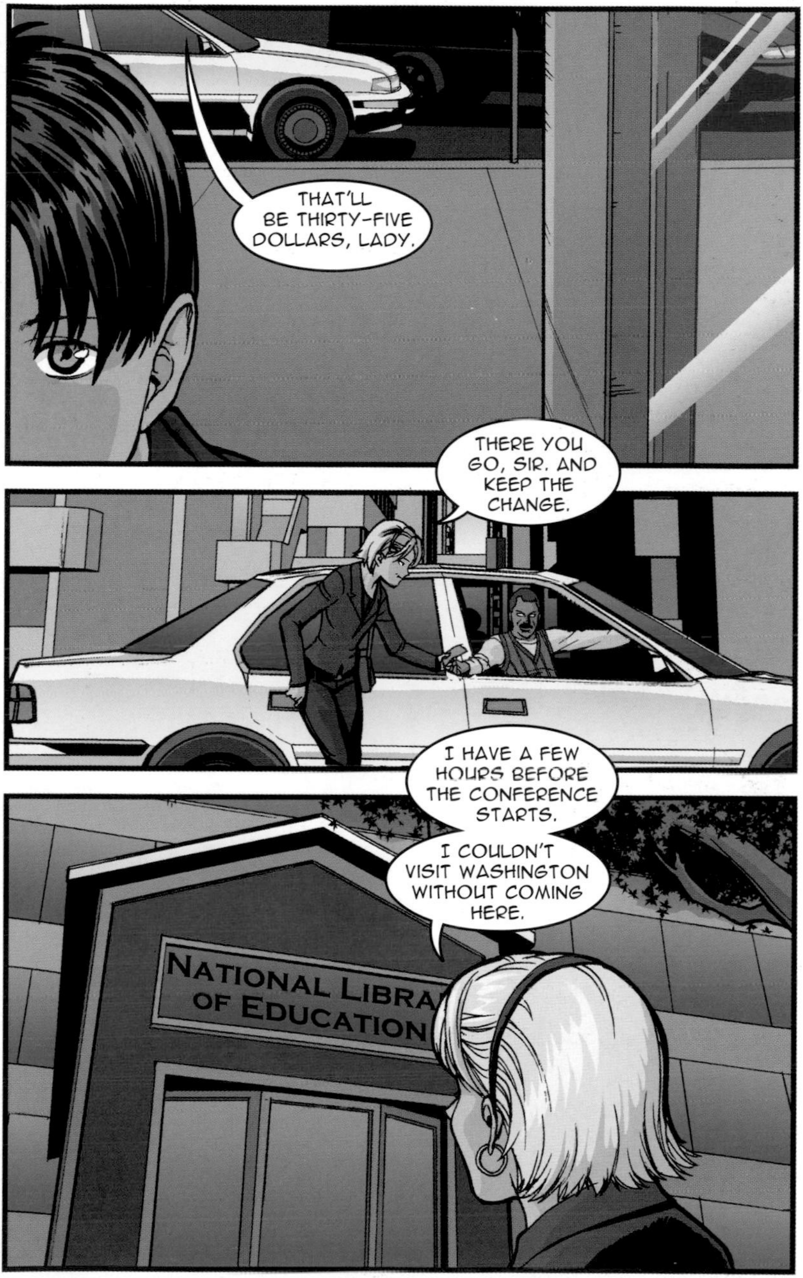
THAT'LL BE THIRTY-FIVE DOLLARS, LADY.
THERE YOU GO, SIR. AND KEEP THE CHANGE.
I HAVE A FEW HOURS BEFORE THE CONFERENCE STARTS.
I COULDN'T VISIT WASHINGTON WITHOUT COMING HERE.
NATIONAL LIBRA
OF EDUCATION

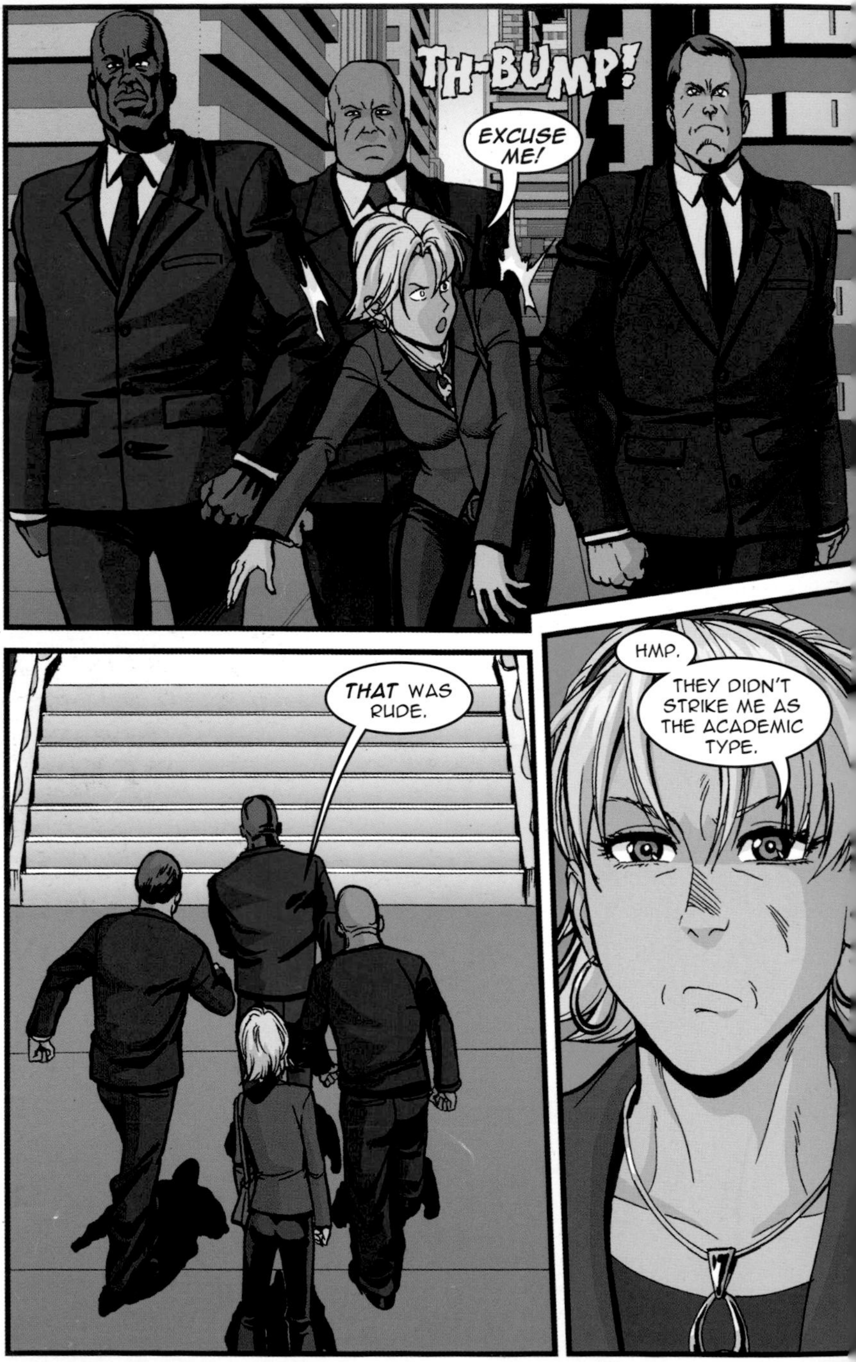
TH-BUMP!
EXCUSE ME!
THAT WAS RUDE.
HMP.
THEY DIDN'T STRIKE ME AS THE ACADEMIC TYPE.

INTERESTING. THE MAIN LOBBY IS TWO FLIGHTS DOWN.

INTERESTING TO WHO?

DO THEY HAVE COMIC-BOOKS HERE?

THAT'S A STUPID QUES-TION.

YEAH. BUT DO THEY?

HELLO.

HI, WE'RE HERE FOR THE LIBRARY TOUR.

UNDER THE NAME "HARDY." PARTY OF FIVE?

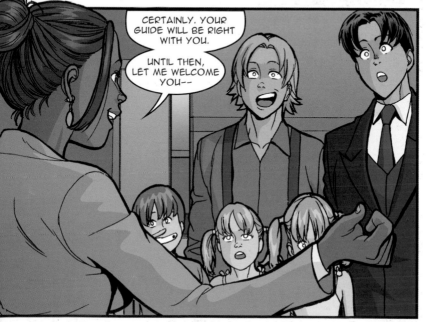

CERTAINLY. YOUR GUIDE WILL BE RIGHT WITH YOU.

UNTIL THEN, LET ME WELCOME YOU--

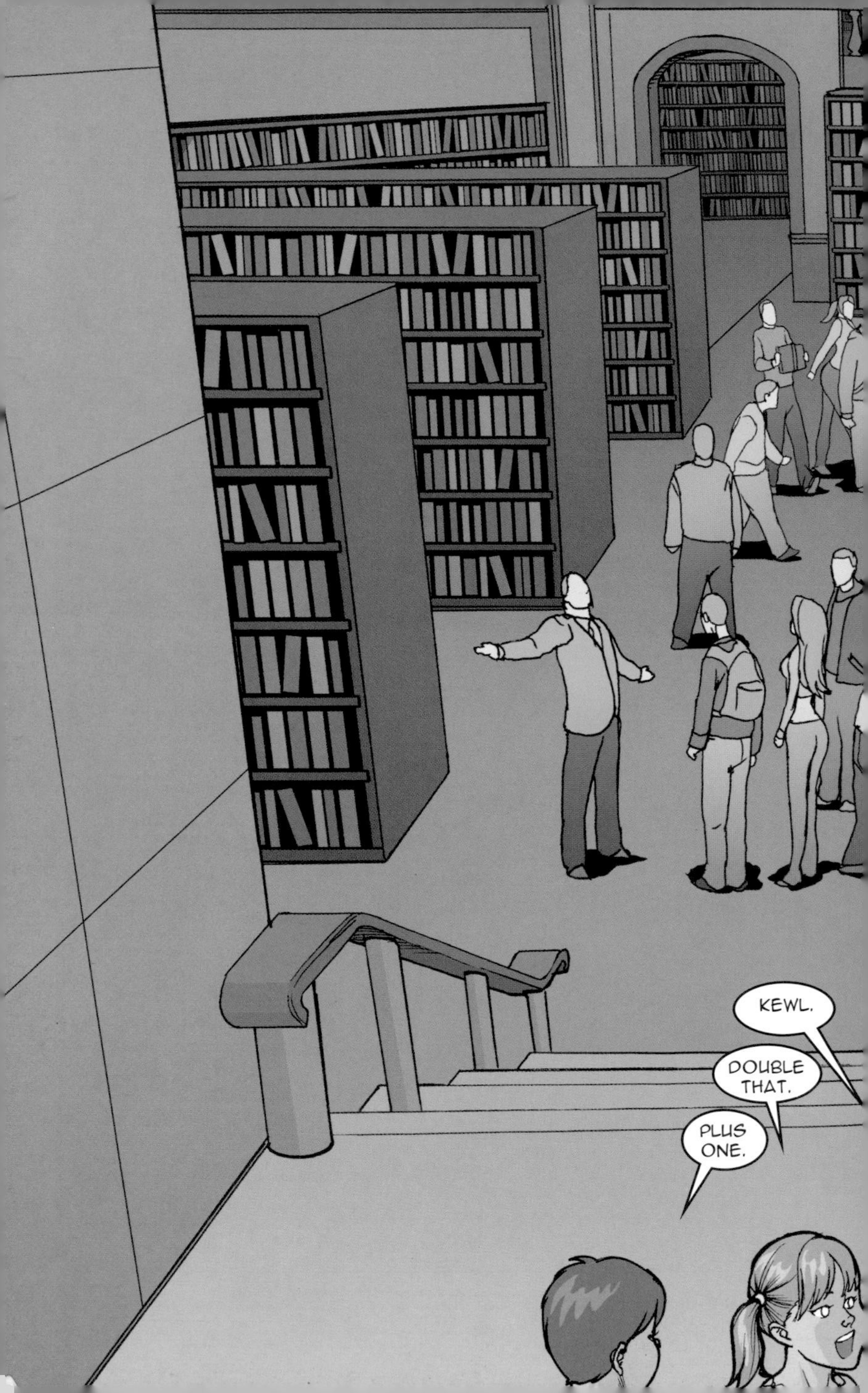
KEWL.
DOUBLE THAT.
PLUS ONE.

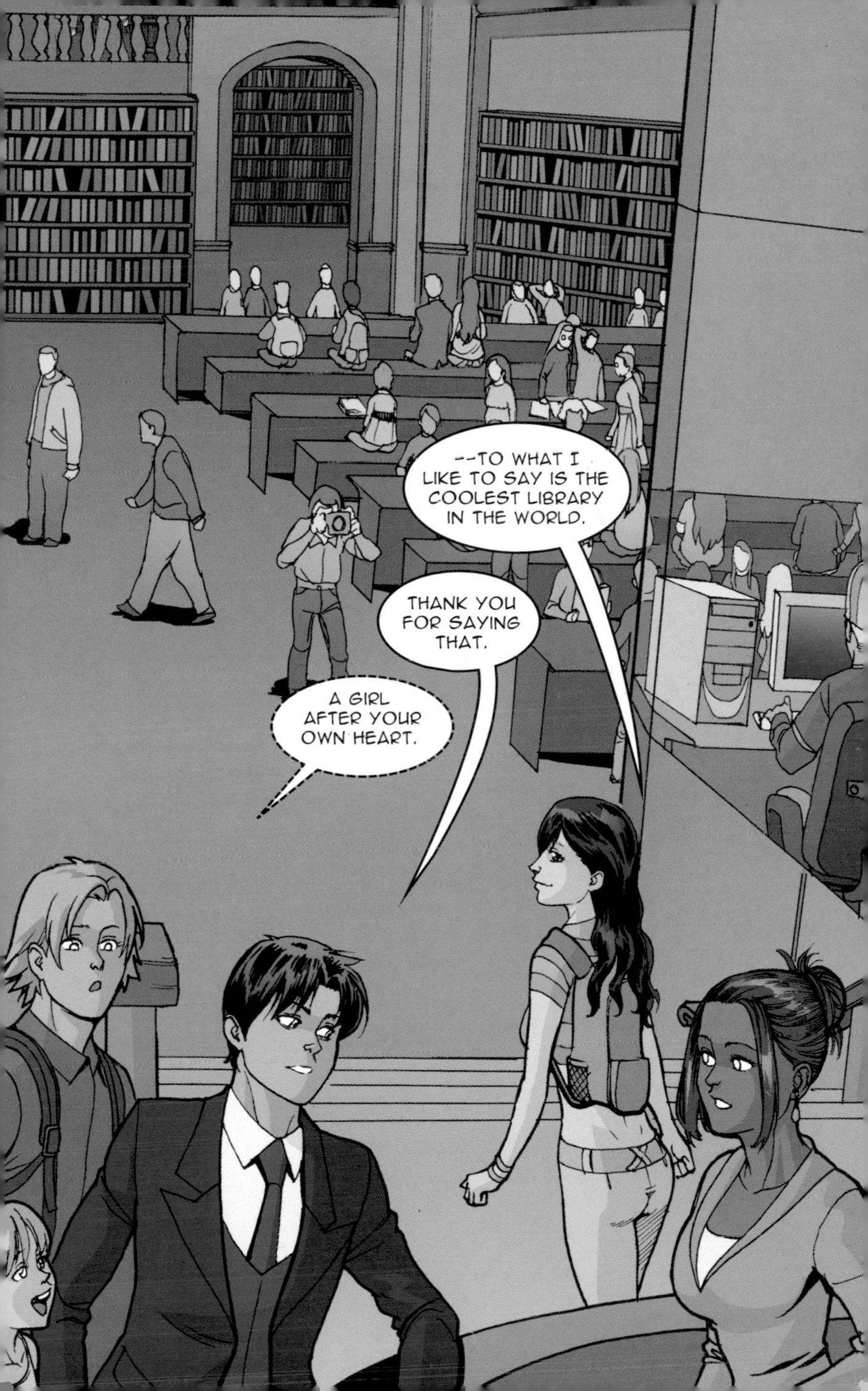
--TO WHAT I LIKE TO SAY IS THE COOLEST LIBRARY IN THE WORLD.
THANK YOU FOR SAYING THAT.
A GIRL AFTER YOUR OWN HEART.

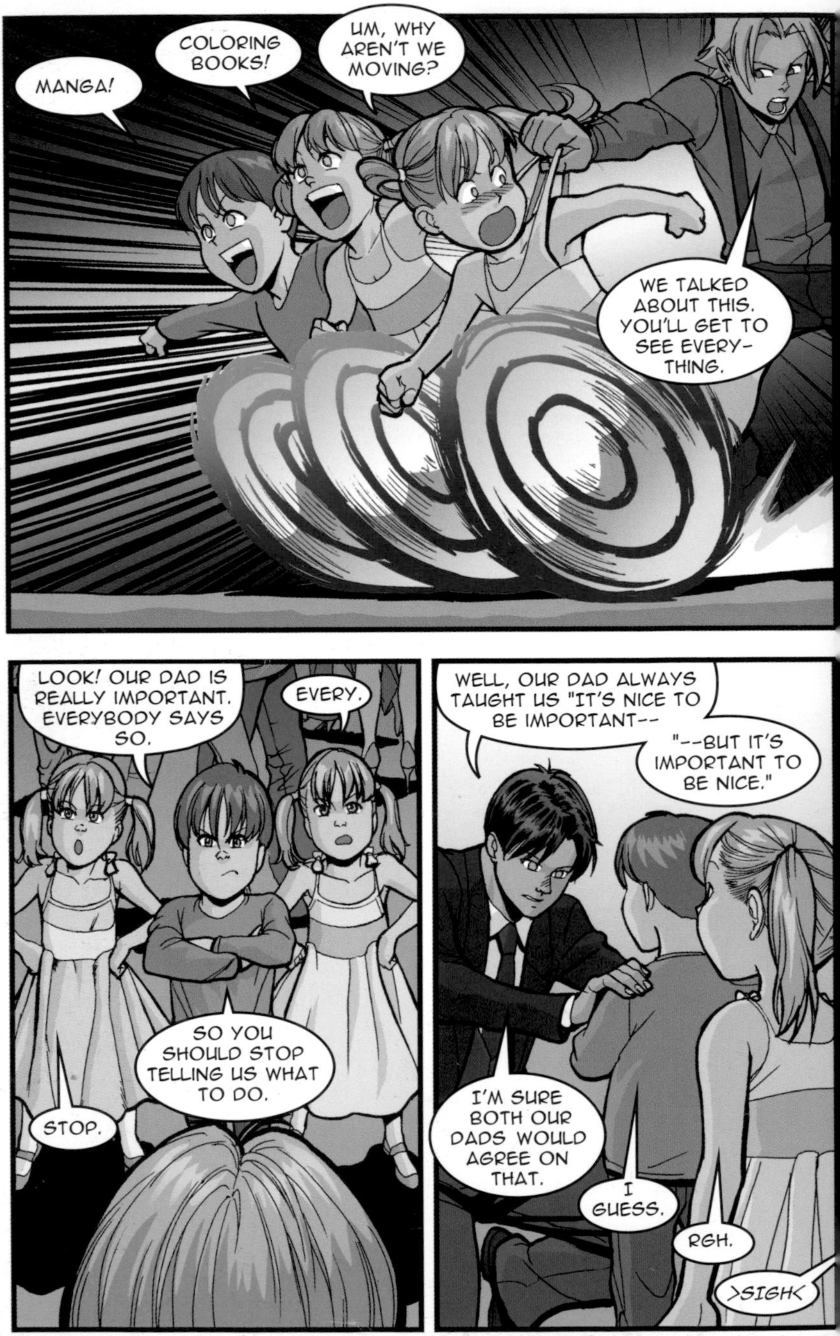
MANGA!
COLORING BOOKS!
UM, WHY AREN'T WE MOVING?
WE TALKED ABOUT THIS. YOU'LL GET TO SEE EVERY-THING.
LOOK! OUR DAD IS REALLY IMPORTANT. EVERYBODY SAYS SO.
EVERY.
STOP.
SO YOU SHOULD STOP TELLING US WHAT TO DO.
WELL, OUR DAD ALWAYS TAUGHT US "IT'S NICE TO BE IMPORTANT--
"--BUT IT'S IMPORTANT TO BE NICE."
I'M SURE BOTH OUR DADS WOULD AGREE ON THAT.
I GUESS.
RGH.
>SIGH<

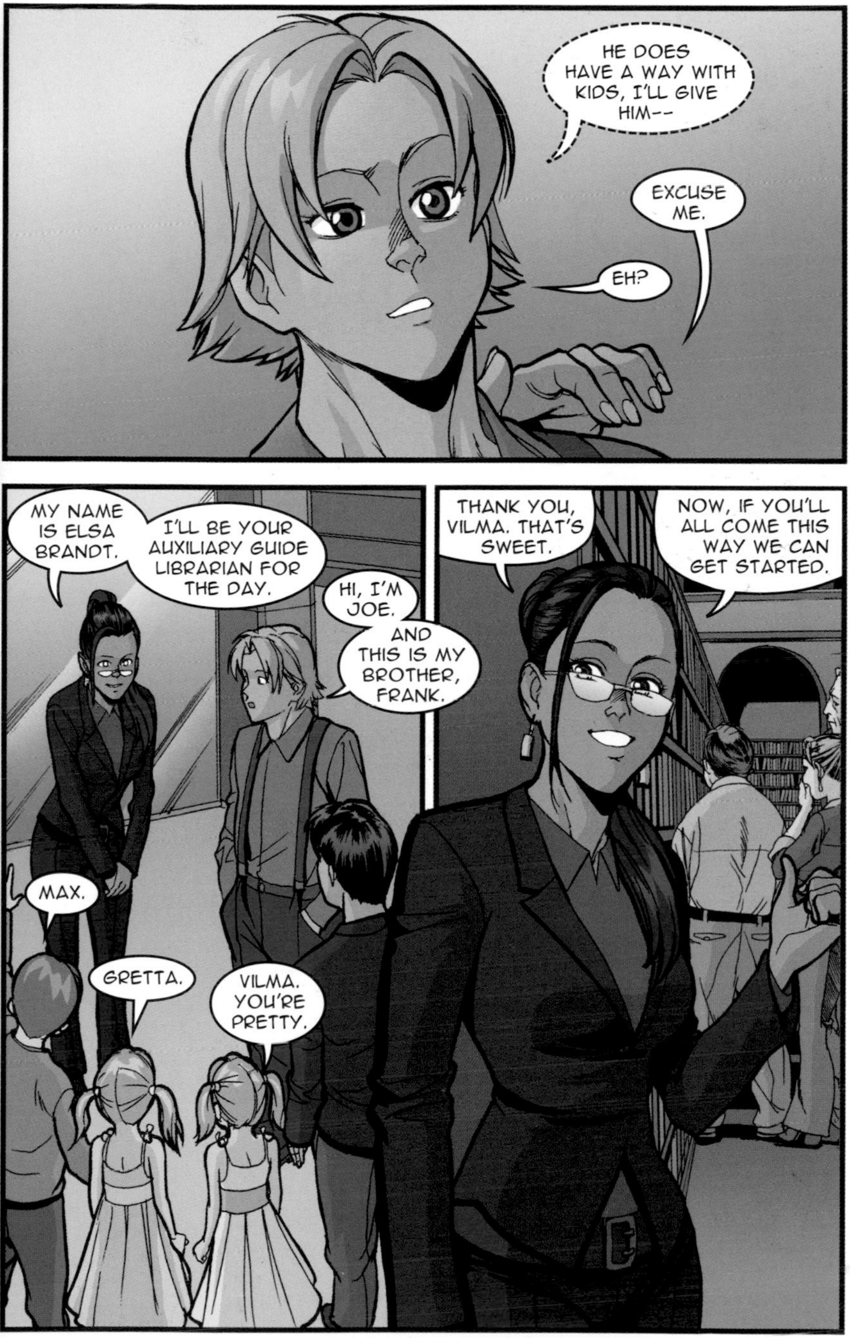
HE DOES HAVE A WAY WITH KIDS, I'LL GIVE HIM--
EXCUSE ME.
EH?
MY NAME IS ELSA BRANDT.
I'LL BE YOUR AUXILIARY GUIDE LIBRARIAN FOR THE DAY.
HI, I'M JOE.
AND THIS IS MY BROTHER, FRANK.
MAX.
GRETTA.
VILMA. YOU'RE PRETTY.
THANK YOU, VILMA. THAT'S SWEET.
NOW, IF YOU'LL ALL COME THIS WAY WE CAN GET STARTED.

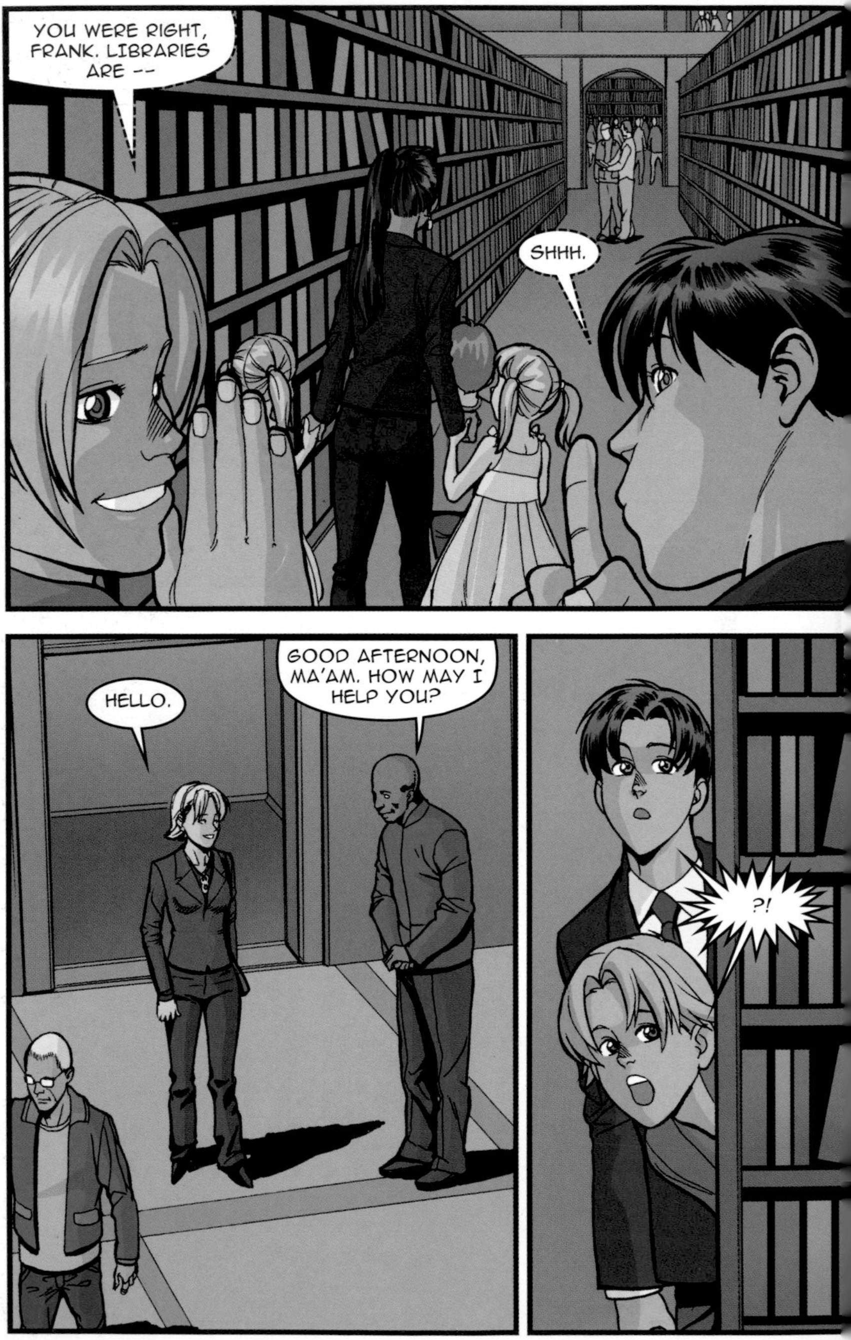
YOU WERE RIGHT, FRANK. LIBRARIES ARE --
SHHH.
HELLO.
GOOD AFTERNOON, MA'AM. HOW MAY I HELP YOU?
?!

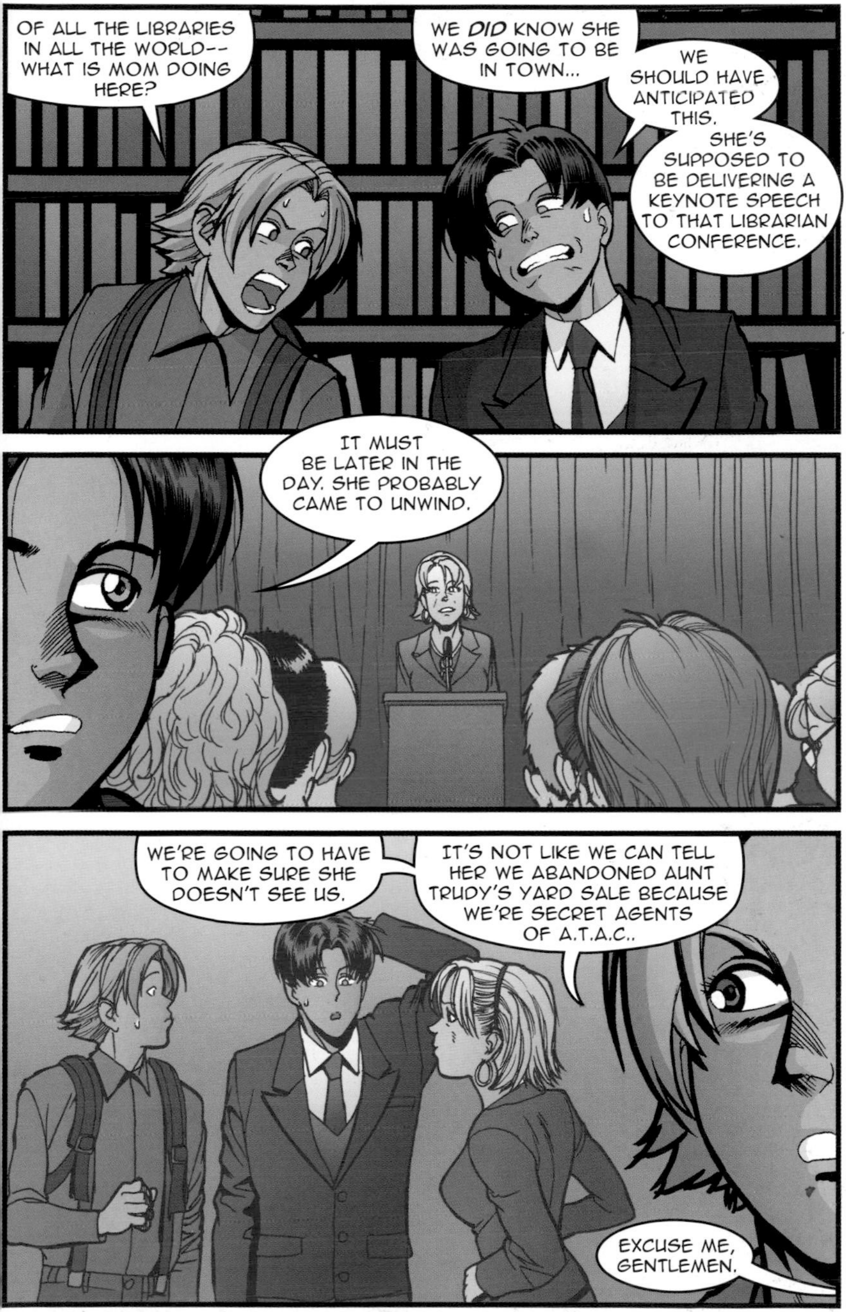
OF ALL THE LIBRARIES IN ALL THE WORLD-- WHAT IS MOM DOING HERE?
WE *DID* KNOW SHE WAS GOING TO BE IN TOWN...
WE SHOULD HAVE ANTICIPATED THIS.
SHE'S SUPPOSED TO BE DELIVERING A KEYNOTE SPEECH TO THAT LIBRARIAN CONFERENCE.
IT MUST BE LATER IN THE DAY. SHE PROBABLY CAME TO UNWIND.
WE'RE GOING TO HAVE TO MAKE SURE SHE DOESN'T SEE US.
IT'S NOT LIKE WE CAN TELL HER WE ABANDONED AUNT TRUDY'S YARD SALE BECAUSE WE'RE SECRET AGENTS OF A.T.A.C..
EXCUSE ME, GENTLEMEN.

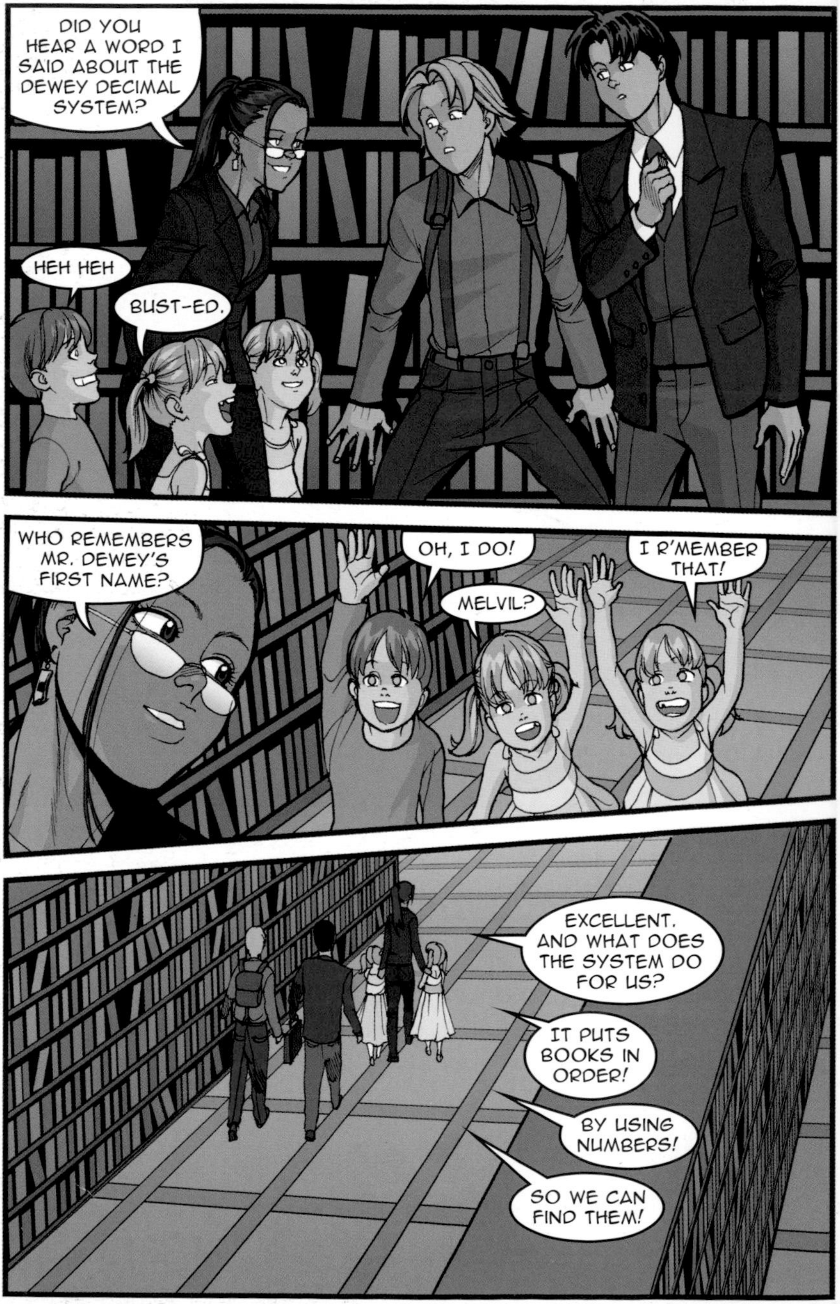
DID YOU HEAR A WORD I SAID ABOUT THE DEWEY DECIMAL SYSTEM?
HEH HEH
BUST-ED.
WHO REMEMBERS MR. DEWEY'S FIRST NAME?
OH, I DO!
MELVIL?
I R'MEMBER THAT!
EXCELLENT. AND WHAT DOES THE SYSTEM DO FOR US?
IT PUTS BOOKS IN ORDER!
BY USING NUMBERS!
SO WE CAN FIND THEM!

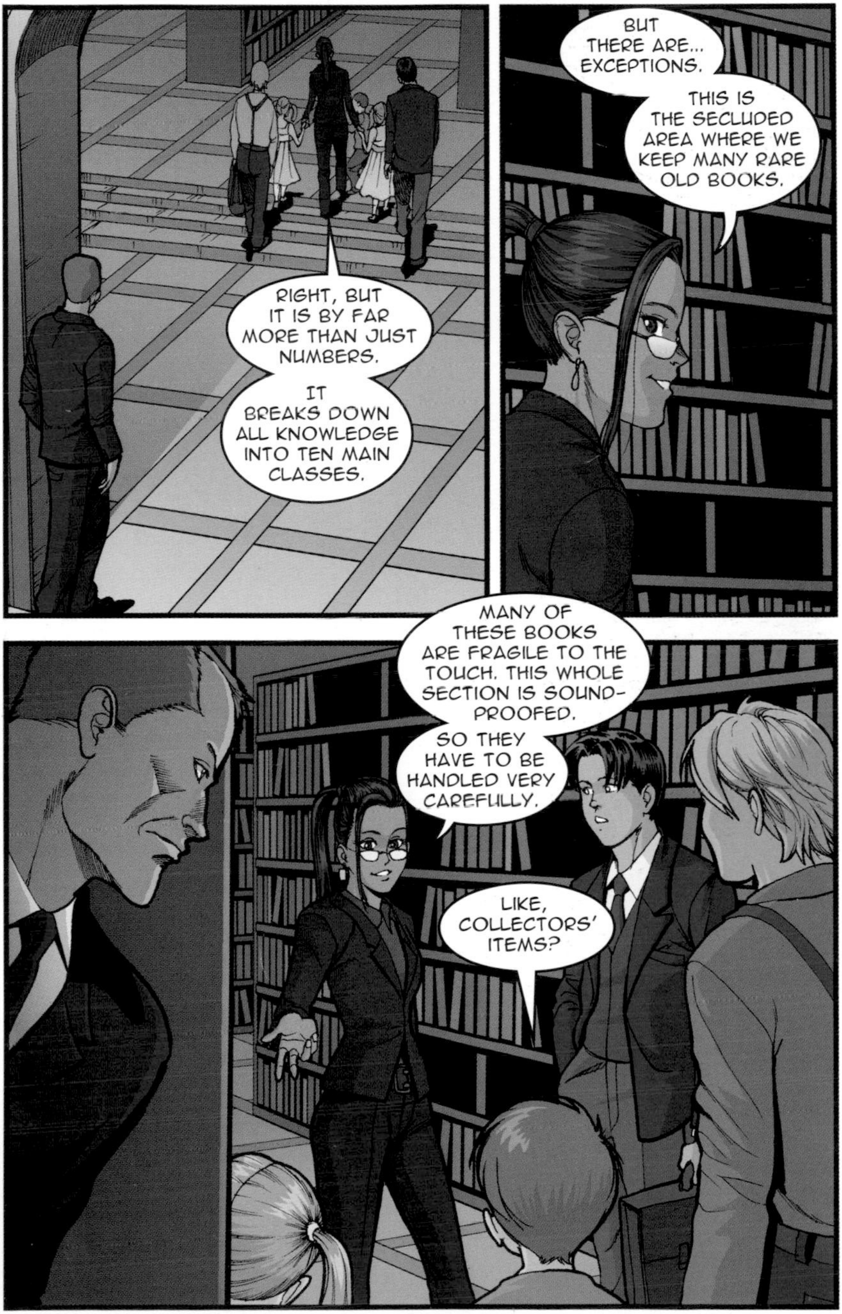
RIGHT, BUT IT IS BY FAR MORE THAN JUST NUMBERS.
IT BREAKS DOWN ALL KNOWLEDGE INTO TEN MAIN CLASSES.
BUT THERE ARE... EXCEPTIONS.
THIS IS THE SECLUDED AREA WHERE WE KEEP MANY RARE OLD BOOKS.
MANY OF THESE BOOKS ARE FRAGILE TO THE TOUCH. THIS WHOLE SECTION IS SOUND-PROOFED.
SO THEY HAVE TO BE HANDLED VERY CAREFULLY.
LIKE, COLLECTORS' ITEMS?

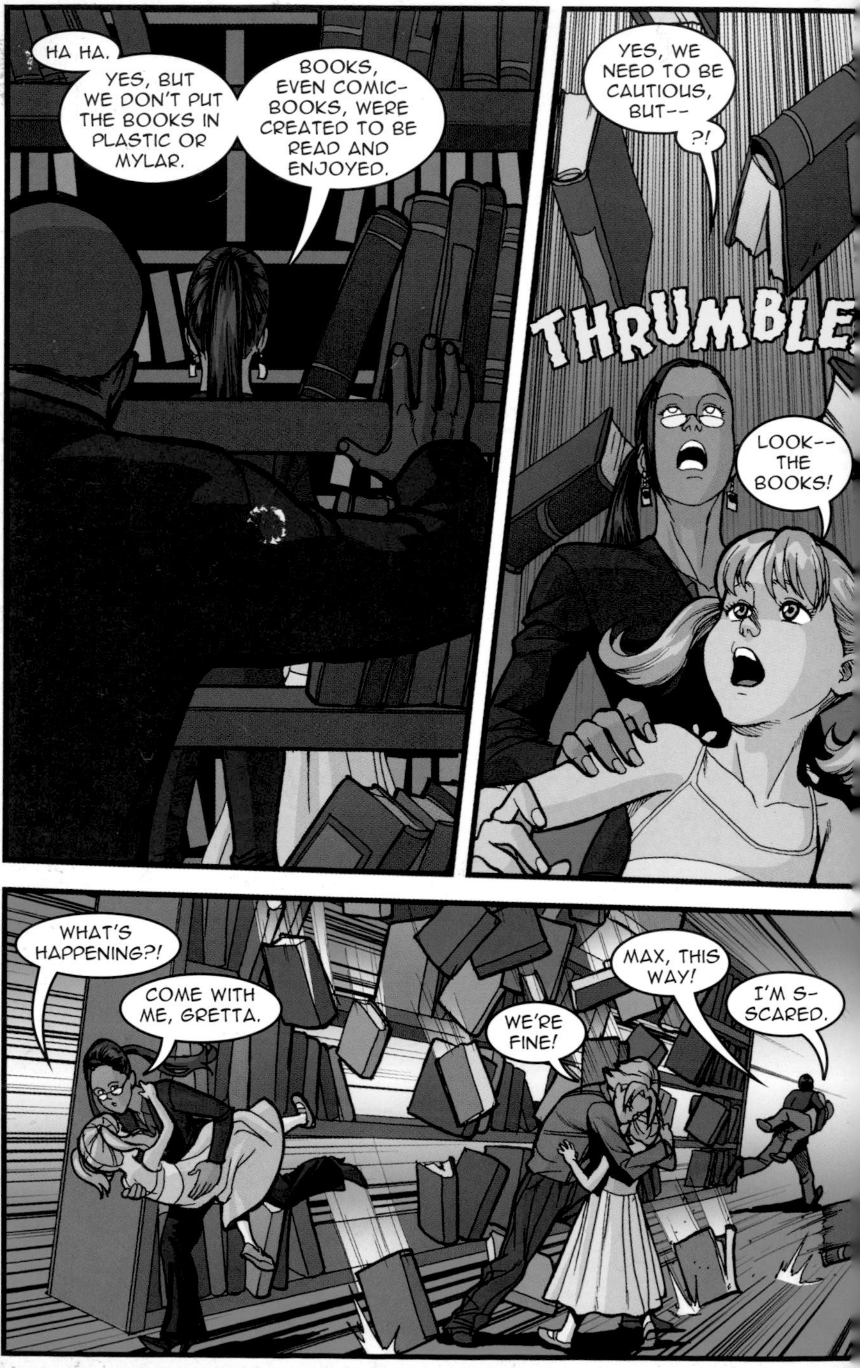
HA HA.
YES, BUT WE DON'T PUT THE BOOKS IN PLASTIC OR MYLAR.
BOOKS, EVEN COMIC-BOOKS, WERE CREATED TO BE READ AND ENJOYED.
YES, WE NEED TO BE CAUTIOUS, BUT--
?!
THRUMBLE
LOOK-- THE BOOKS!
WHAT'S HAPPENING?!
COME WITH ME, GRETTA.
WE'RE FINE!
MAX, THIS WAY!
I'M S-SCARED.

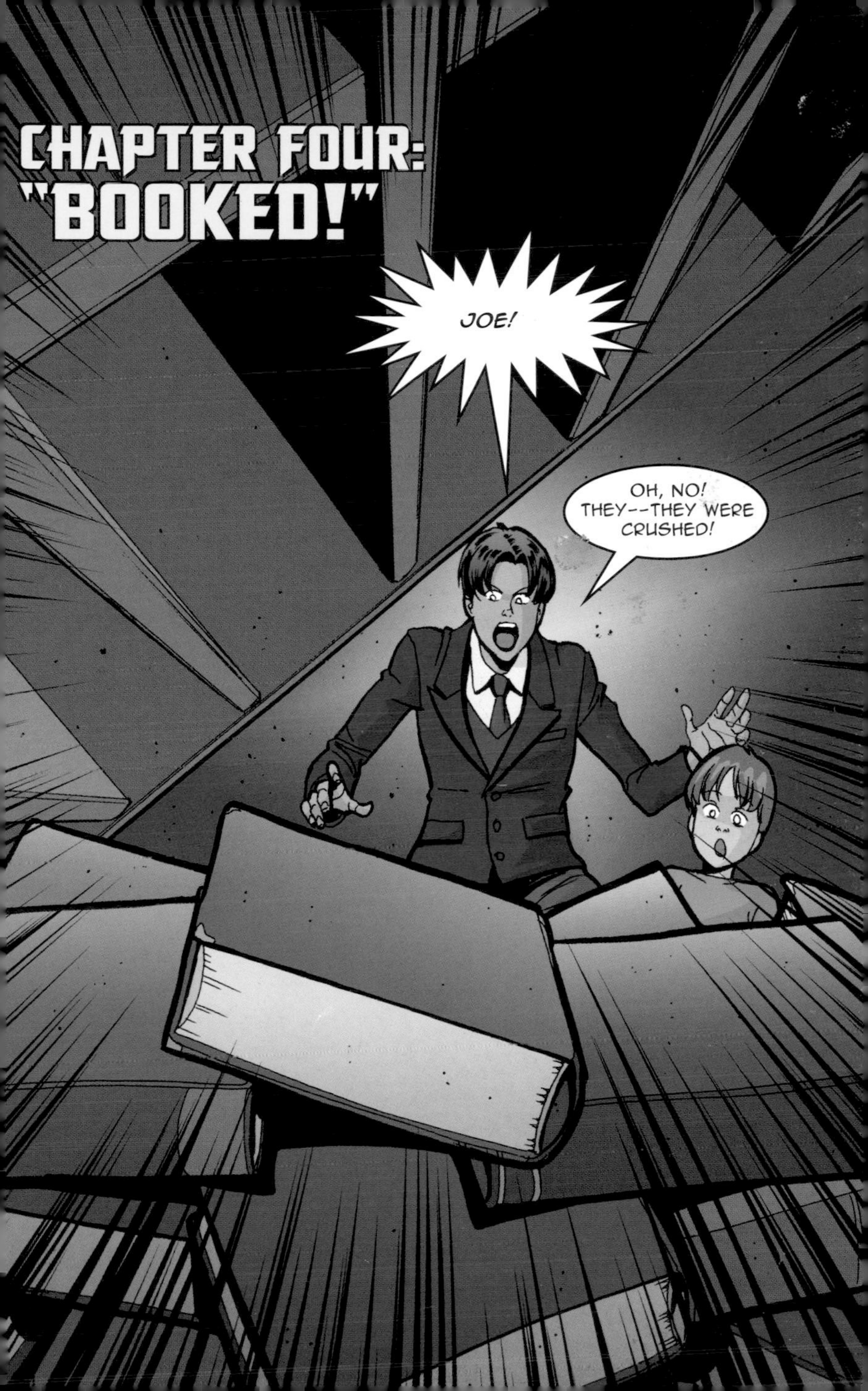
CHAPTER FOUR:
"BOOKED!"
JOE!
OH, NO! THEY--THEY WERE CRUSHED!

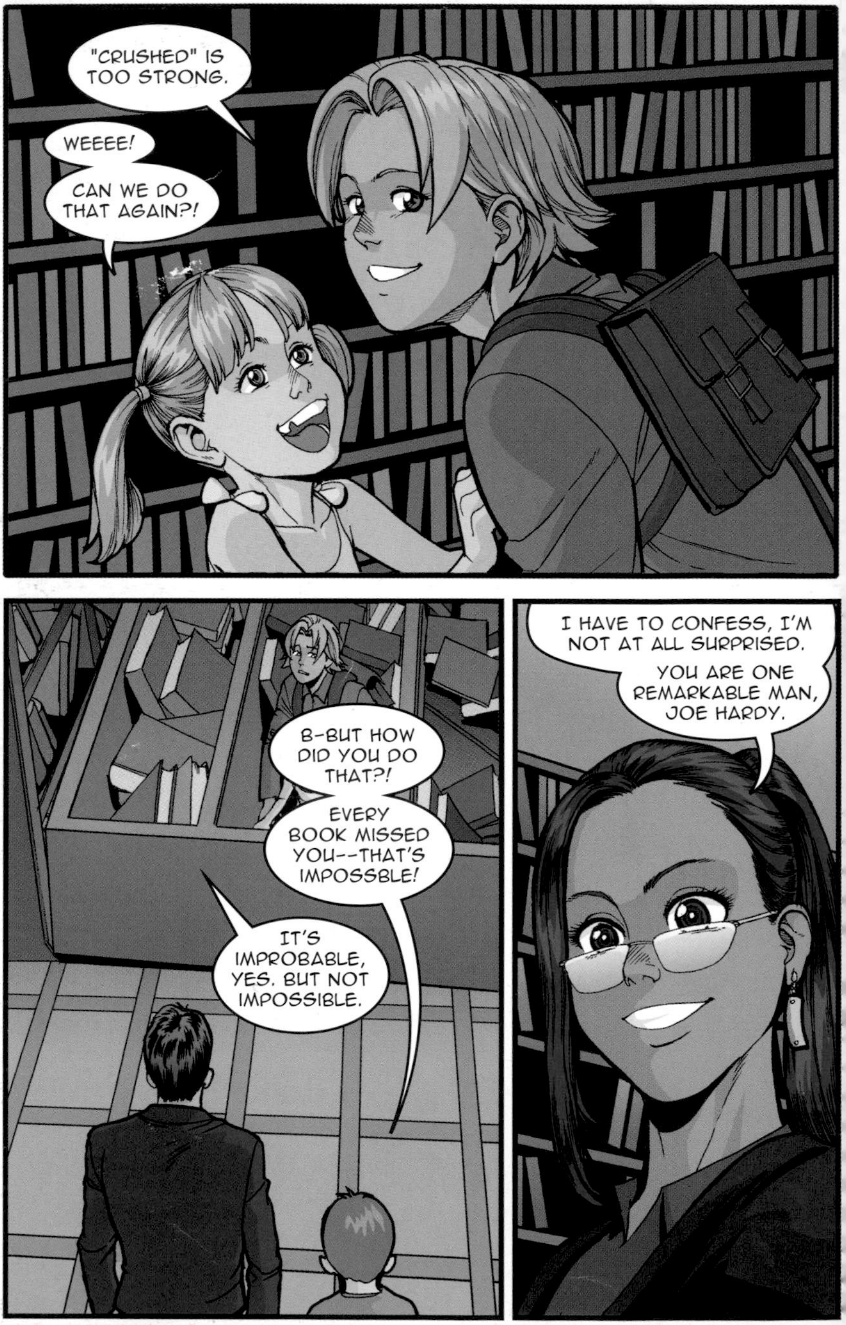
"CRUSHED" IS TOO STRONG.
WEEEE!
CAN WE DO THAT AGAIN?!
B-BUT HOW DID YOU DO THAT?!
EVERY BOOK MISSED YOU--THAT'S IMPOSSBLE!
IT'S IMPROBABLE, YES. BUT NOT IMPOSSIBLE.
I HAVE TO CONFESS, I'M NOT AT ALL SURPRISED.
YOU ARE ONE REMARKABLE MAN, JOE HARDY.

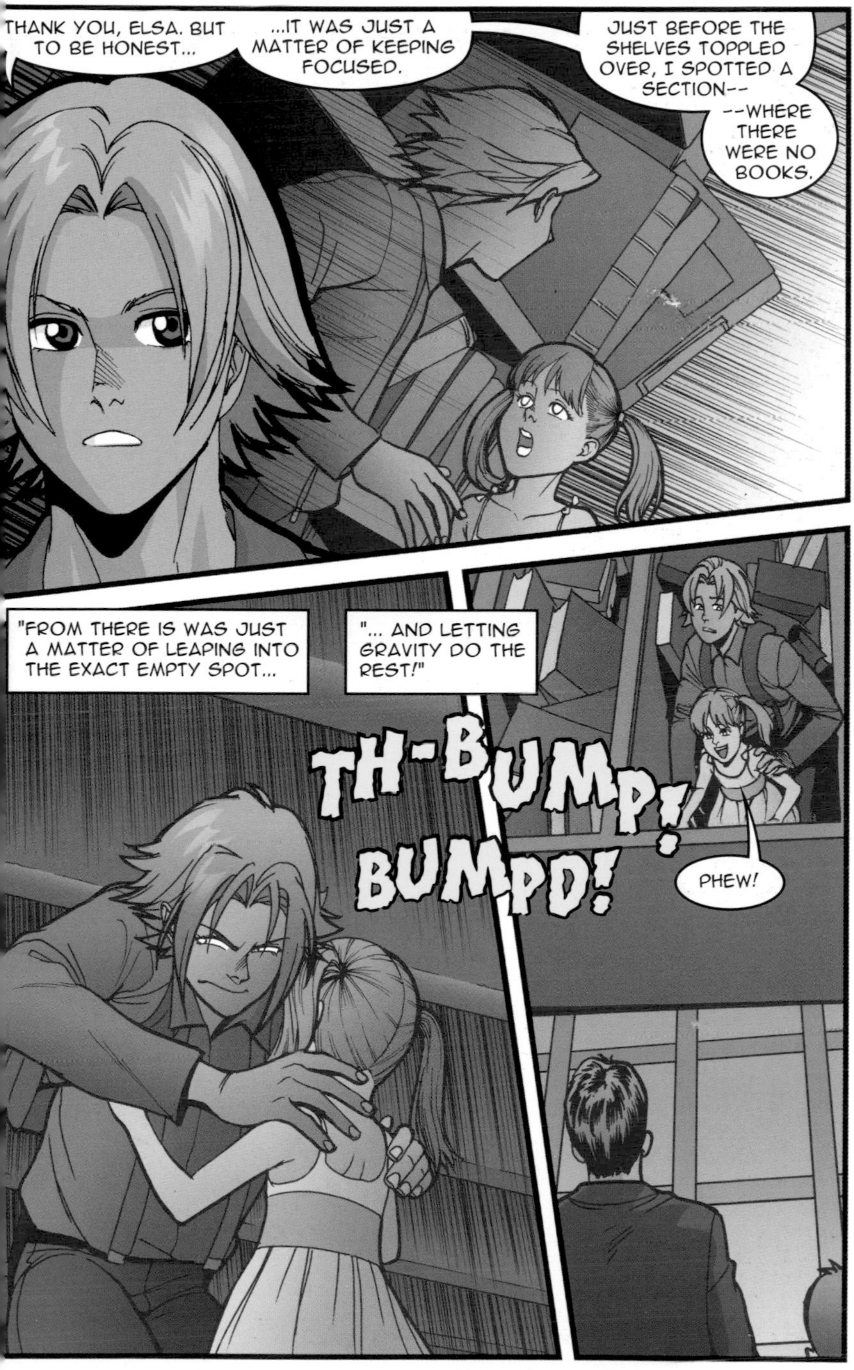
THANK YOU, ELSA. BUT TO BE HONEST...
...IT WAS JUST A MATTER OF KEEPING FOCUSED.
JUST BEFORE THE SHELVES TOPPLED OVER, I SPOTTED A SECTION--
--WHERE THERE WERE NO BOOKS.
"FROM THERE IS WAS JUST A MATTER OF LEAPING INTO THE EXACT EMPTY SPOT...
"... AND LETTING GRAVITY DO THE REST!"
TH-BUMP!
BUMPD!
PHEW!

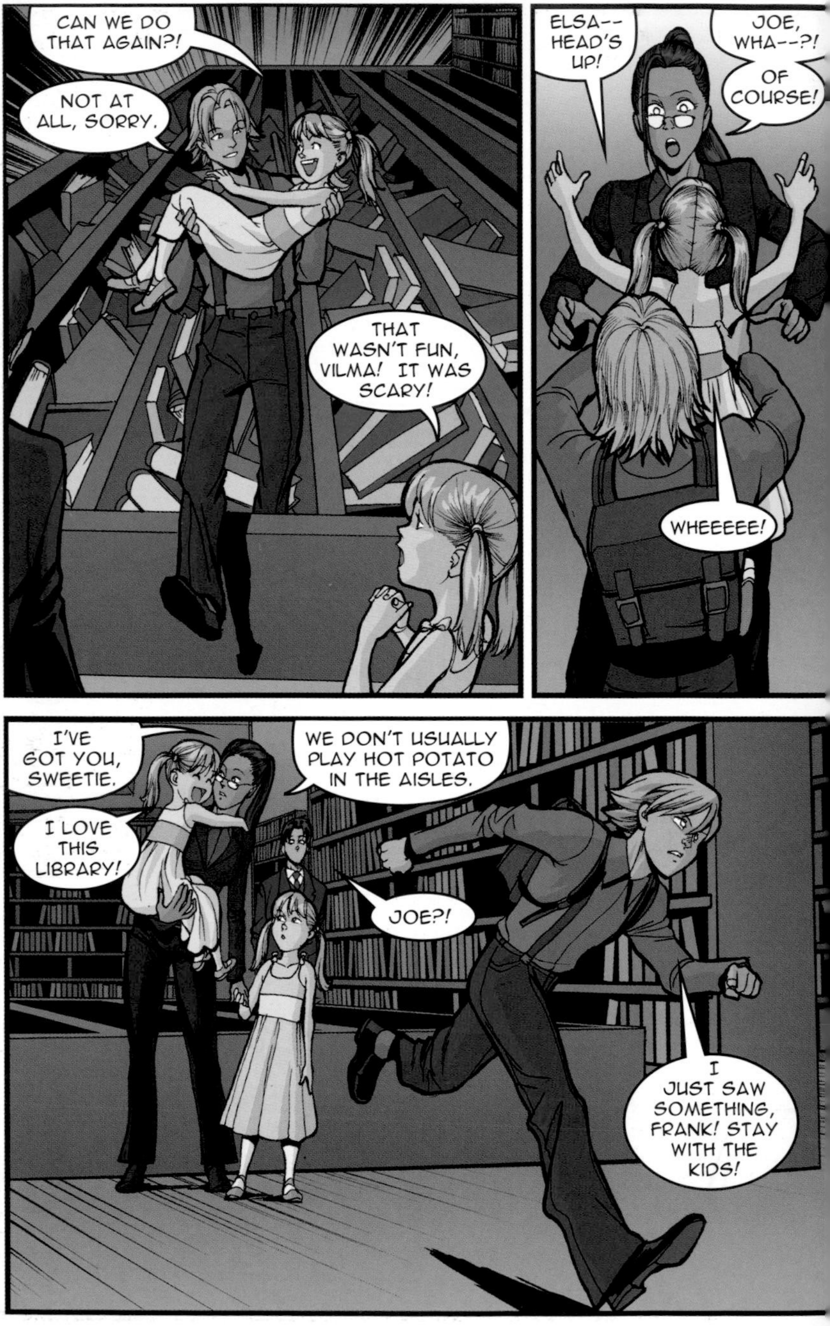
CAN WE DO THAT AGAIN?!
NOT AT ALL, SORRY.
THAT WASN'T FUN, VILMA! IT WAS SCARY!
ELSA-- HEAD'S UP!
JOE, WHA--?!
OF COURSE!
WHEEEEE!
I'VE GOT YOU, SWEETIE.
I LOVE THIS LIBRARY!
WE DON'T USUALLY PLAY HOT POTATO IN THE AISLES.
JOE?!
I JUST SAW SOMETHING, FRANK! STAY WITH THE KIDS!

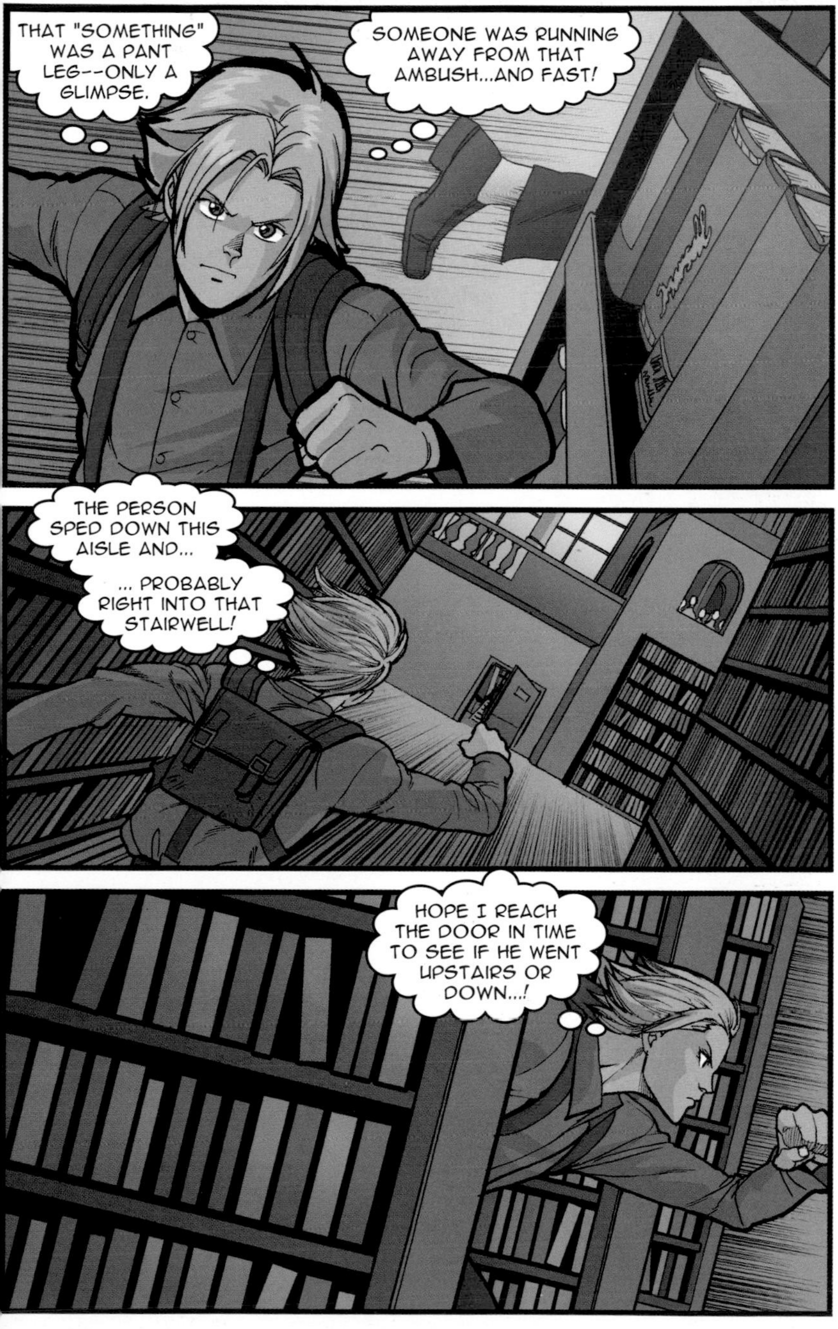
THAT "SOMETHING" WAS A PANT LEG--ONLY A GLIMPSE.
SOMEONE WAS RUNNING AWAY FROM THAT AMBUSH...AND FAST!
THE PERSON SPED DOWN THIS AISLE AND...
... PROBABLY RIGHT INTO THAT STAIRWELL!
HOPE I REACH THE DOOR IN TIME TO SEE IF HE WENT UPSTAIRS OR DOWN...!

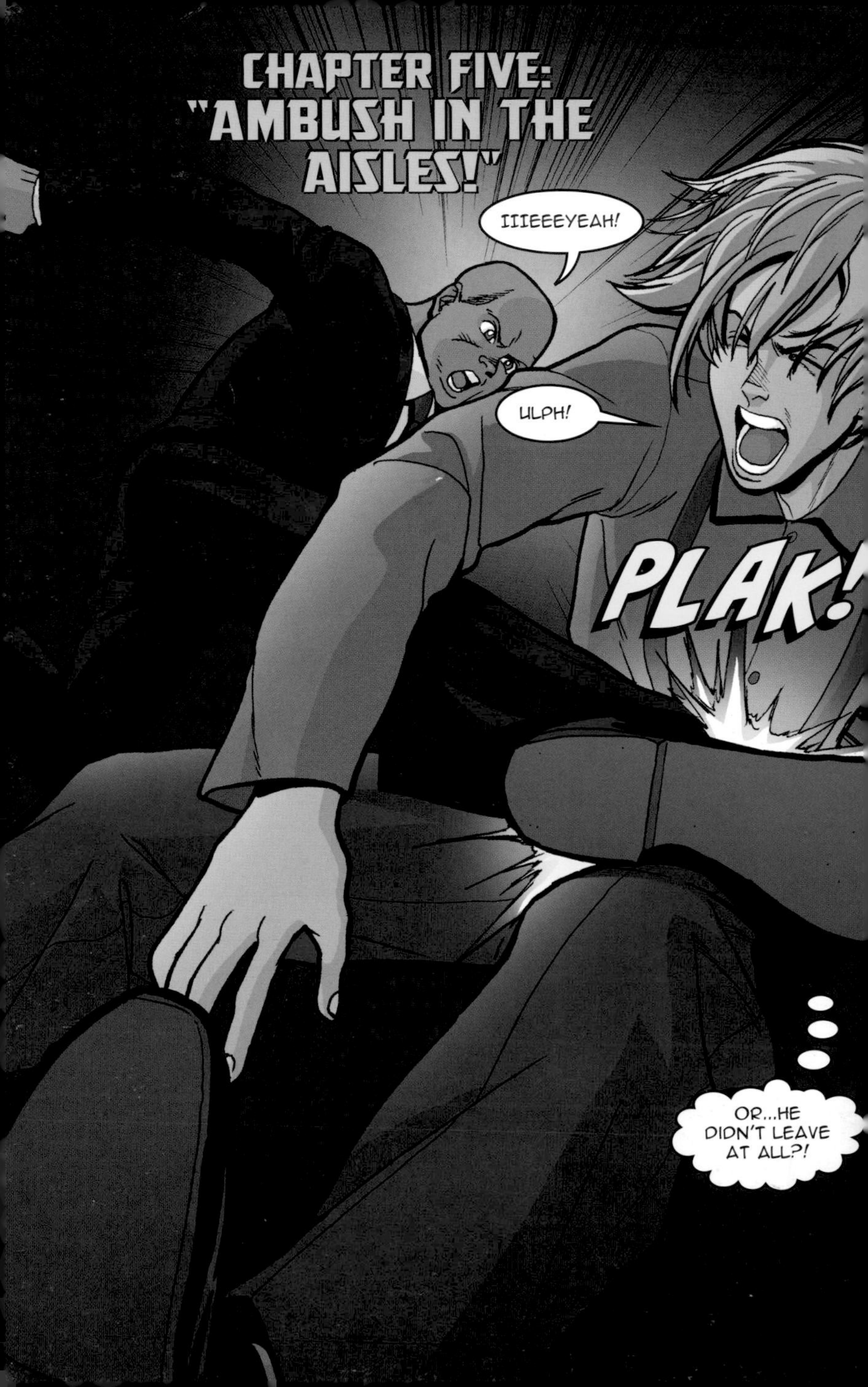
CHAPTER FIVE:
"AMBUSH IN THE AISLES!"
IIIEEEYEAH!
ULPH!
PLAK!
OR...HE DIDN'T LEAVE AT ALL?!

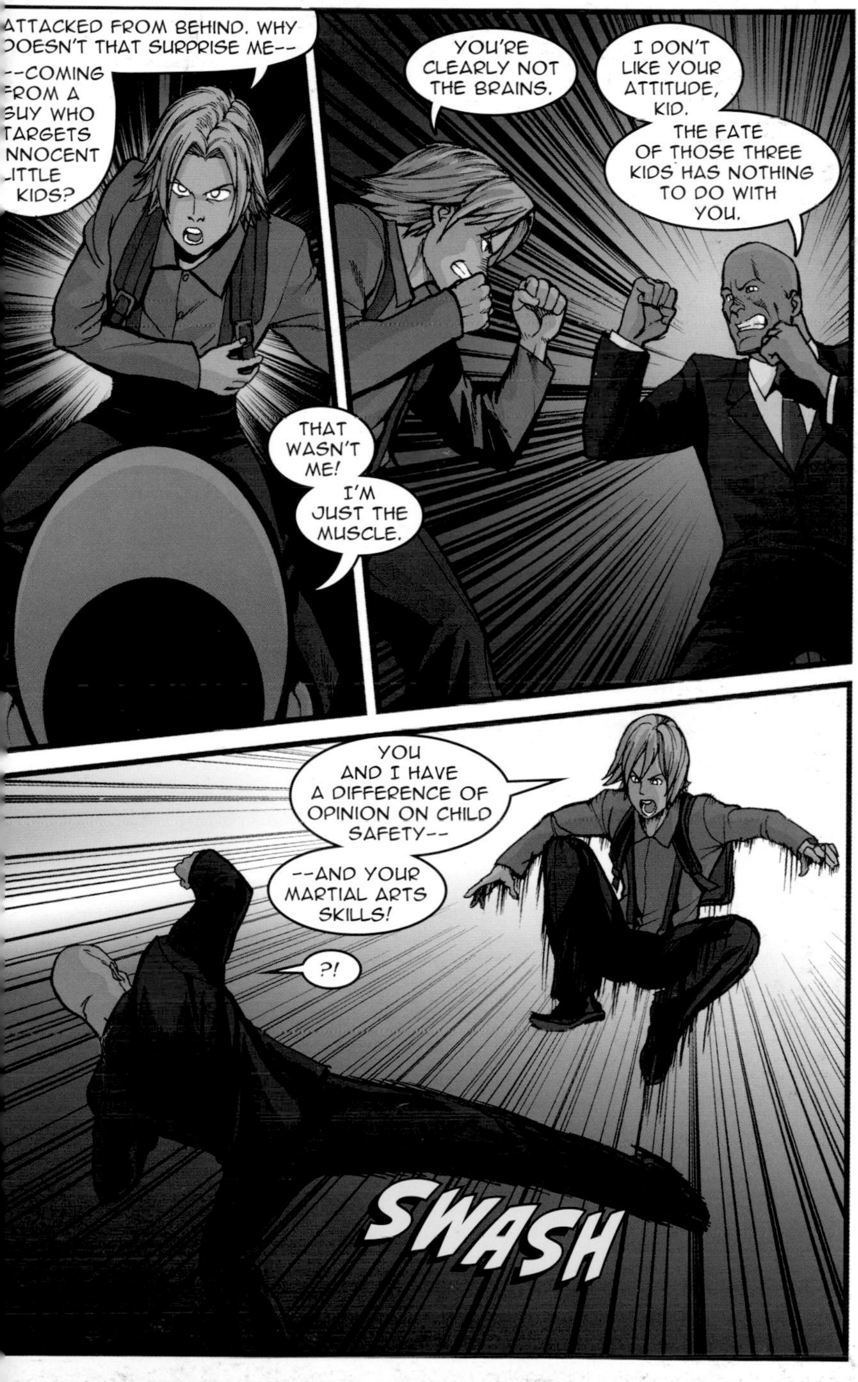
ATTACKED FROM BEHIND. WHY DOESN'T THAT SURPRISE ME--
--COMING FROM A GUY WHO TARGETS INNOCENT LITTLE KIDS?
THAT WASN'T ME!
I'M JUST THE MUSCLE.
YOU'RE CLEARLY NOT THE BRAINS.
I DON'T LIKE YOUR ATTITUDE, KID.
THE FATE OF THOSE THREE KIDS HAS NOTHING TO DO WITH YOU.
YOU AND I HAVE A DIFFERENCE OF OPINION ON CHILD SAFETY--
--AND YOUR MARTIAL ARTS SKILLS!
?!
SWASH

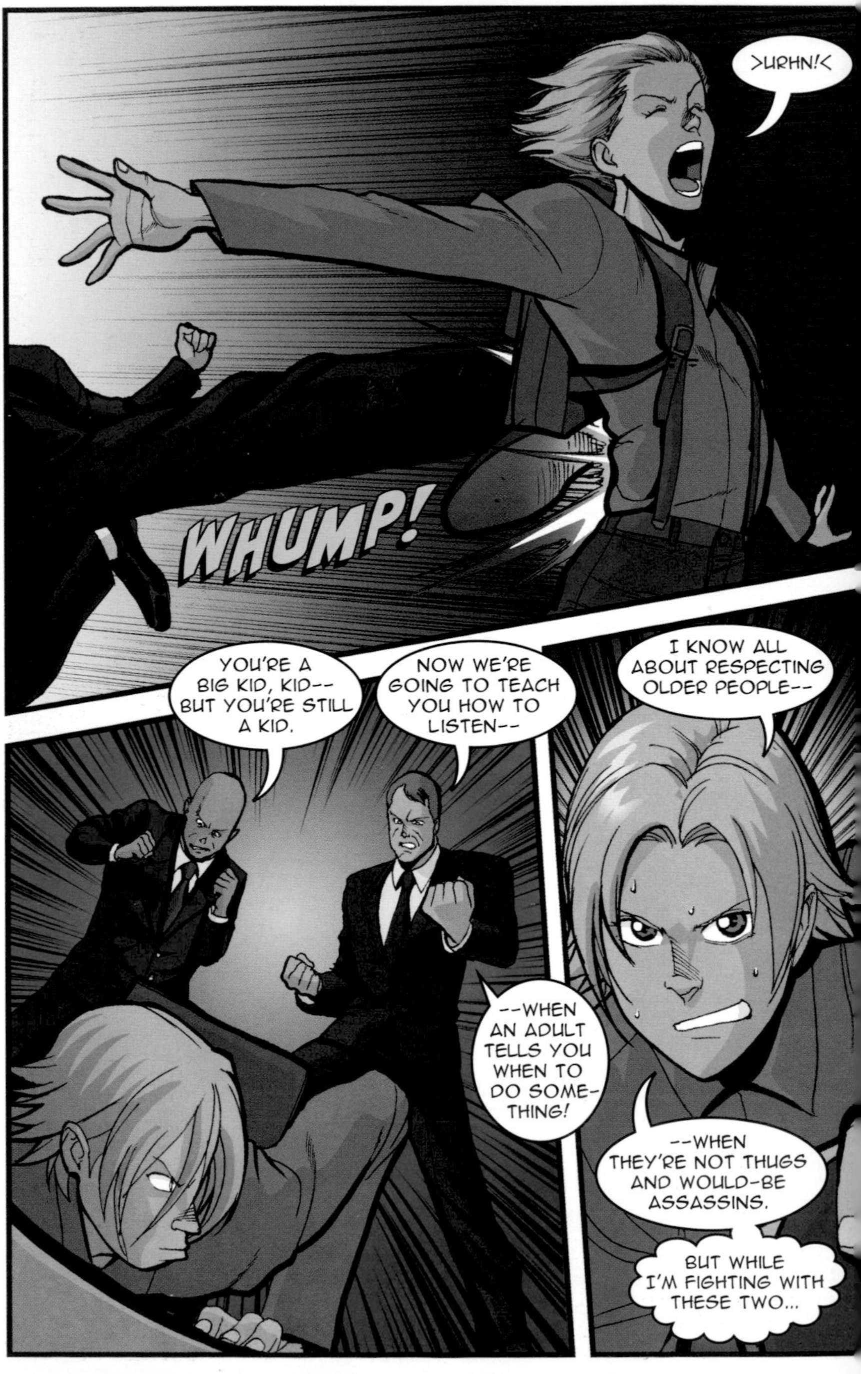
>URHN!<
WHUMP!
YOU'RE A BIG KID, KID-- BUT YOU'RE STILL A KID.
NOW WE'RE GOING TO TEACH YOU HOW TO LISTEN--
--WHEN AN ADULT TELLS YOU WHEN TO DO SOME-THING!
I KNOW ALL ABOUT RESPECTING OLDER PEOPLE--
--WHEN THEY'RE NOT THUGS AND WOULD-BE ASSASSINS.
BUT WHILE I'M FIGHTING WITH THESE TWO...

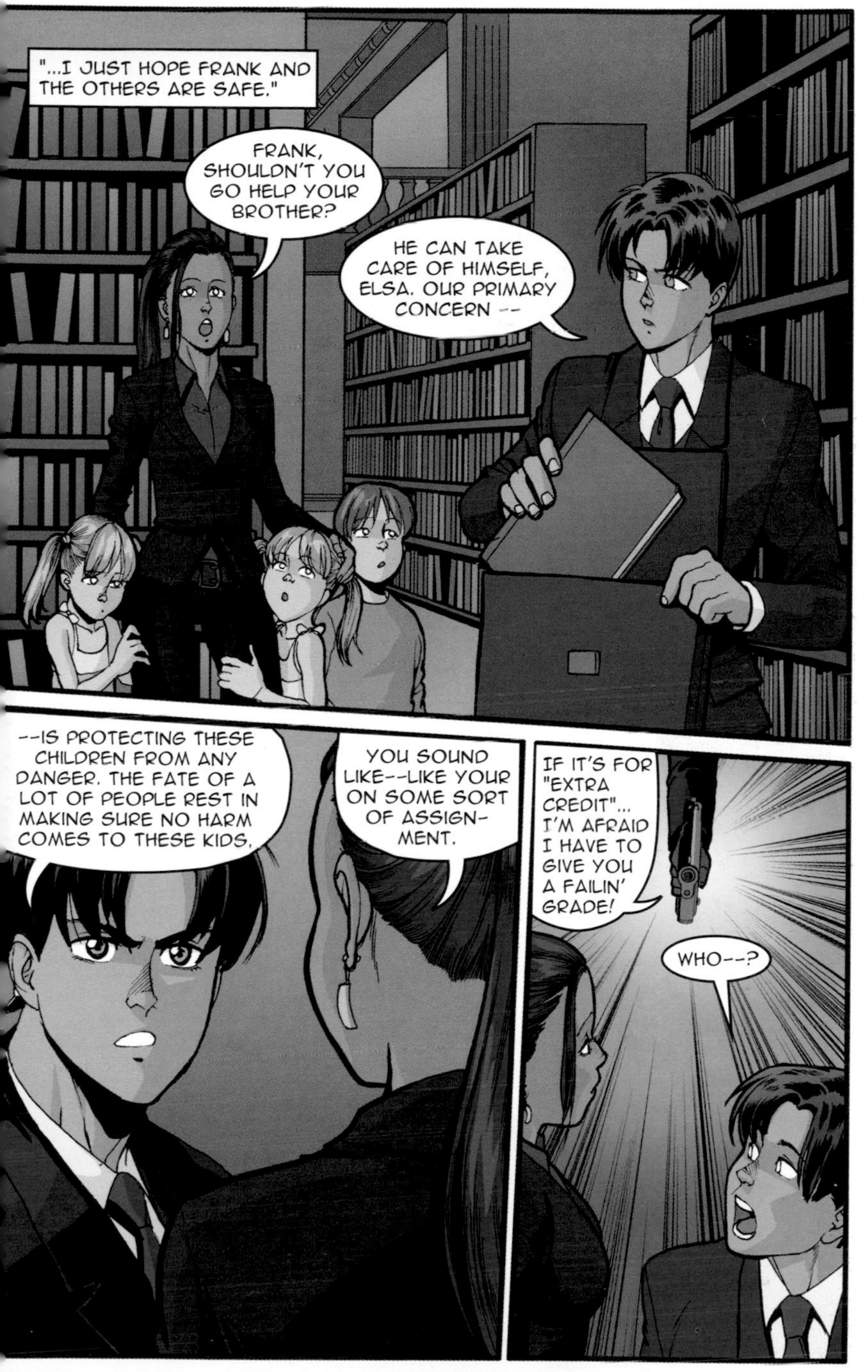
"...I JUST HOPE FRANK AND THE OTHERS ARE SAFE."
FRANK, SHOULDN'T YOU GO HELP YOUR BROTHER?
HE CAN TAKE CARE OF HIMSELF, ELSA. OUR PRIMARY CONCERN --
--IS PROTECTING THESE CHILDREN FROM ANY DANGER. THE FATE OF A LOT OF PEOPLE REST IN MAKING SURE NO HARM COMES TO THESE KIDS.
YOU SOUND LIKE--LIKE YOUR ON SOME SORT OF ASSIGN-MENT.
IF IT'S FOR "EXTRA CREDIT"... I'M AFRAID I HAVE TO GIVE YOU A FAILIN' GRADE!
WHO--?

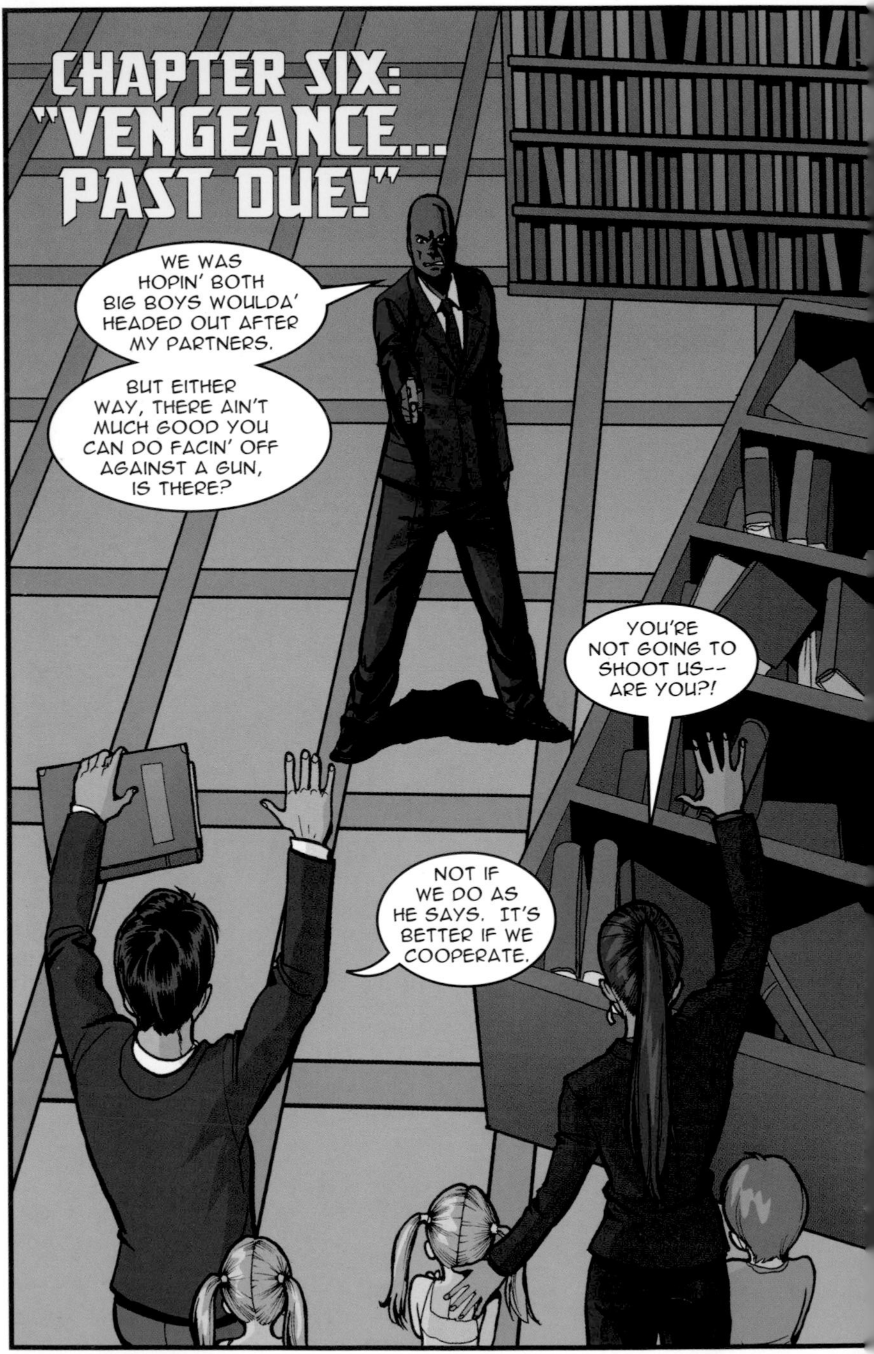
CHAPTER SIX: "VENGEANCE... PAST DUE!"
WE WAS HOPIN' BOTH BIG BOYS WOULDA' HEADED OUT AFTER MY PARTNERS.
BUT EITHER WAY, THERE AIN'T MUCH GOOD YOU CAN DO FACIN' OFF AGAINST A GUN, IS THERE?
YOU'RE NOT GOING TO SHOOT US-- ARE YOU?!
NOT IF WE DO AS HE SAYS. IT'S BETTER IF WE COOPERATE.

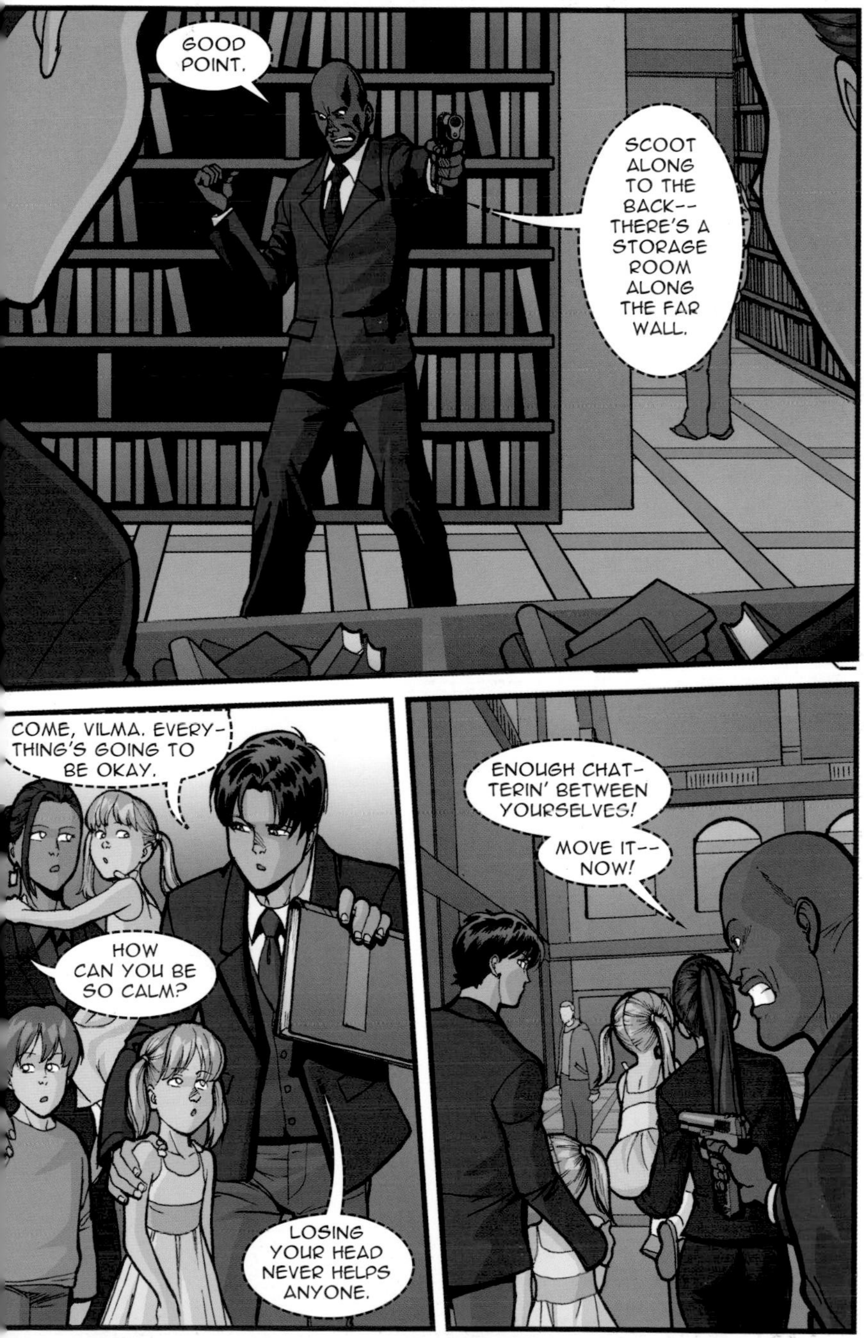
GOOD POINT.
SCOOT ALONG TO THE BACK-- THERE'S A STORAGE ROOM ALONG THE FAR WALL.
COME, VILMA. EVERY-THING'S GOING TO BE OKAY.
HOW CAN YOU BE SO CALM?
LOSING YOUR HEAD NEVER HELPS ANYONE.
ENOUGH CHAT-TERIN' BETWEEN YOURSELVES!
MOVE IT-- NOW!

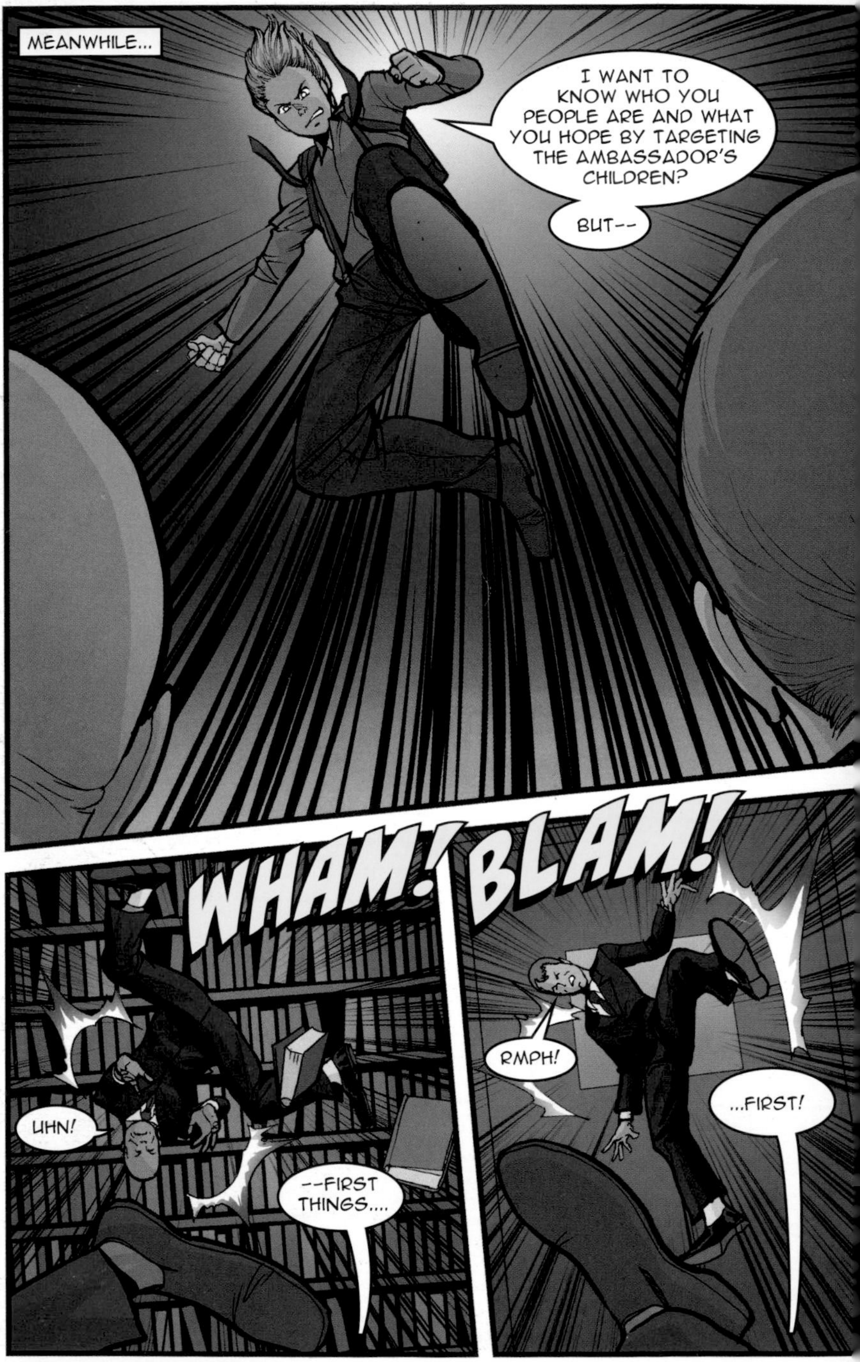
MEANWHILE...
I WANT TO KNOW WHO YOU PEOPLE ARE AND WHAT YOU HOPE BY TARGETING THE AMBASSADOR'S CHILDREN?
BUT--
WHAM!
UHN!
--FIRST THINGS....
BLAM!
RMPH!
...FIRST!

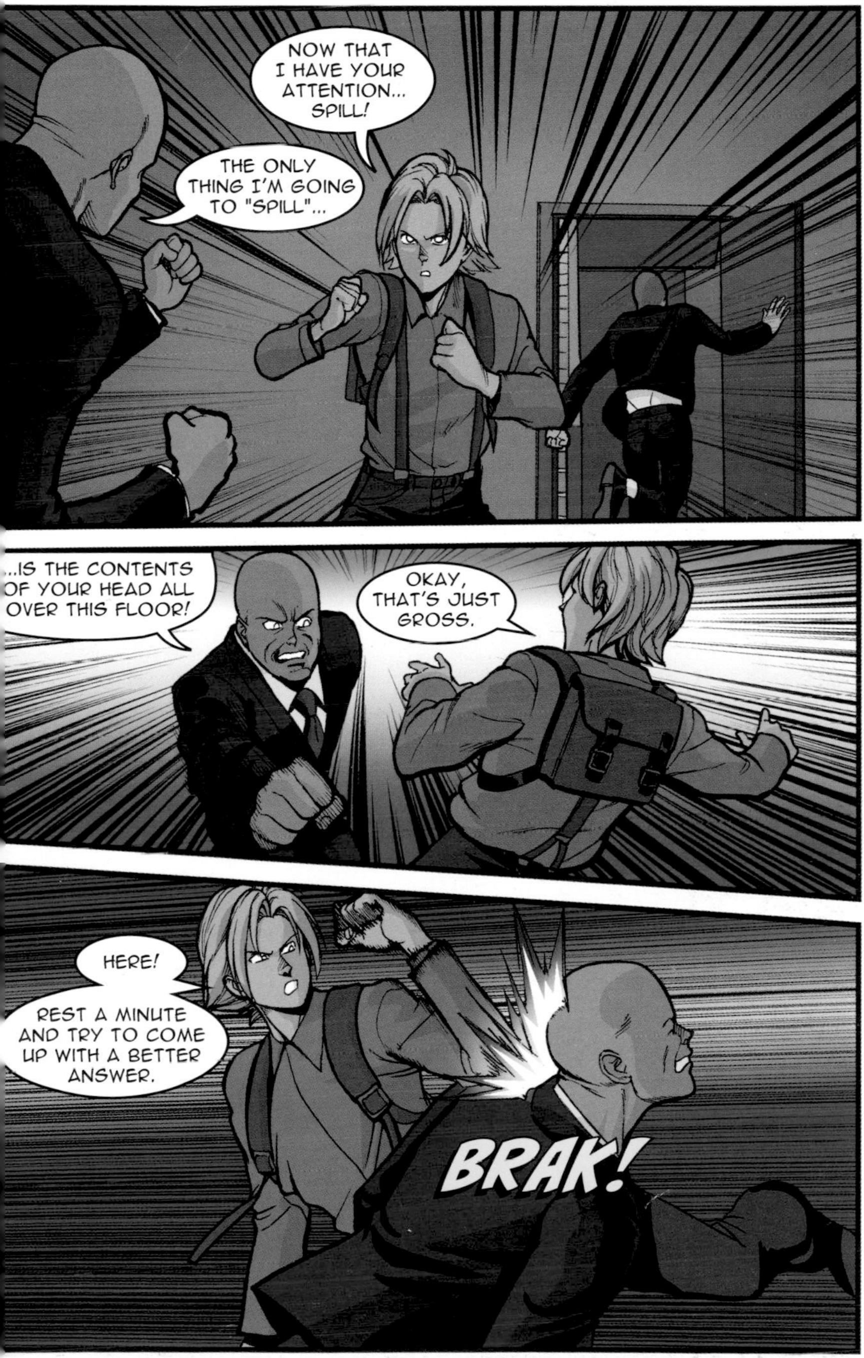
NOW THAT I HAVE YOUR ATTENTION... SPILL!
THE ONLY THING I'M GOING TO "SPILL"...
...IS THE CONTENTS OF YOUR HEAD ALL OVER THIS FLOOR!
OKAY, THAT'S JUST GROSS.
HERE!
REST A MINUTE AND TRY TO COME UP WITH A BETTER ANSWER.
BRAK!

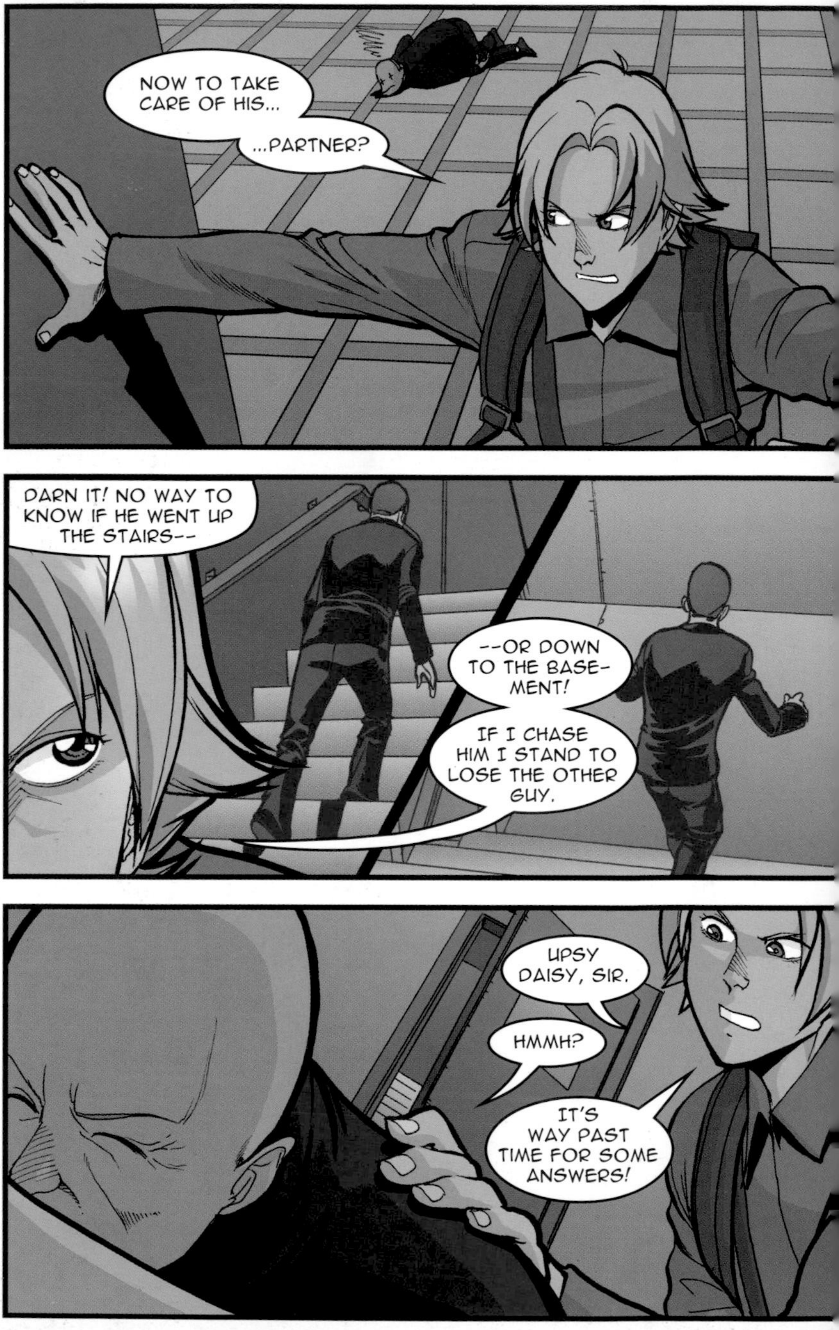
NOW TO TAKE CARE OF HIS...
...PARTNER?
DARN IT! NO WAY TO KNOW IF HE WENT UP THE STAIRS--
--OR DOWN TO THE BASE-MENT!
IF I CHASE HIM I STAND TO LOSE THE OTHER GUY.
UPSY DAISY, SIR.
HMMH?
IT'S WAY PAST TIME FOR SOME ANSWERS!

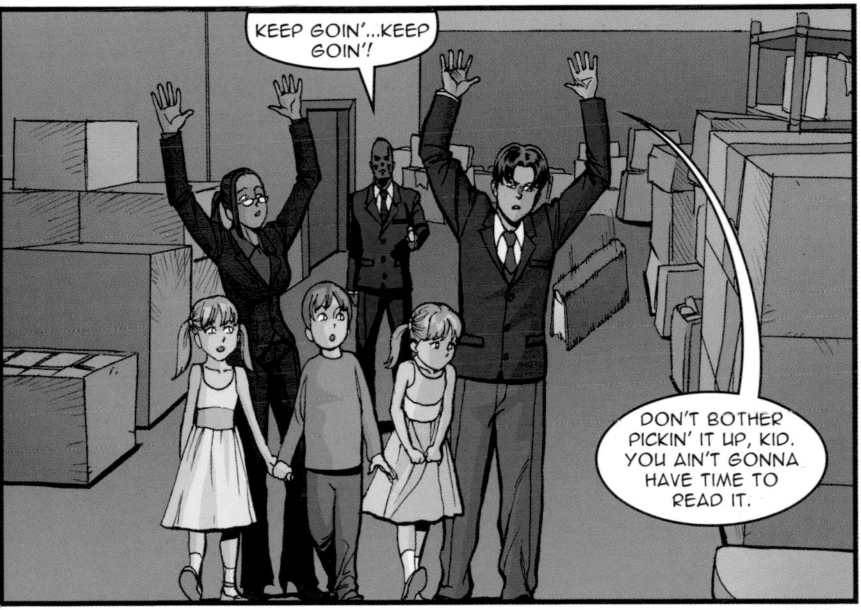
KEEP GOIN'...KEEP GOIN'!
DON'T BOTHER PICKIN' IT UP, KID. YOU AIN'T GONNA HAVE TIME TO READ IT.

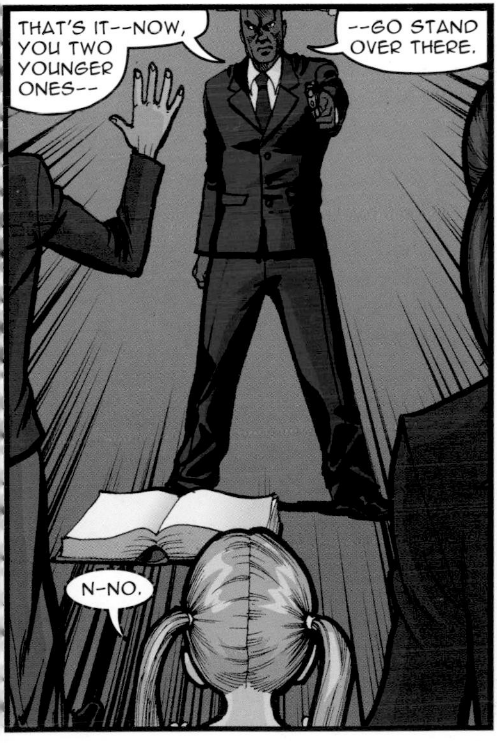
THAT'S IT--NOW, YOU TWO YOUNGER ONES--
--GO STAND OVER THERE.
N-NO.

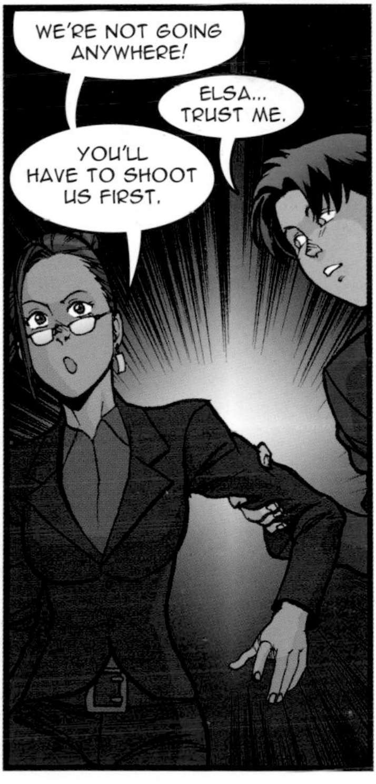
WE'RE NOT GOING ANYWHERE!
YOU'LL HAVE TO SHOOT US FIRST.
ELSA... TRUST ME.

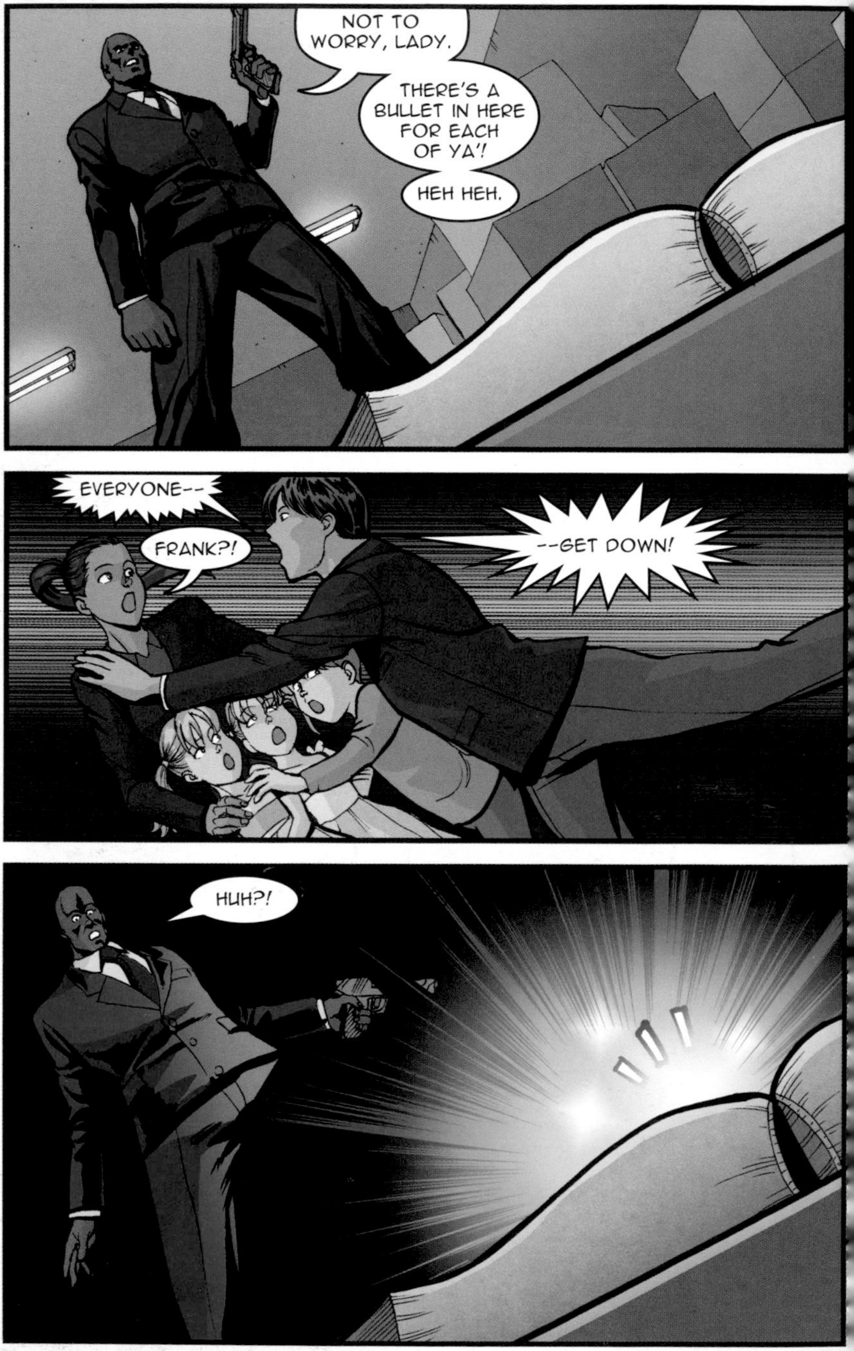
NOT TO WORRY, LADY.
THERE'S A BULLET IN HERE FOR EACH OF YA'!
HEH HEH.
EVERYONE--
FRANK?!
--GET DOWN!
HUH?!

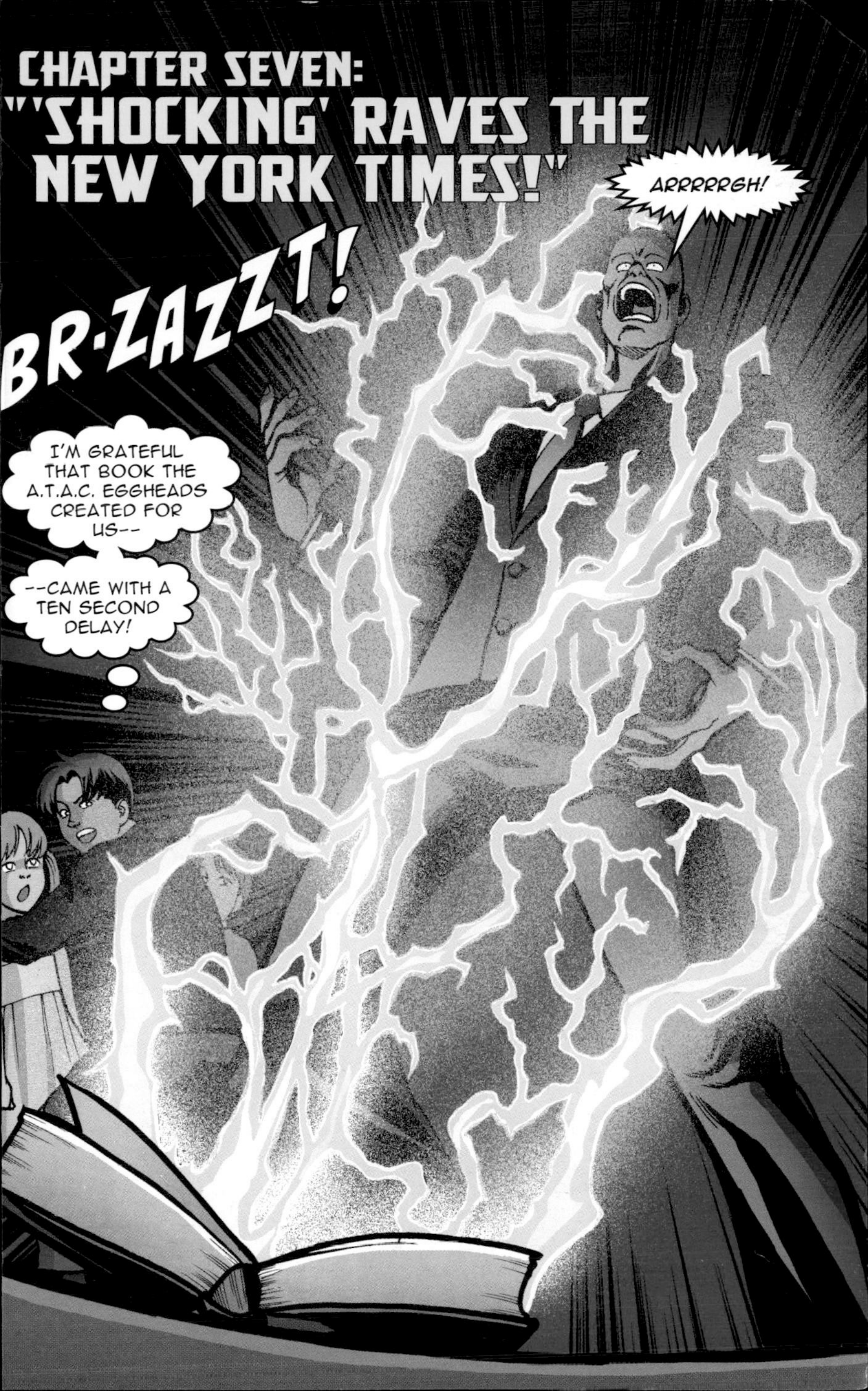
CHAPTER SEVEN:
"'SHOCKING' RAVES THE NEW YORK TIMES!"
ARRRRRGH!
BR-ZAZZT!
I'M GRATEFUL THAT BOOK THE A.T.A.C. EGGHEADS CREATED FOR US--
--CAME WITH A TEN SECOND DELAY!

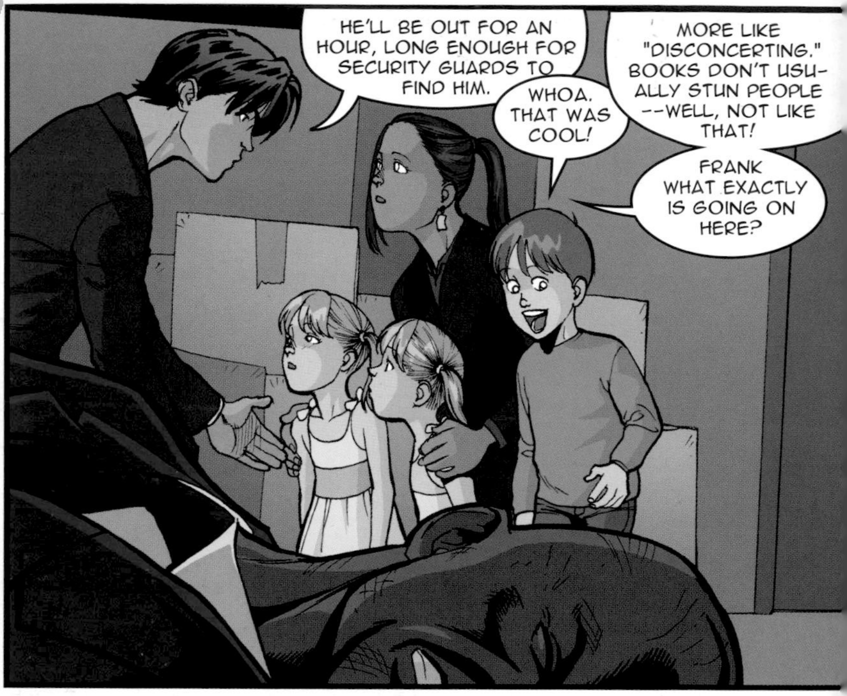
HE'LL BE OUT FOR AN HOUR, LONG ENOUGH FOR SECURITY GUARDS TO FIND HIM.
WHOA. THAT WAS COOL!
MORE LIKE "DISCONCERTING." BOOKS DON'T USU-ALLY STUN PEOPLE --WELL, NOT LIKE THAT!
FRANK WHAT EXACTLY IS GOING ON HERE?

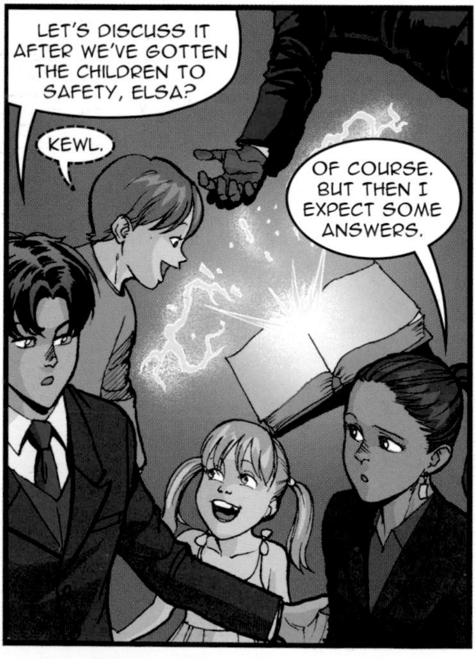
LET'S DISCUSS IT AFTER WE'VE GOTTEN THE CHILDREN TO SAFETY, ELSA?
KEWL.
OF COURSE. BUT THEN I EXPECT SOME ANSWERS.

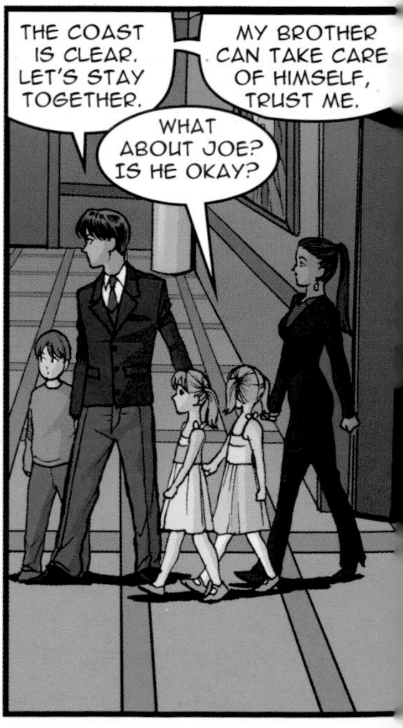
THE COAST IS CLEAR. LET'S STAY TOGETHER.
MY BROTHER CAN TAKE CARE OF HIMSELF, TRUST ME.
WHAT ABOUT JOE? IS HE OKAY?

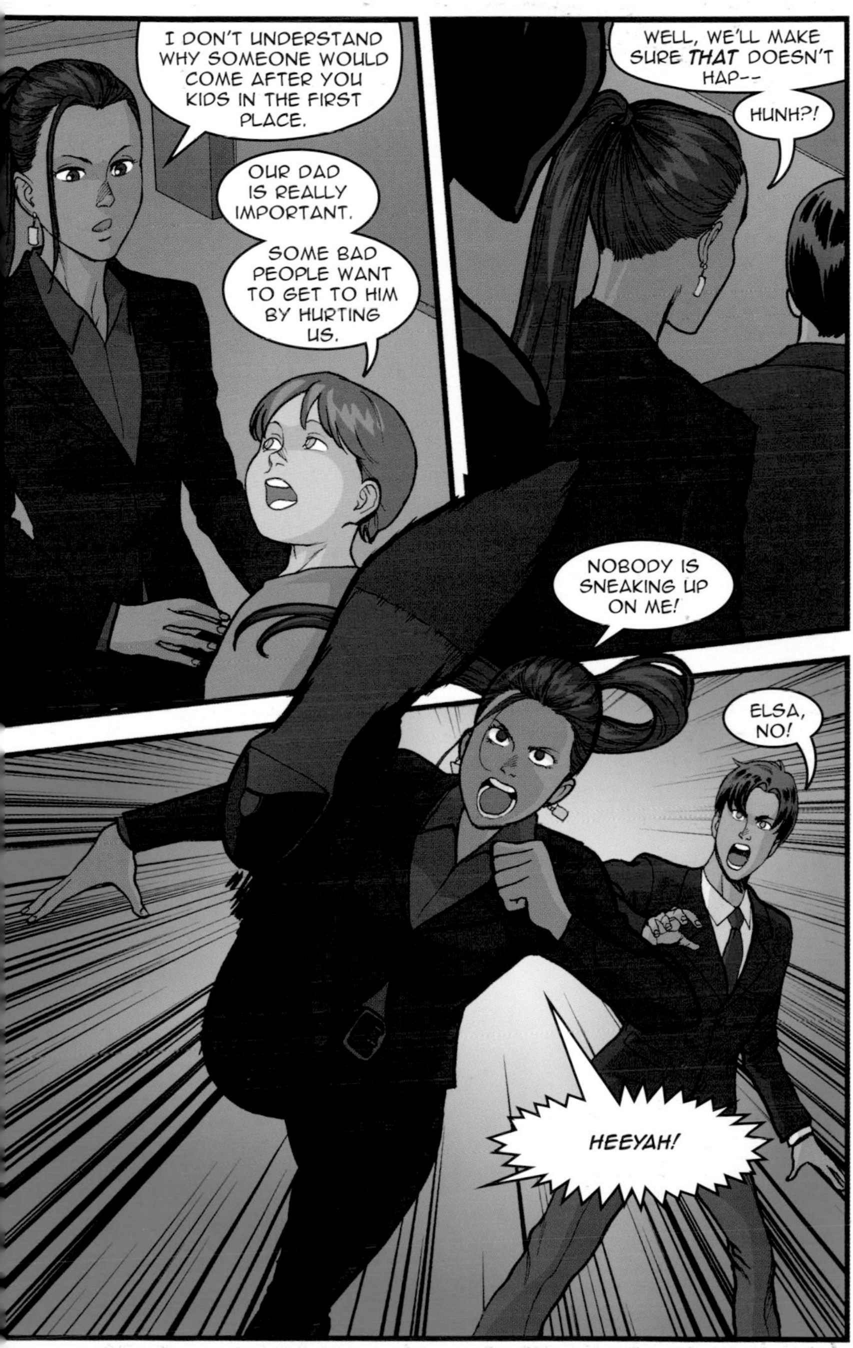
I DON'T UNDERSTAND WHY SOMEONE WOULD COME AFTER YOU KIDS IN THE FIRST PLACE.
OUR DAD IS REALLY IMPORTANT.
SOME BAD PEOPLE WANT TO GET TO HIM BY HURTING US.
WELL, WE'LL MAKE SURE *THAT* DOESN'T HAP--
HUNH?!
NOBODY IS SNEAKING UP ON ME!
ELSA, NO!
HEEYAH!

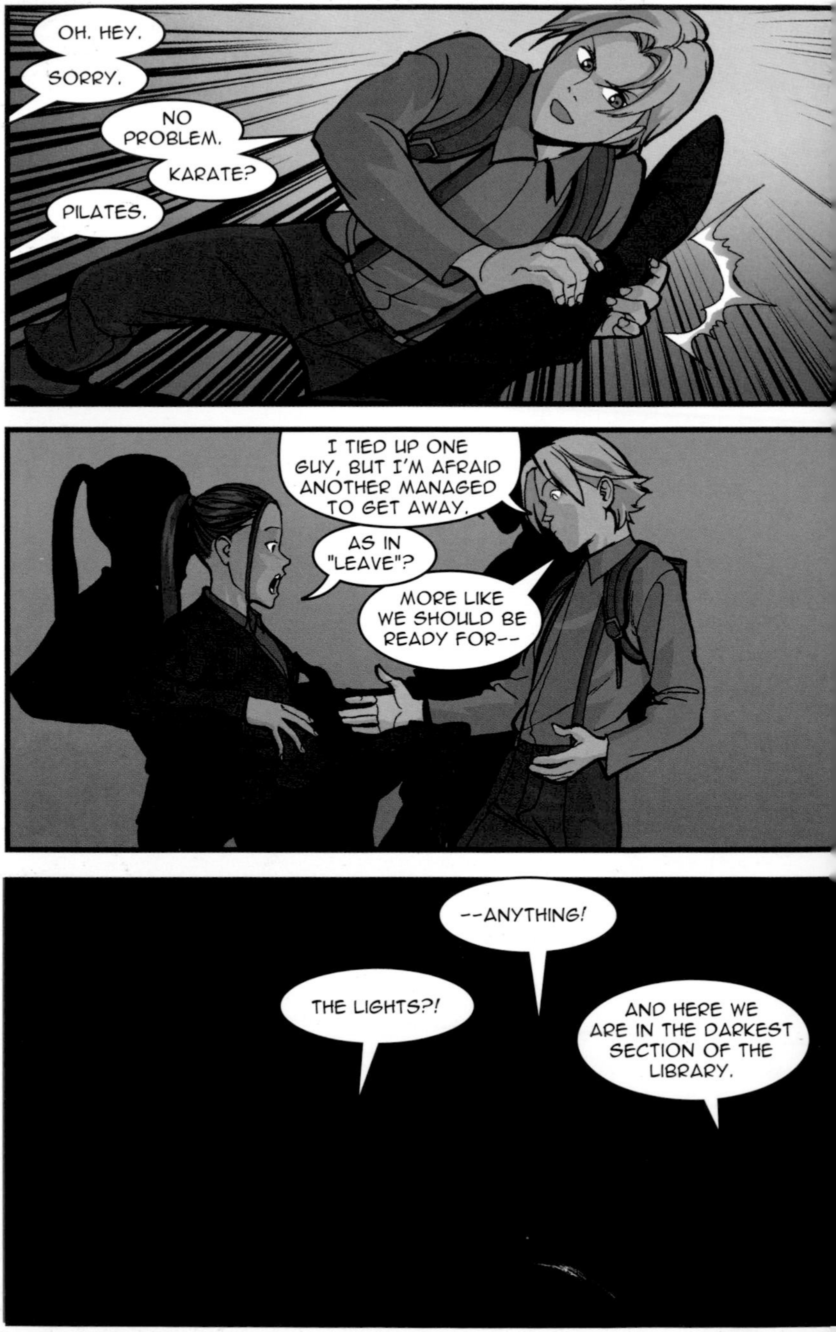
OH. HEY.
SORRY.
NO PROBLEM.
KARATE?
PILATES.
I TIED UP ONE GUY, BUT I'M AFRAID ANOTHER MANAGED TO GET AWAY.
AS IN "LEAVE"?
MORE LIKE WE SHOULD BE READY FOR--
--ANYTHING!
THE LIGHTS?!
AND HERE WE ARE IN THE DARKEST SECTION OF THE LIBRARY.

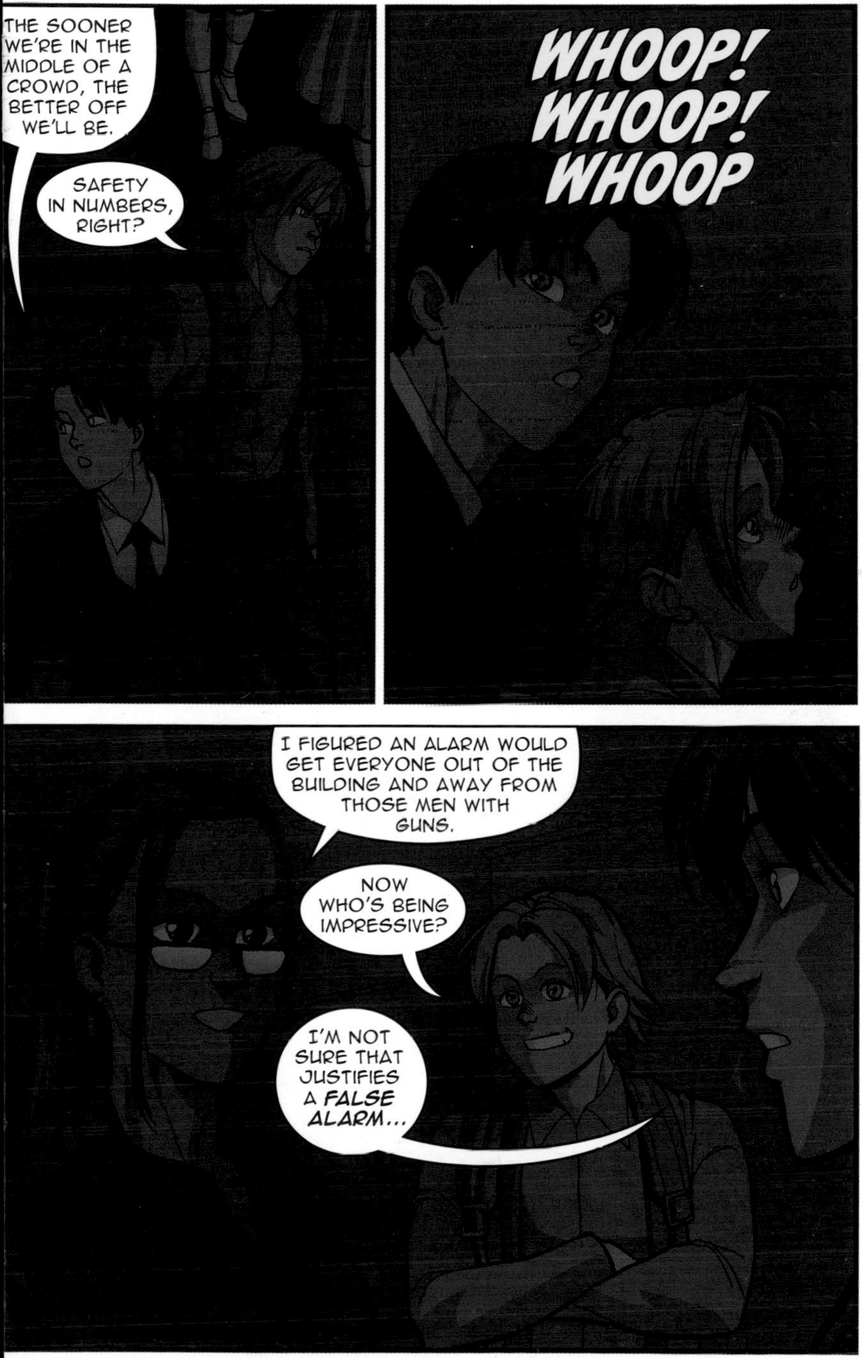
THE SOONER WE'RE IN THE MIDDLE OF A CROWD, THE BETTER OFF WE'LL BE.
SAFETY IN NUMBERS, RIGHT?
WHOOP! WHOOP! WHOOP
I FIGURED AN ALARM WOULD GET EVERYONE OUT OF THE BUILDING AND AWAY FROM THOSE MEN WITH GUNS.
NOW WHO'S BEING IMPRESSIVE?
I'M NOT SURE THAT JUSTIFIES A FALSE ALARM...

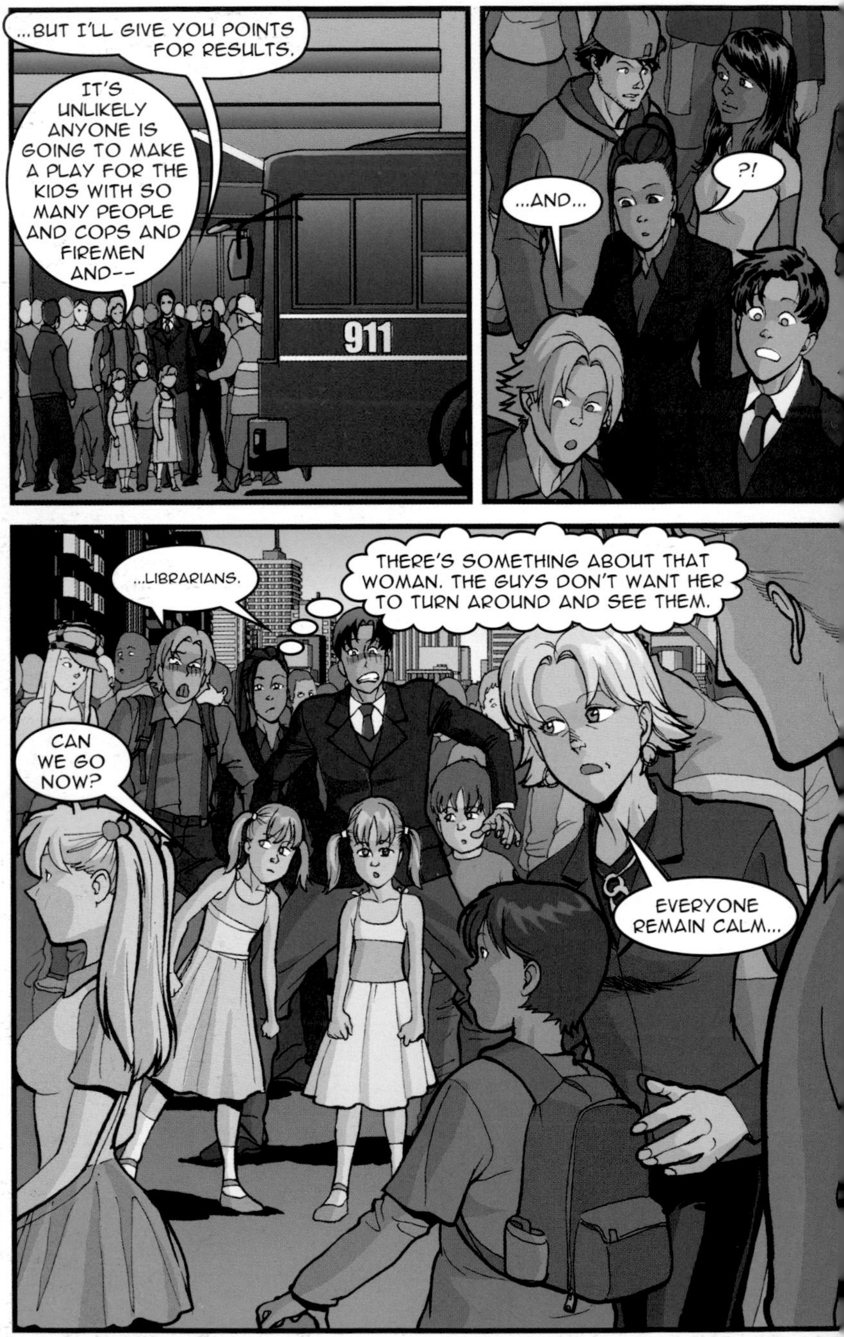
...BUT I'LL GIVE YOU POINTS FOR RESULTS.
IT'S UNLIKELY ANYONE IS GOING TO MAKE A PLAY FOR THE KIDS WITH SO MANY PEOPLE AND COPS AND FIREMEN AND--
911
...AND...
?!
...LIBRARIANS.
THERE'S SOMETHING ABOUT THAT WOMAN. THE GUYS DON'T WANT HER TO TURN AROUND AND SEE THEM.
CAN WE GO NOW?
EVERYONE REMAIN CALM...

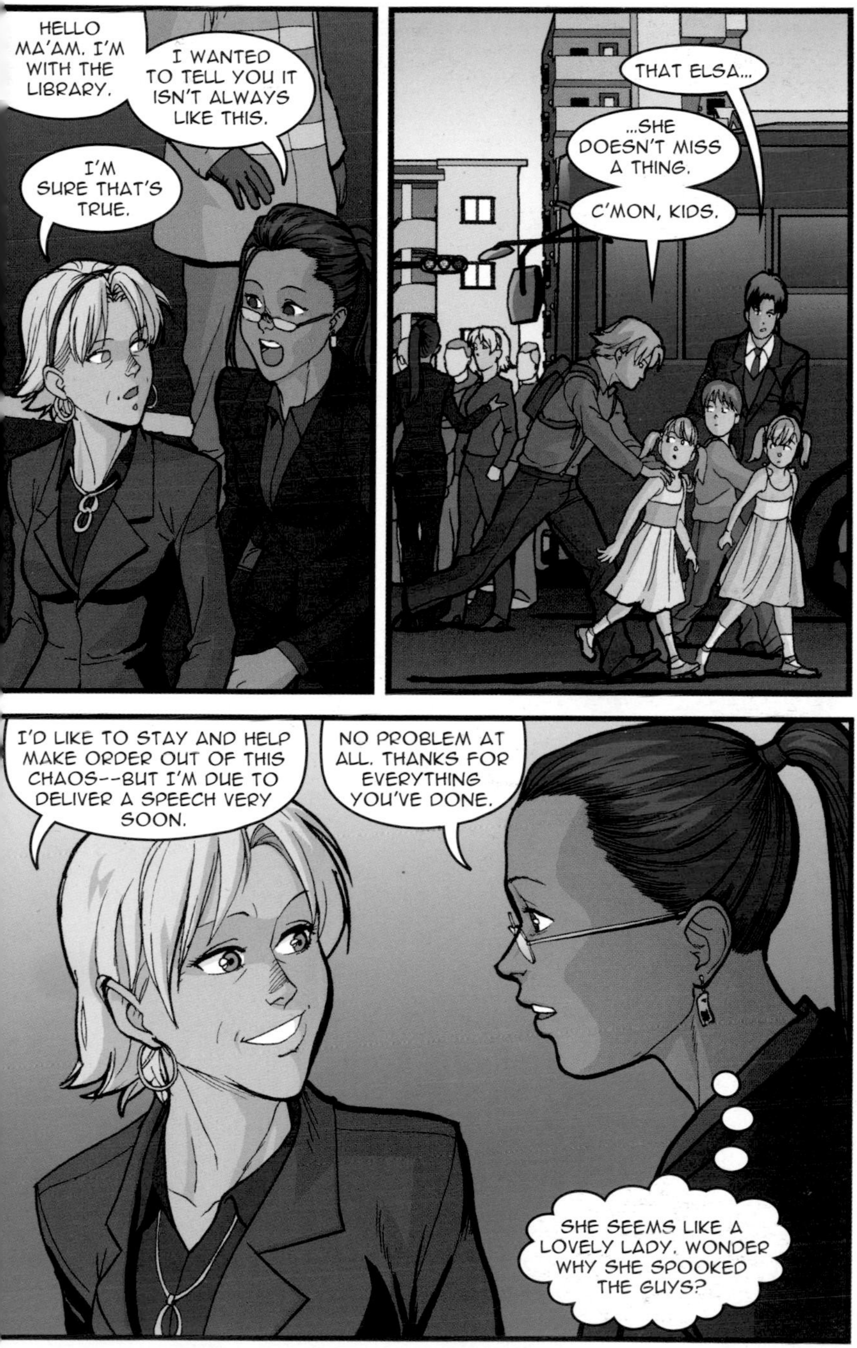
HELLO MA'AM. I'M WITH THE LIBRARY.
I WANTED TO TELL YOU IT ISN'T ALWAYS LIKE THIS.
I'M SURE THAT'S TRUE.
THAT ELSA...
...SHE DOESN'T MISS A THING.
C'MON, KIDS.
I'D LIKE TO STAY AND HELP MAKE ORDER OUT OF THIS CHAOS--BUT I'M DUE TO DELIVER A SPEECH VERY SOON.
NO PROBLEM AT ALL. THANKS FOR EVERYTHING YOU'VE DONE.
SHE SEEMS LIKE A LOVELY LADY. WONDER WHY SHE SPOOKED THE GUYS?

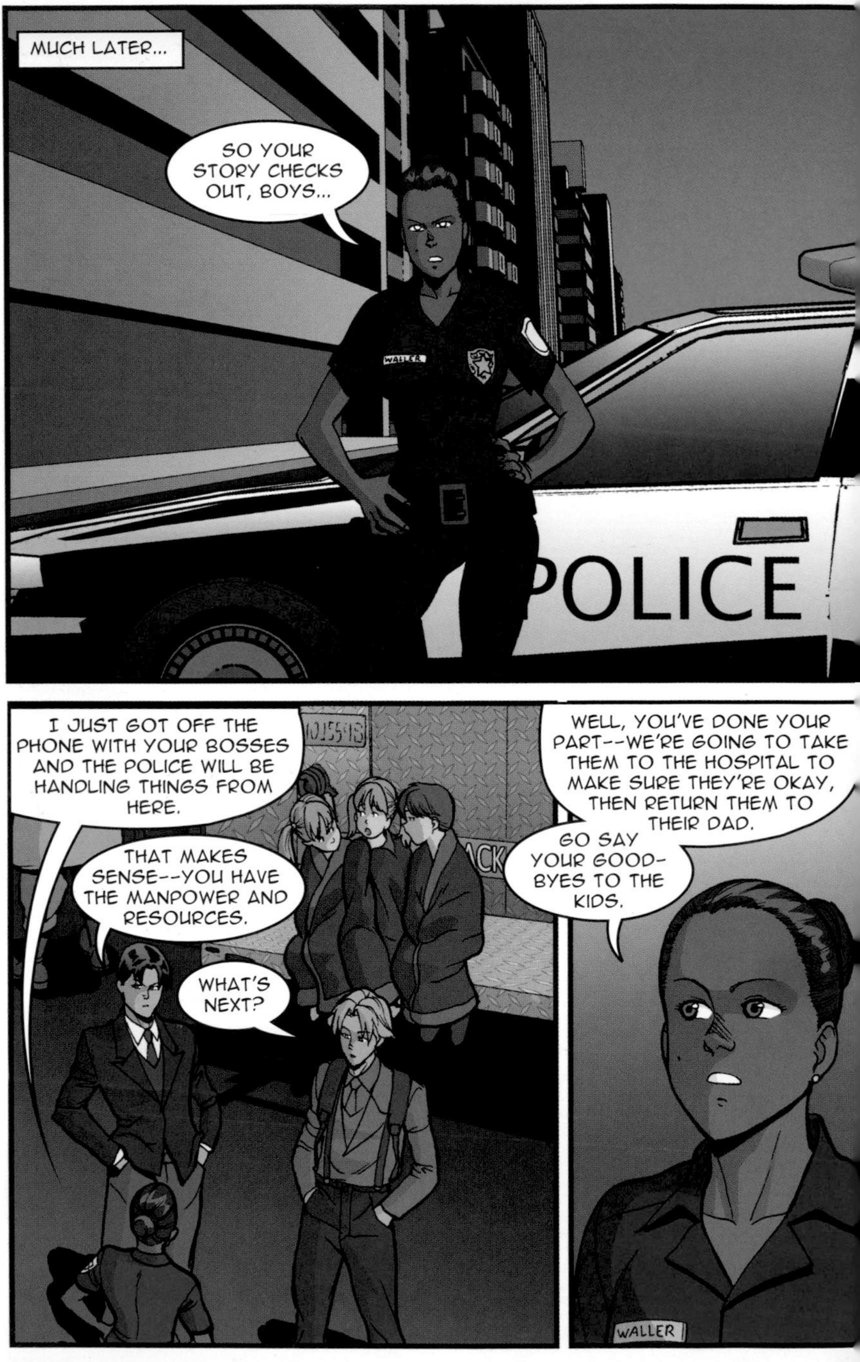
MUCH LATER...
SO YOUR STORY CHECKS OUT, BOYS...
WALLER
POLICE
I JUST GOT OFF THE PHONE WITH YOUR BOSSES AND THE POLICE WILL BE HANDLING THINGS FROM HERE.
THAT MAKES SENSE--YOU HAVE THE MANPOWER AND RESOURCES.
WHAT'S NEXT?
WELL, YOU'VE DONE YOUR PART--WE'RE GOING TO TAKE THEM TO THE HOSPITAL TO MAKE SURE THEY'RE OKAY, THEN RETURN THEM TO THEIR DAD.
GO SAY YOUR GOOD-BYES TO THE KIDS.
WALLER

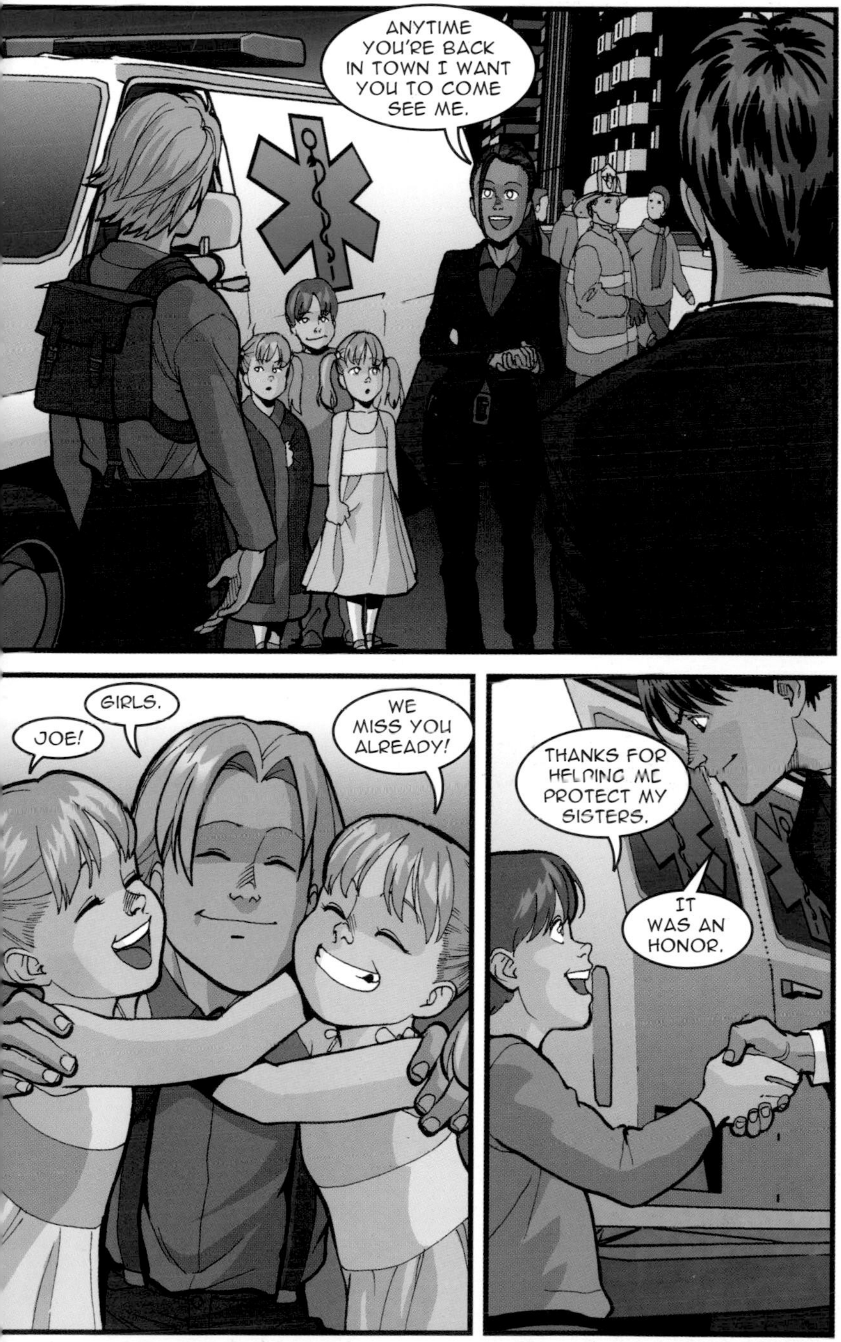
ANYTIME YOU'RE BACK IN TOWN I WANT YOU TO COME SEE ME.
JOE!
GIRLS.
WE MISS YOU ALREADY!
THANKS FOR HELPING ME PROTECT MY SISTERS.
IT WAS AN HONOR.

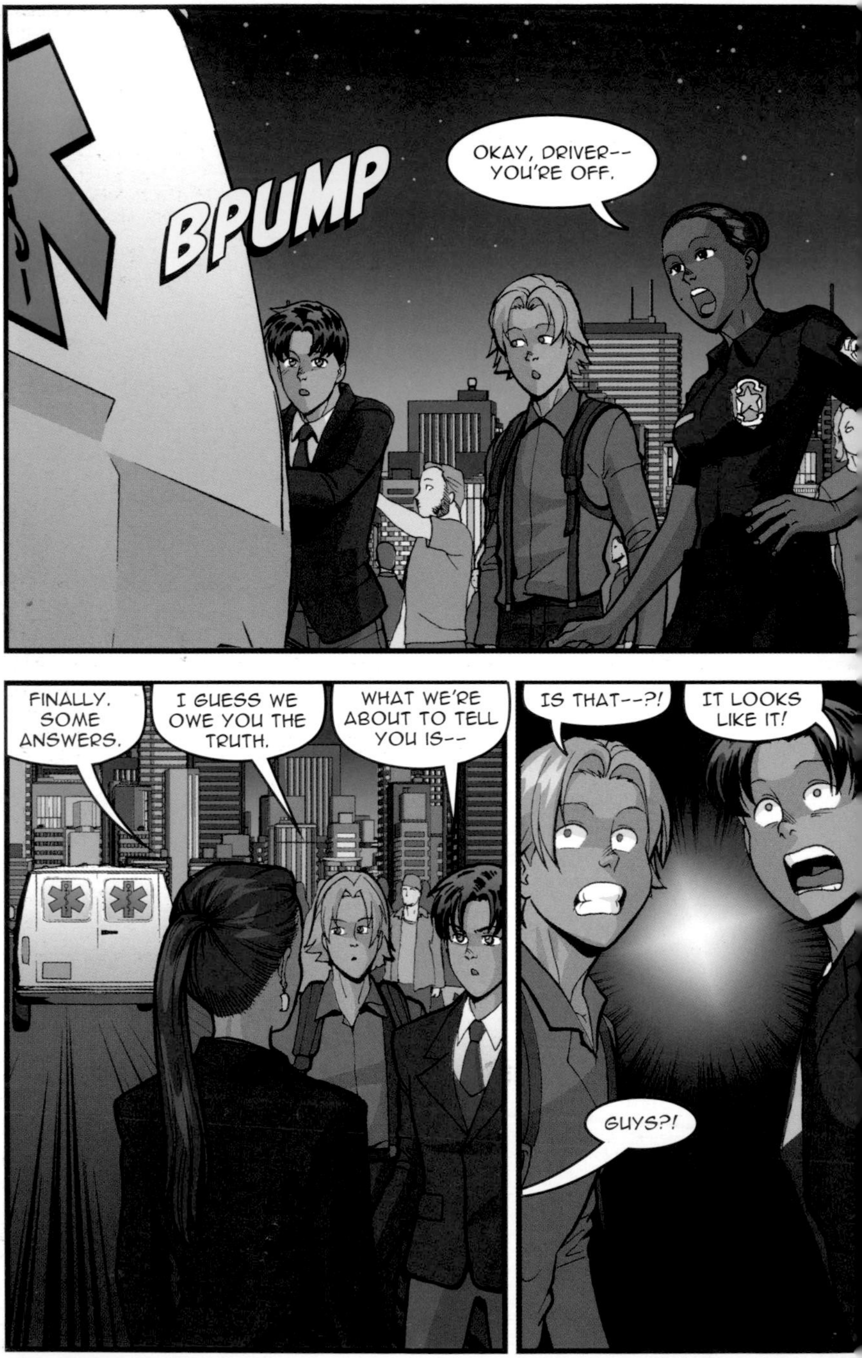
BPUMP
OKAY, DRIVER-- YOU'RE OFF.
FINALLY. SOME ANSWERS.
I GUESS WE OWE YOU THE TRUTH.
WHAT WE'RE ABOUT TO TELL YOU IS--
IS THAT--?!
IT LOOKS LIKE IT!
GUYS?!

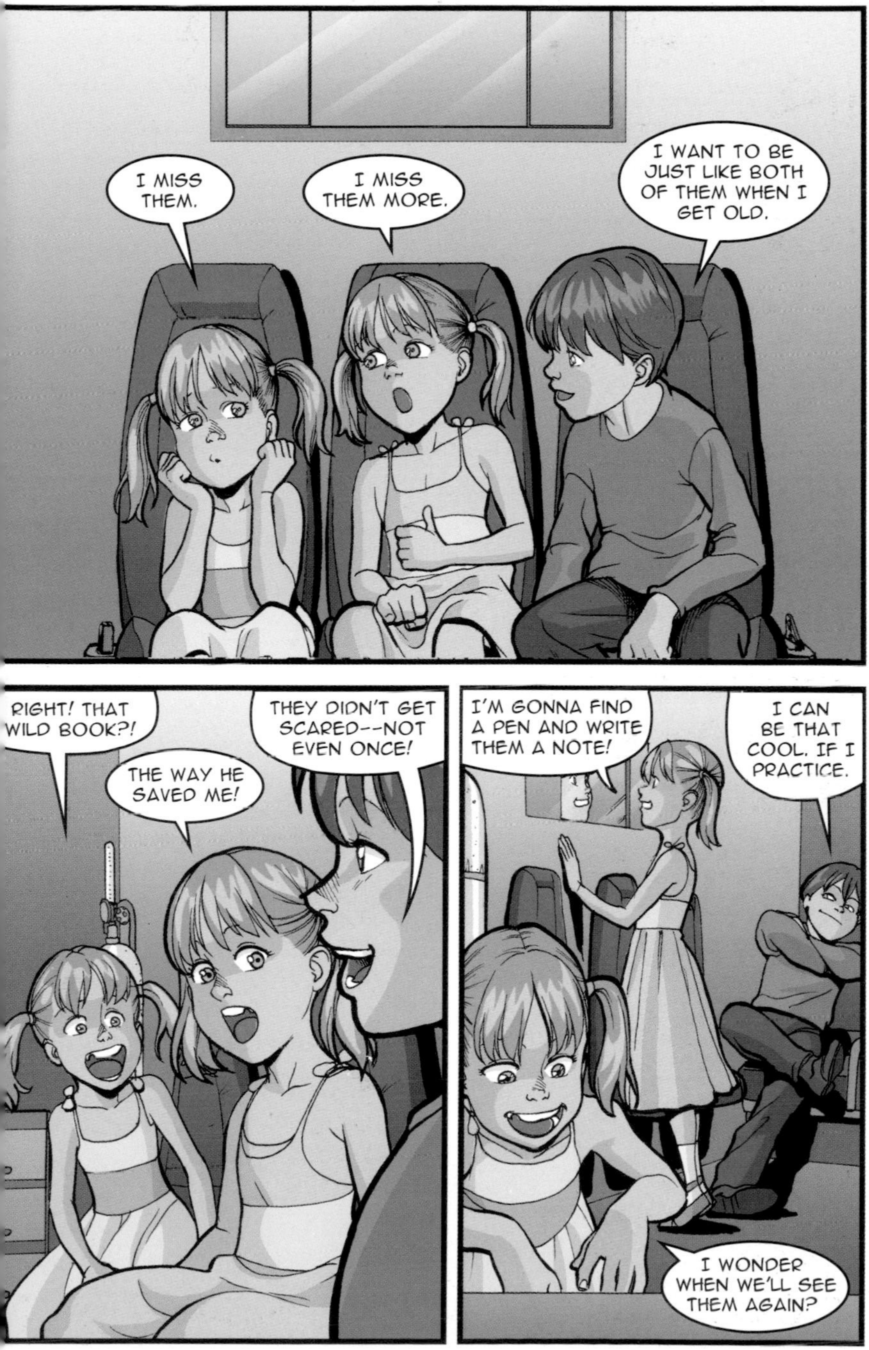
I MISS THEM.
I MISS THEM MORE.
I WANT TO BE JUST LIKE BOTH OF THEM WHEN I GET OLD.
RIGHT! THAT WILD BOOK?!
THE WAY HE SAVED ME!
THEY DIDN'T GET SCARED--NOT EVEN ONCE!
I'M GONNA FIND A PEN AND WRITE THEM A NOTE!
I CAN BE THAT COOL. IF I PRACTICE.
I WONDER WHEN WE'LL SEE THEM AGAIN?

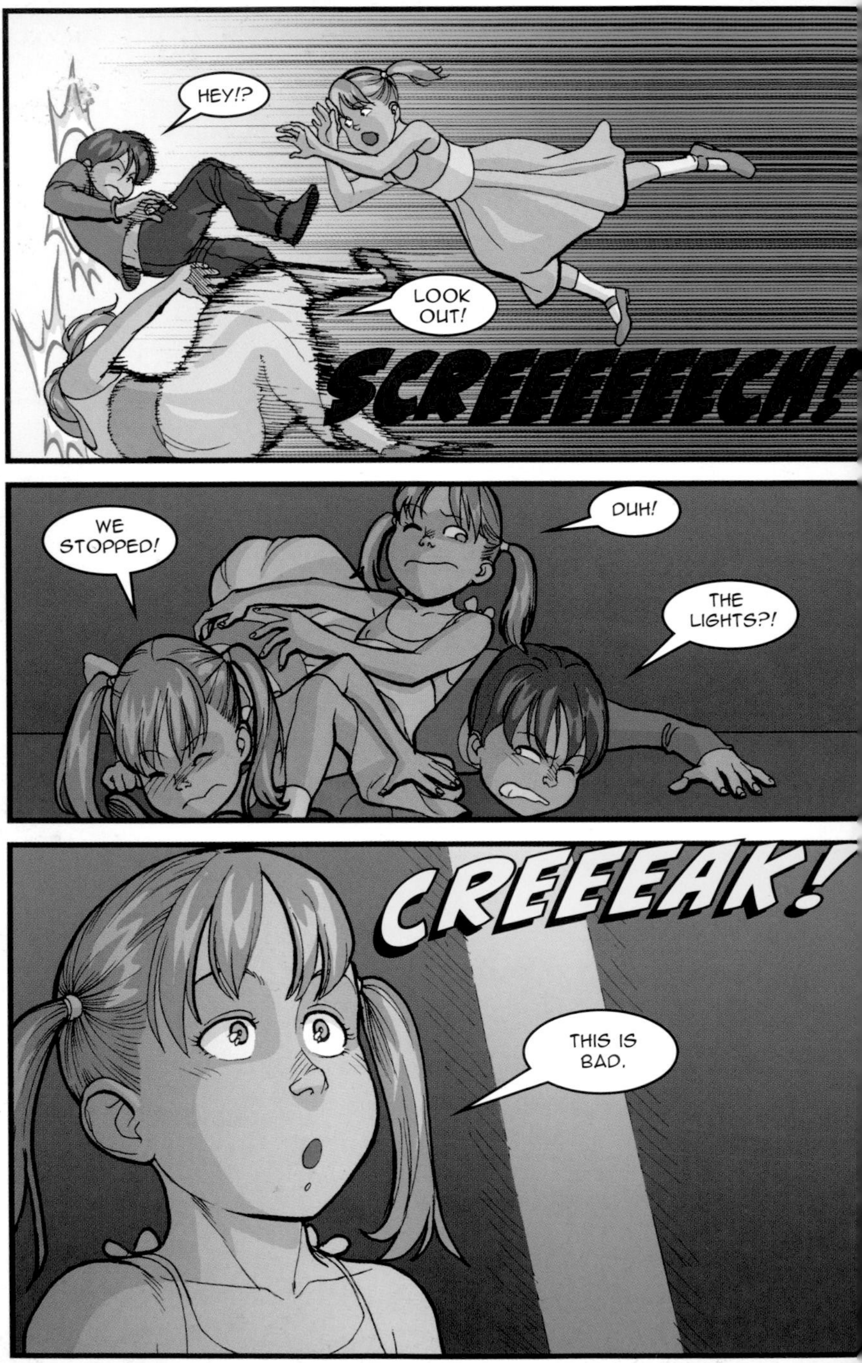
HEY!?
LOOK OUT!
SCREEEEEECH!
WE STOPPED!
DUH!
THE LIGHTS?!
CREEEAK!
THIS IS BAD.

CHAPTER EIGHT: "A GOOD BOOK ALWAYS ILLUMINATES!"

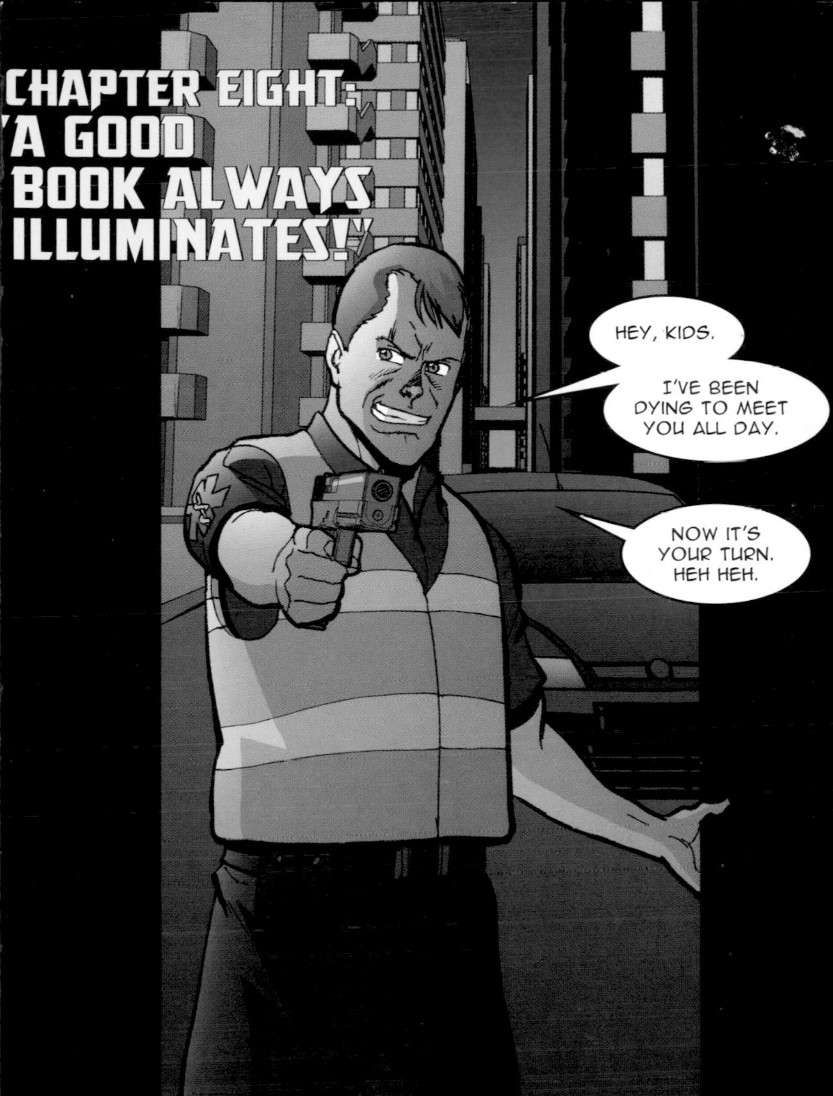
HEY, KIDS.
I'VE BEEN DYING TO MEET YOU ALL DAY.
NOW IT'S YOUR TURN. HEH HEH.

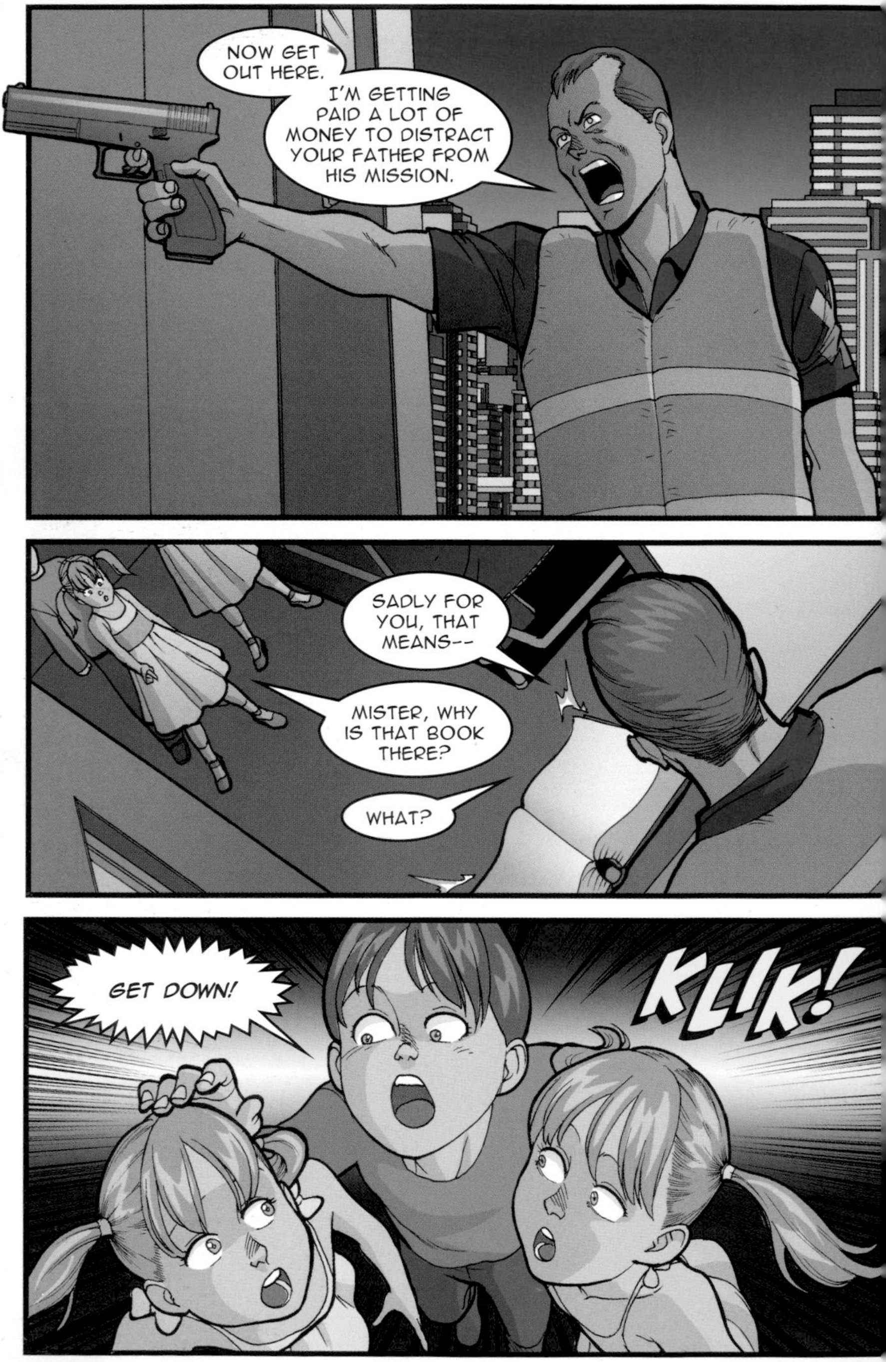
NOW GET OUT HERE.
I'M GETTING PAID A LOT OF MONEY TO DISTRACT YOUR FATHER FROM HIS MISSION.
SADLY FOR YOU, THAT MEANS--
MISTER, WHY IS THAT BOOK THERE?
WHAT?
GET DOWN!
KLIK!

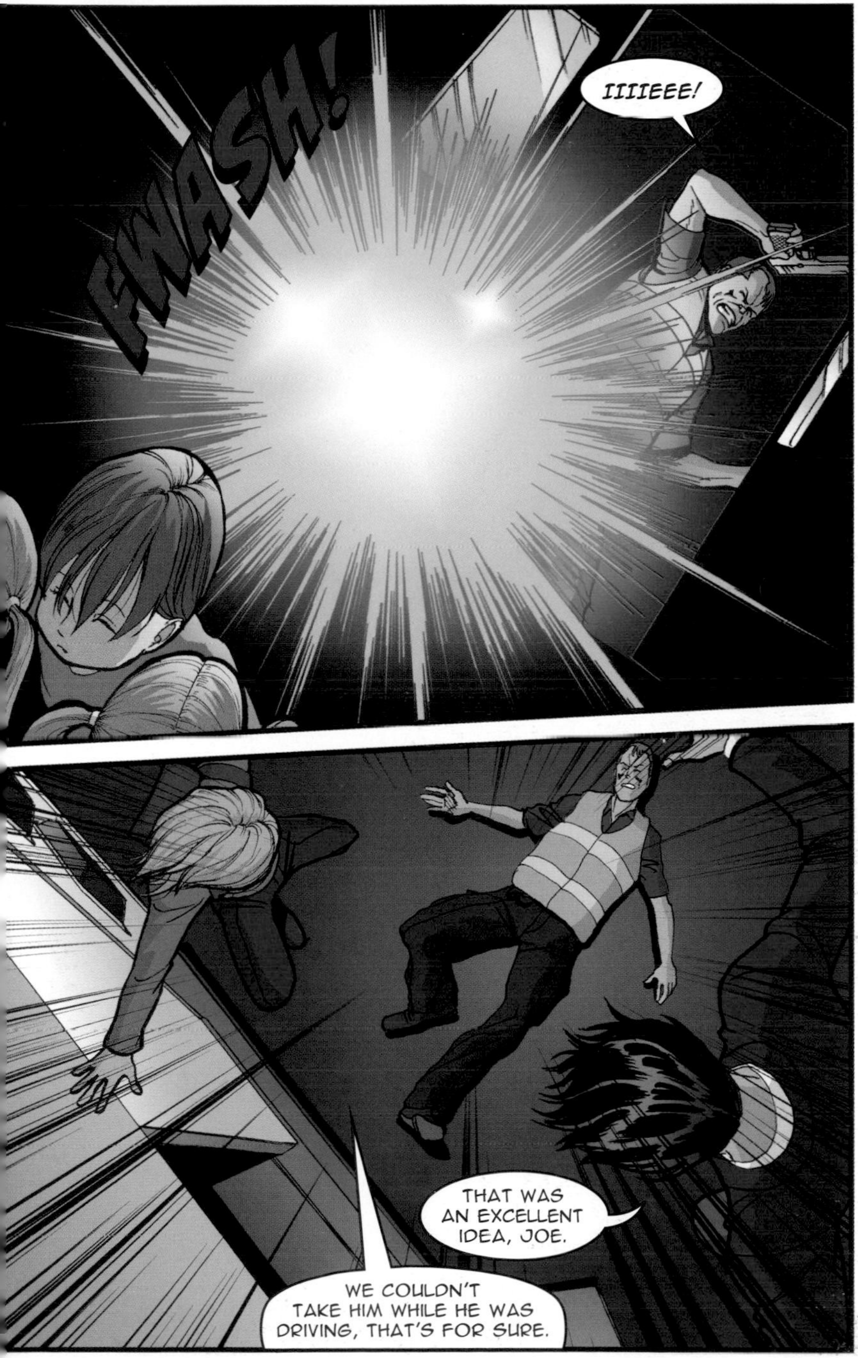
FWASH!
IIIIEEE!
THAT WAS AN EXCELLENT IDEA, JOE.
WE COULDN'T TAKE HIM WHILE HE WAS DRIVING, THAT'S FOR SURE.

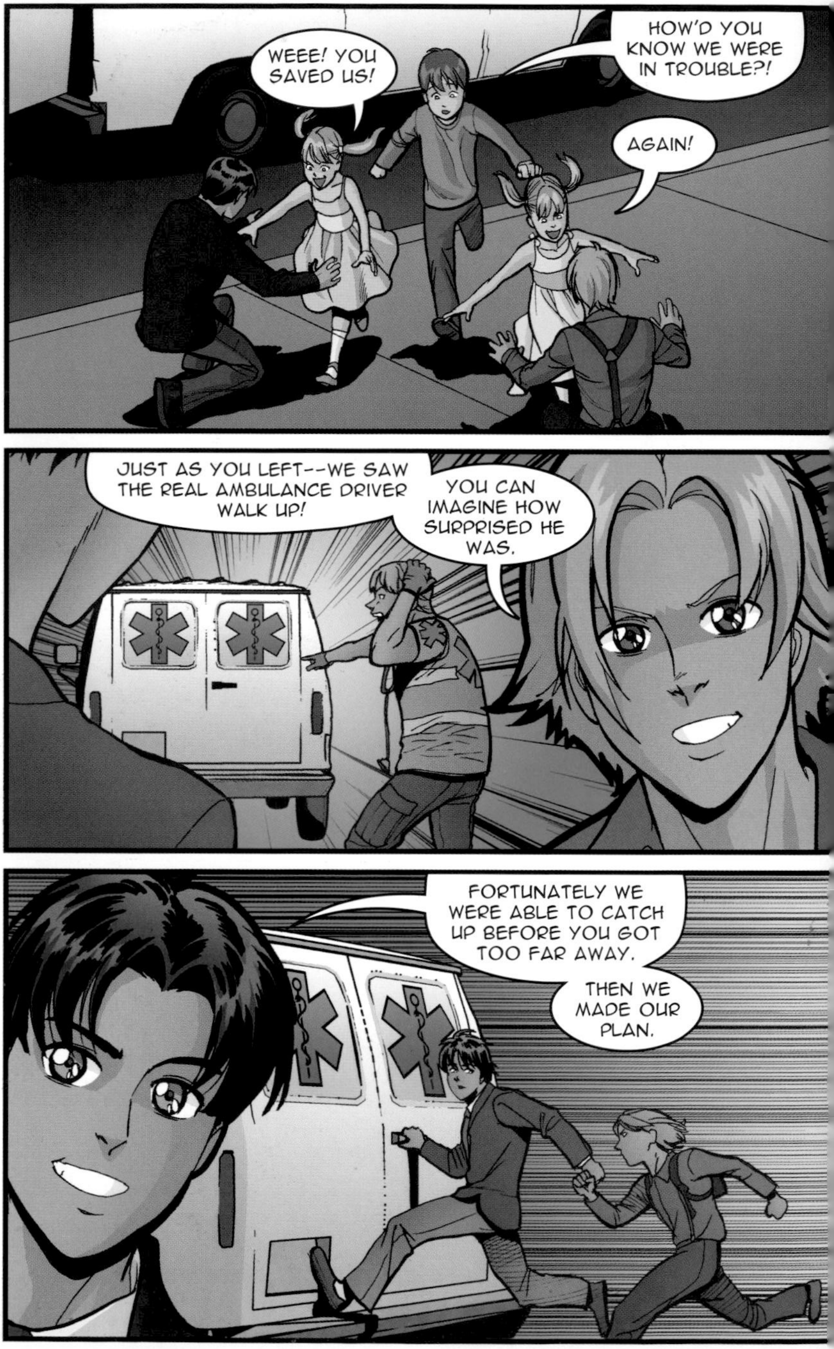
WEEE! YOU SAVED US!
HOW'D YOU KNOW WE WERE IN TROUBLE?!
AGAIN!
JUST AS YOU LEFT--WE SAW THE REAL AMBULANCE DRIVER WALK UP!
YOU CAN IMAGINE HOW SURPRISED HE WAS.
FORTUNATELY WE WERE ABLE TO CATCH UP BEFORE YOU GOT TOO FAR AWAY.
THEN WE MADE OUR PLAN.

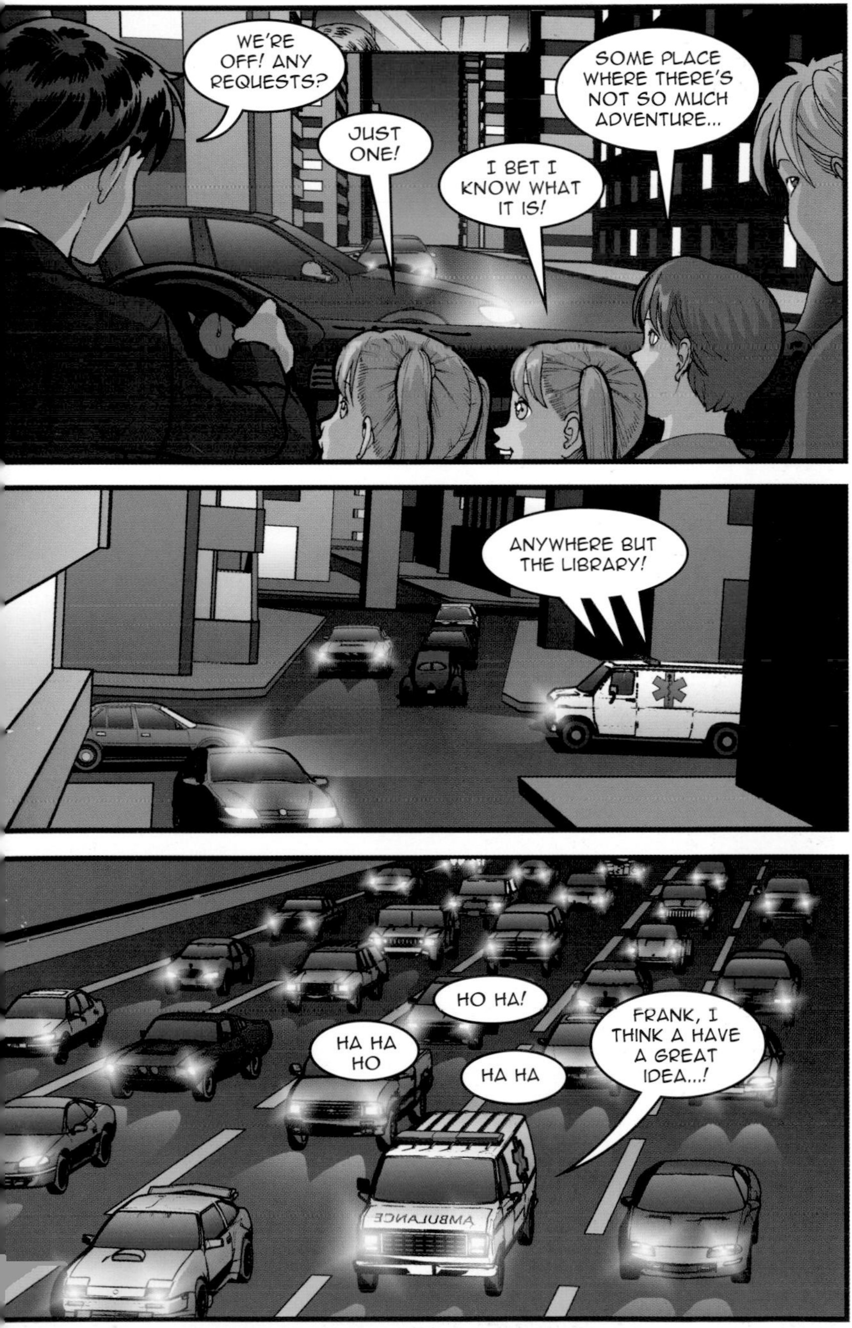
WE'RE OFF! ANY REQUESTS?
JUST ONE!
I BET I KNOW WHAT IT IS!
SOME PLACE WHERE THERE'S NOT SO MUCH ADVENTURE...
ANYWHERE BUT THE LIBRARY!
HO HA!
HA HA HO
HA HA
FRANK, I THINK A HAVE A GREAT IDEA...!
AMBULANCE

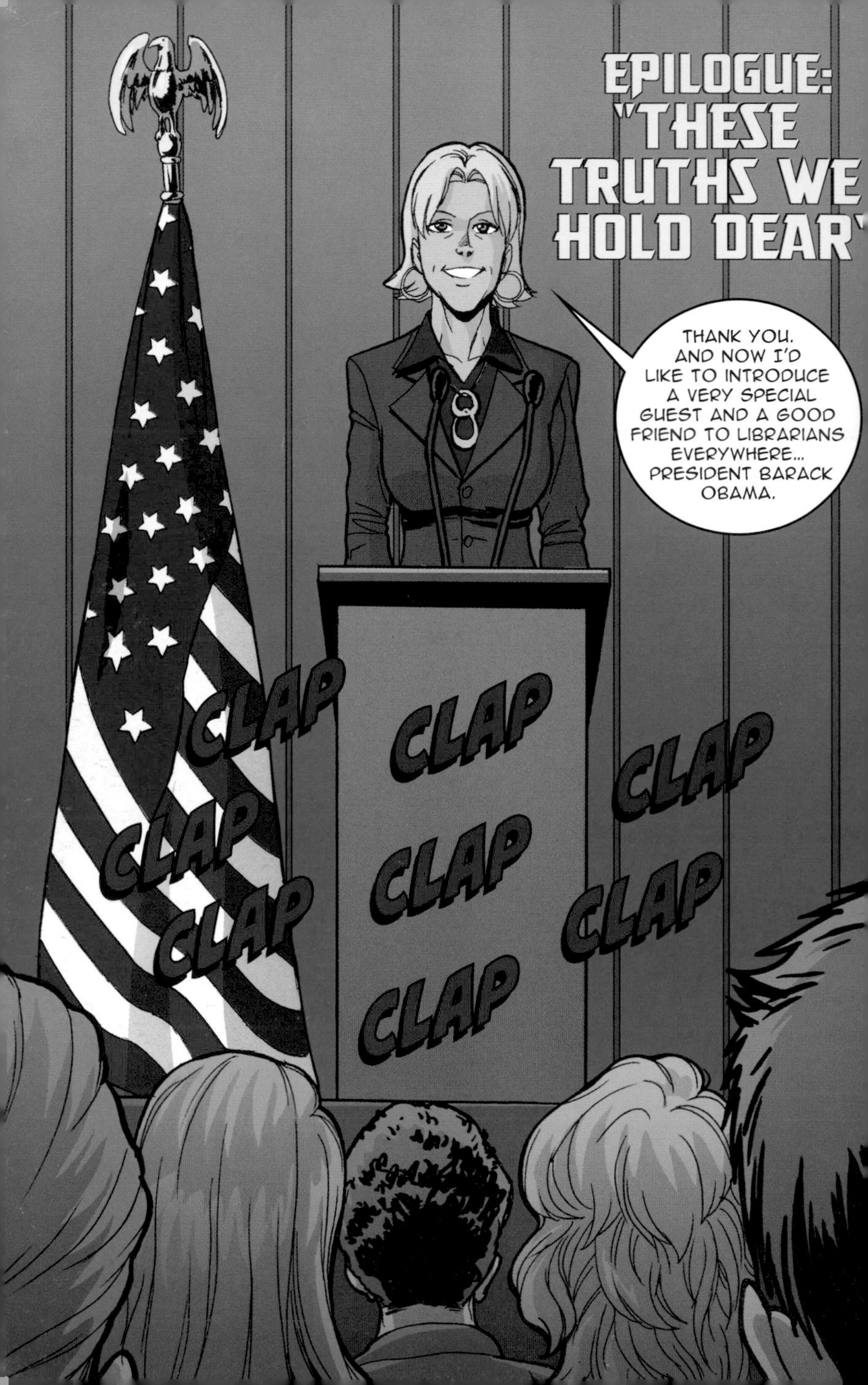
EPILOGUE: "THESE TRUTHS WE HOLD DEAR"
THANK YOU. AND NOW I'D LIKE TO INTRODUCE A VERY SPECIAL GUEST AND A GOOD FRIEND TO LIBRARIANS EVERYWHERE... PRESIDENT BARACK OBAMA.
CLAP CLAP CLAP CLAP CLAP CLAP CLAP CLAP

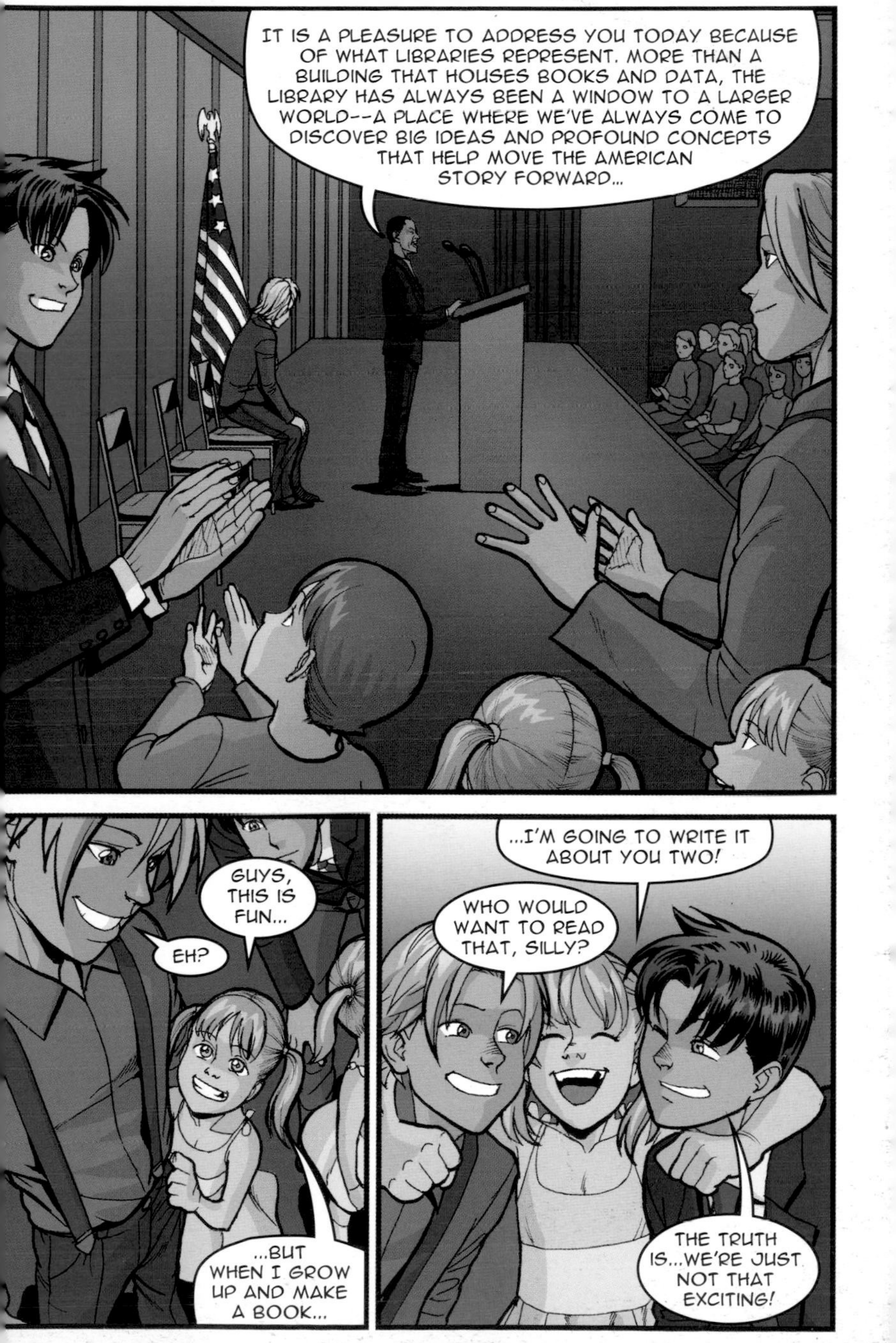
IT IS A PLEASURE TO ADDRESS YOU TODAY BECAUSE OF WHAT LIBRARIES REPRESENT. MORE THAN A BUILDING THAT HOUSES BOOKS AND DATA, THE LIBRARY HAS ALWAYS BEEN A WINDOW TO A LARGER WORLD--A PLACE WHERE WE'VE ALWAYS COME TO DISCOVER BIG IDEAS AND PROFOUND CONCEPTS THAT HELP MOVE THE AMERICAN STORY FORWARD...
GUYS, THIS IS FUN...
EH?
...BUT WHEN I GROW UP AND MAKE A BOOK...
...I'M GOING TO WRITE IT ABOUT YOU TWO!
WHO WOULD WANT TO READ THAT, SILLY?
THE TRUTH IS...WE'RE JUST NOT THAT EXCITING!

Special Preview of THE HARDY BOYS Graphic Novel #17 – "Word Up!"

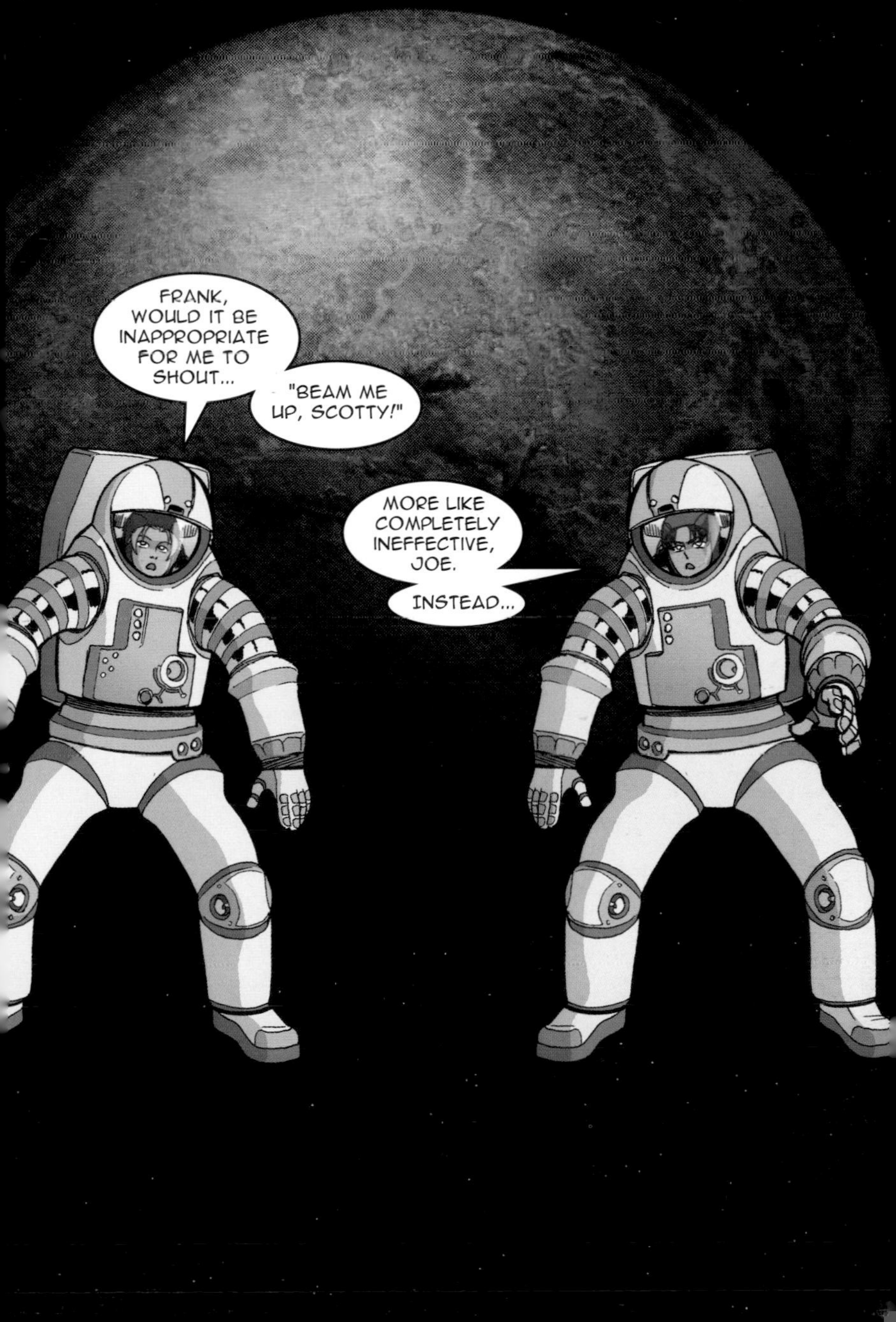
FRANK, WOULD IT BE INAPPROPRIATE FOR ME TO SHOUT...
"BEAM ME UP, SCOTTY!"
MORE LIKE COMPLETELY INEFFECTIVE, JOE.
INSTEAD...

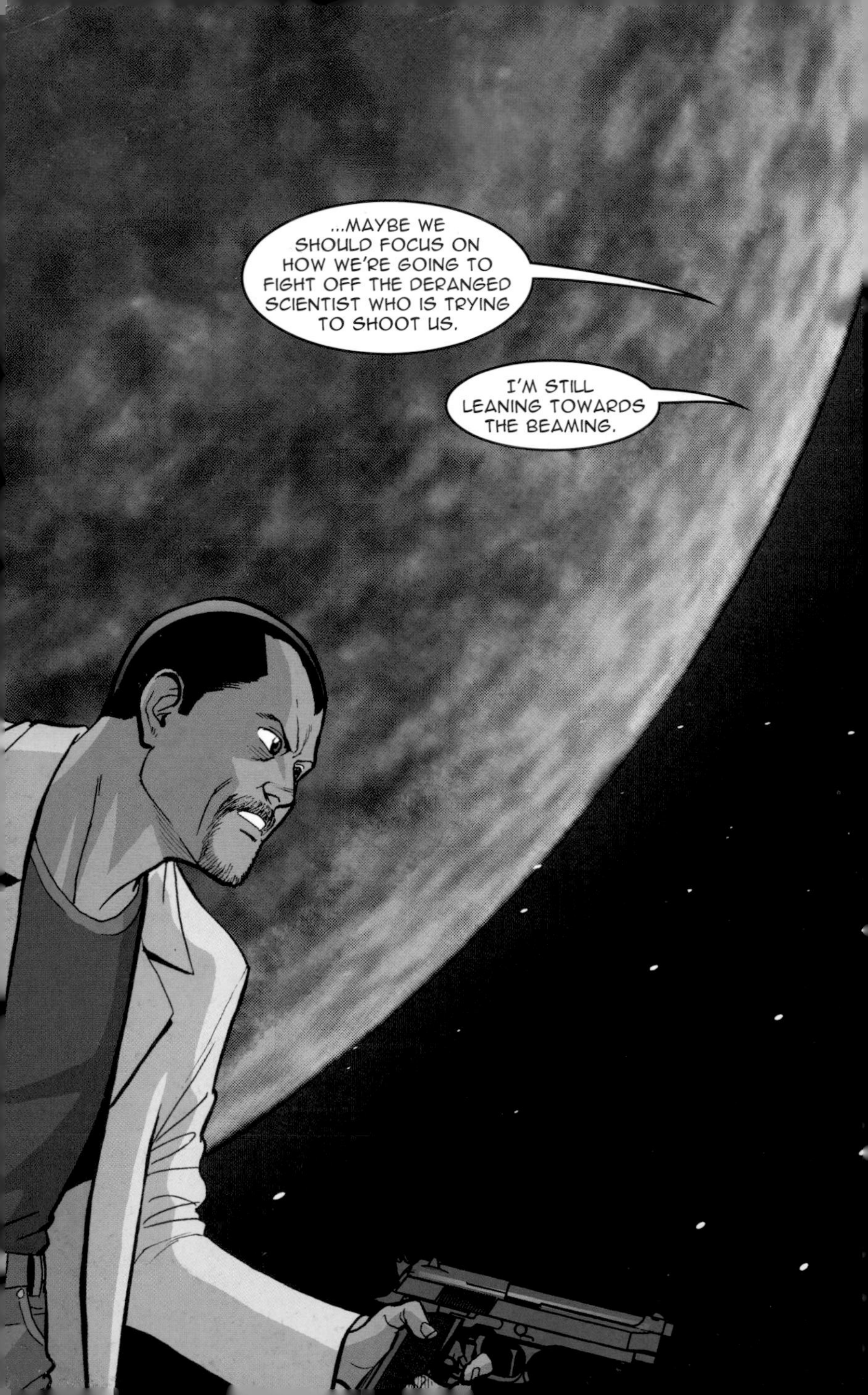
...MAYBE WE SHOULD FOCUS ON HOW WE'RE GOING TO FIGHT OFF THE DERANGED SCIENTIST WHO IS TRYING TO SHOOT US.
I'M STILL LEANING TOWARDS THE BEAMING.

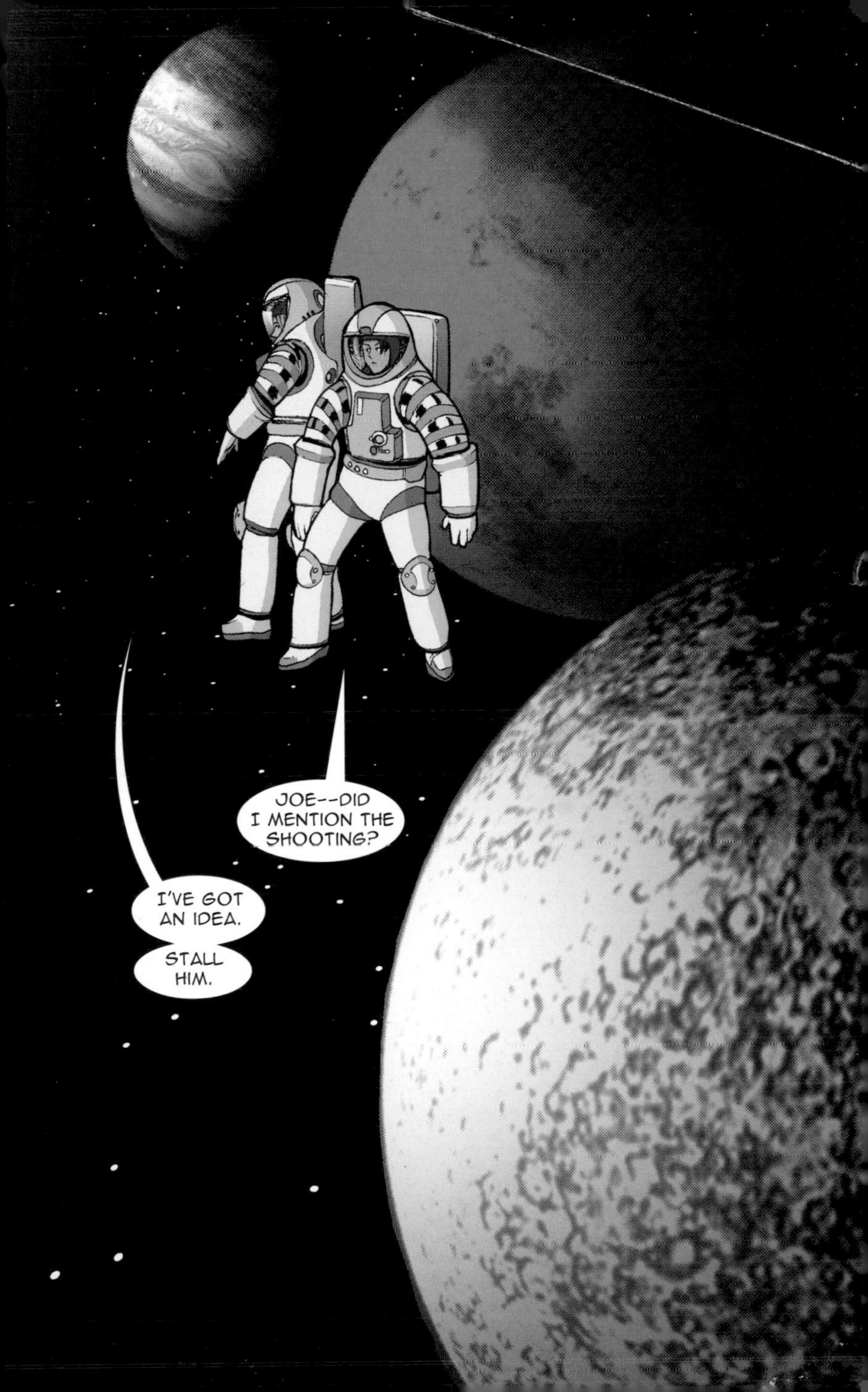
JOE--DID I MENTION THE SHOOTING?
I'VE GOT AN IDEA.
STALL HIM.

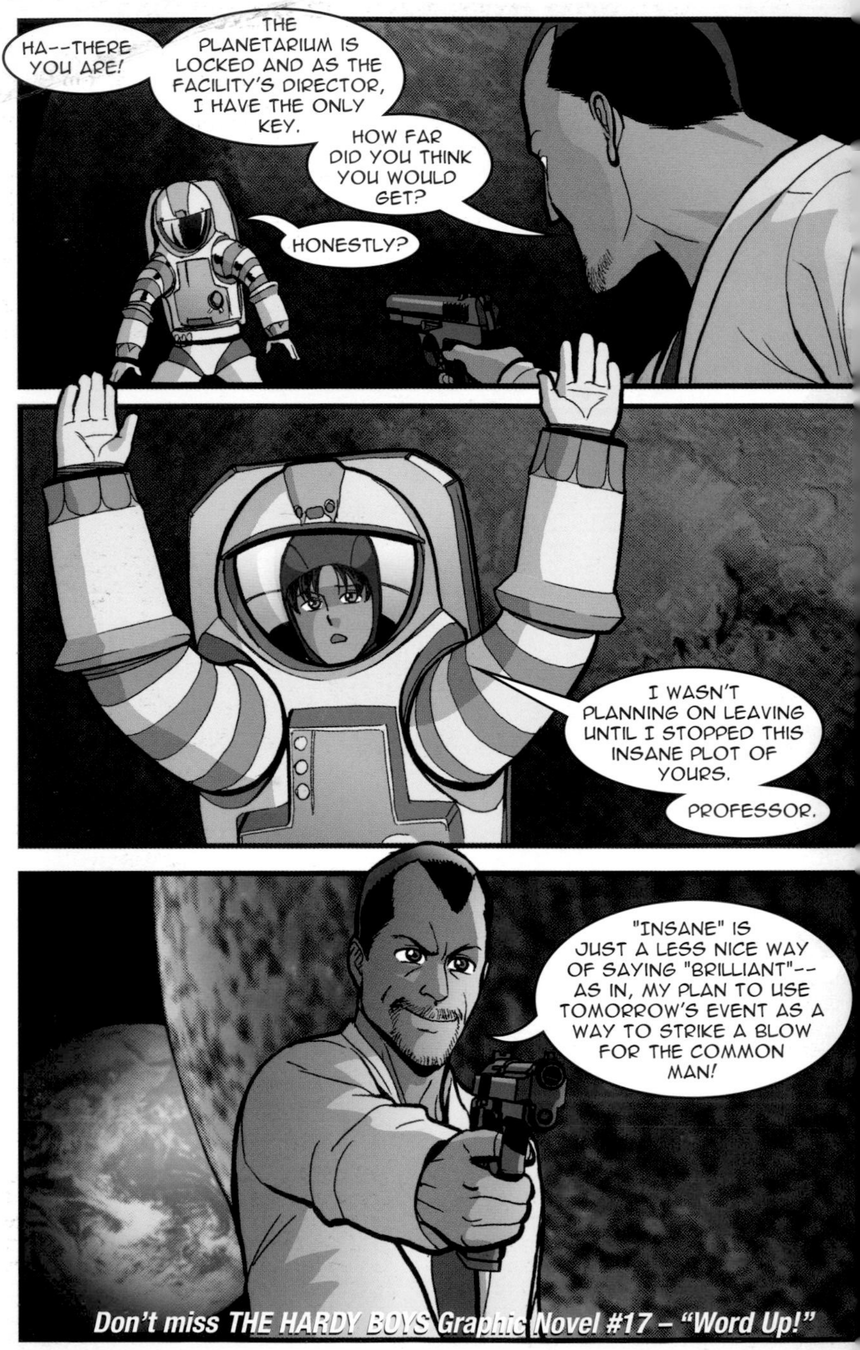
HA--THERE YOU ARE!
THE PLANETARIUM IS LOCKED AND AS THE FACILITY'S DIRECTOR, I HAVE THE ONLY KEY.
HOW FAR DID YOU THINK YOU WOULD GET?
HONESTLY?
I WASN'T PLANNING ON LEAVING UNTIL I STOPPED THIS INSANE PLOT OF YOURS.
PROFESSOR.
"INSANE" IS JUST A LESS NICE WAY OF SAYING "BRILLIANT"--AS IN, MY PLAN TO USE TOMORROW'S EVENT AS A WAY TO STRIKE A BLOW FOR THE COMMON MAN!
Don't miss THE HARDY BOYS Graphic Novel #17 – "Word Up!"

WATCH OUT FOR PAPERCUT**Z**

Hey, Papercutz people, it's me your ol pal, Papercutz Editor-in-Chief Jim Salicrup, here with a couple of thoughts to share...

We really hope you enjoyed this very special edition of THE HARDY BOYS dedicated to librarians everywhere. We hope you enjoyed President Obama's cameo appearance, and thought you should know that in real life it was Senator Barack Obama who addressed the American Library Association on June 27, 2005, and you can go to: http://obama.senate.gov/speech/050627-us_senator_barack_obama_addres/ to read his entire speech. All we can possibly add is that we at Papercutz fully agree and support libraries every way we possibly can.

We also have an extra bonus for Hardy Boys fans – a special excerpt of Book One in the Murder House trilogy, "Deprivation House" by Franklin W. Dixon.

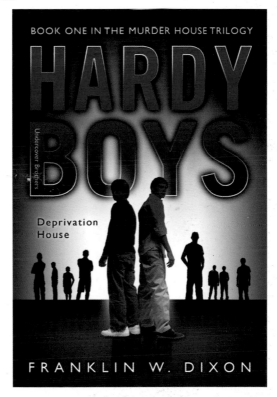

BOOK ONE IN THE MURDER HOUSE TRILOGY

HARDY BOYS

Undercover Brothers

Deprivation House

FRANKLIN W. DIXON

As you all know, in addition to the graphic novels from Papercutz, Frank and Joe Hardy appear every other month in all-new novels, and by special arrangement with our good friends at Simon & Schuster we're able to offer this special excerpt of the latest and greatest Hardy Boys mystery. But I warn you, after you read this special excerpt, you'll want to read the rest of the book! I mean, how can you possibly resist?

Thanks, Jim

Avalanche!

Frank and I carefully picked our way through the cave. The walls glowed with ghostly green phosphorescence. The eerie light made my brother look like a stranger.

I consulted our map. It had taken four days to find someone who would allow us to make a copy with no questions asked. "I think we turn left up here," I said. Frank nodded.

The ground began to quiver beneath our feet. The quiver became a rumble. I looked at Frank. I knew what he was thinking. I was thinking the same thing.

Avalanche!

Boulders the size of Volkswagens tumbled around us. I dove for the cave floor, but I still managed to get smacked by one. It stung, too. The things might have been made of painted Styrofoam, but they were still pretty humongous masses of painted Styrofoam.

I stayed low as the mining cars chugged by on the track. Once they rounded the bend—slooowly—the wires holding the "boulders" retracted, pulling them back up to the ceiling. Ready to terrify the next group of kids who dared to get on the Lost Dutchman's Mine Ride. Heh, heh, heh.

I stood up once I was sure I couldn't be seen by the kids. I didn't want to spoil the magic.

"I don't know why you thought we needed a map, anyway. This place is about the size of a mini-mart," I complained.

"I want to find the evidence fast and get out of here," Frank told me, shoving himself to his feet. "We don't know how many times the thieves make drops, and I'd rather not run into them if we can help it."

Frank started forward, then made a left. I followed him. We hit a dingy room away from the sight line of the tracks. It was filled with junk that had clearly been part of the ride, but needed repairs.

"You don't think...?" I asked, staring at a wheelbarrow full of chipped "gold nuggets." They all had a lot of white showing through the gold.

"Why not?" Frank asked.

"Because it's so incredibly cheesy," I answered. "Hiding the stuff you steal from tourists with the fake gold."

"Maybe when you work at Frontier Village, the cheesiness rubs off," he suggested. He started unloading Styrofoam chunks.

I spotted something silver partway down. A large lockbox. I tried the lid. Unlocked. Because who would be looking for it in here, back where the props from the ride were repaired?

Frank opened the lid. I immediately recognized several pieces of jewelry. "I don't know why an East Asian diplomat would bring his family here," I said.

"Well, he did. And this hilariously expensive owl pendant was stolen. But now it can be returned to its rightful owner. Case closed." Frank shut the lockbox and picked it up.

"Put it down."

I turned around and saw a guy dressed like a cowboy standing behind me. A sheriff with a handlebar mustache had his back.

"Wait. Isn't it supposed to be, 'Stop right thar, pardner'?" I asked. Sometimes I try to be funny at the wrong times. This was one of them. The cowboy responded to my attempt at humor by sucker punching me in the gut.

"It's over," Frank said. "You've been caught. We know exactly how your operation works. Exactly who's involved. That's how we knew where to find your stash."

"Right," I added, my voice coming in that just-punched woof.

The cowboy and the sheriff moved in on Frank. "Put the box down," the cowboy repeated.

Frank did. Which could only mean one thing.

Fight!

I grabbed a full-size plastic skeleton by the feet. I swung it like it was a baseball bat and the cowboy's head was the ball.

Didn't get a home run. It's hard to hit a homer with a plastic bat. But I did connect.

And now the cowboy was coming at me. That was basically my plan. Why should Frank get to fight two guys?

The cowboy gave a quick spin and caught me in the back of the knee with his boot. I stumbled forward. He took advantage of my position and grabbed me in a headlock.

You want to play that? Okay, I thought.

I rotated my shoulder and got my arm in front of the cowboy's body. I slid my leg behind both of his. Then I let myself fall backward, taking him with me. I slammed my elbow into his chest as we hit the ground.

I also leaned my head forward as we were falling. That's important. Otherwise, you can injure the all-important noggin.

Before the cowboy could recover, I twisted around and sat on him. I pressed his forearms to the ground with my hands. He struggled, but I had him pinned.

"Want some of this?" Frank asked. He held up some rope. There's always a bunch of rope around at Frontier Village. I realized he already had the sheriff tied up.

By the time the next mining cars went by the avalanche, we were ready to roll. We loaded cowboy and sheriff on board—the cars don't move at warp speed or anything—and took them to justice.

The lockbox held enough evidence to get them locked away. Heh, heh, heh.

If You Win, You Lose

Ahh. A little downtime. Signing on as an agent with American Teens Against Crime (ATAC) is basically the coolest thing I've ever done. Knowing that I've helped bring in murderers and thieves and arsonists is a rush. Doing that with an organization my dad started up after he retired is even better.

But once in a while, it's good to be able to kick back in one of my favorite places—the school library. The biggest crime that's going to go down in here is somebody turning a book in late. And that's not my department.

Plus, I'm an information junkie, and this place has all the facts you need. If not in one of the books, then on one of the computers. I—

 JOE

Joe here. You want to know the real reason Frank loves the library so much? It's because he's compulsively organized. I'm talking compulsive as in a psychiatric disorder. His label maker is one of his favorite things in the world. The library, with that whole Dewey decimal system to keep things in order, is paradise for him. Which is pretty pathetic. My paradise would have—

FRANK

Not in my section, Joe. Out. Anyway, as I was saying, I was hanging out in the library before first period, catching up on some homework. Joe was catching up on some *Z's*.

My neurons started firing a little faster as I spotted a dark-haired guy pushing a cart full of books our way. Vijay Patel. There was only one reason for him to be at our school. We were about to get our next ATAC assignment.

I gave Joe a kick to wake him up. "You're Frank Hardy, right?" Vijay asked. He knows who I am. Vijay's been with ATAC almost as long as Joe and I have. He's one of the intel guys, but he's trying to get moved up to fieldwork.

"That's me," I answered.

"Here's the book you requested." Vijay slapped a bright blue book down in front of me, then rolled his cart away with a big grin on his face. I knew what the grin was about as soon as I read the book's title: The Bonehead's Guide to Talking to Girls.

Joe gave a snort-laugh. "You so need that."

Okay, so I sometimes have a tendency to blush when I'm talking to female types. But blushing is partially controlled by the automatic nervous system, although some volitional somatic control comes into play. So basically, a blush is not completely under the blusher's control. So I decided not to even answer Joe. Sometimes the best thing you can do with my younger brother is ignore him.

I cracked the cover of the book enough to see that the pages had been hollowed out. A game cartridge—our ATAC assignments always came in the form of game cartridges—some cash, and some ID and other background stuff were inside.

"Let's get out of here," I told Joe. He swung his backpack over one shoulder and followed me out of the library, through the quad, and out into the parking lot. I figured we could sit in the car and watch the "game" on Joe's portable player.

"Conrad at three o' clock," Joe warned me.

I adjusted the book Vijay had just given me so the title was absolutely hidden. If Brian Conrad saw it, I'd be hearing about it at least until graduation. So would everybody else at school. Including the girls I already had enough trouble talking to!

"Thanks," I said as I slid behind the wheel. I flipped Joe the game cartridge and he slid it into the player. We both stared at the blank screen expectantly. Hundred-dollar bills began to float from the top of the screen and land in piles at the bottom. To a ka-ching, ka-ching sound, a counter in the lower left tallied up the cash.

"Hello, Mr. Franklin." Joe let out a low whistle when the counter reached $1,000,000.

"One million dollars could be yours—for living in this Mediterranean villa tucked away in exclusive Beverly Hills," a woman's voice purred as the pile of money faded and was replaced by a photo of a mansion.

"Do you think there's a catch?" asked Joe. He scratched his head. "I'm thinkin' maybe there's a catch."

"Maybe one million dollars could be yours," I suggested, taking in the fountain out front, the palm trees, the balconies on all levels, the arched doorways, the red tile roofs. "Except there'd still be a catch. That place has to be worth multiple millions. I'm guessing double-digit millions."

"Send us a tape showing us why you think you're special enough to compete. Teenagers only, please. And don't bother asking for more details. You won't get them." I could almost hear the woman smirking as she said that.

"Thousands of teens sent in tapes," the deep voice of our ATAC contact told us. Different views of the mansion flicked across the screen. A massive room with a fireplace big enough to walk into that I thought might be a living room. A home theater. A kitchen that looked like it belonged in a five-star restaurant.

"Twelve were chosen to live at the villa beginning this weekend," our contact continued. "And at least one of the twelve has received a death threat."

The screen blackened for a minute, then the Gossip Tonight logo flashed on. A film clip of a tall girl strutting down a red carpet started up. Short dress. Big smile.

"The list of people who want her dead has got to be pretty long," Joe commented.

"Why?" I asked. "And who is she anyway?" She looked sort of familiar. And she clearly had fans, but I couldn't come up with a name or what she had fans for.

"Ripley Lansing," Joe answered. He did his trademark my-big-brother-is-a-big-dork eye roll. "Her father's the drummer for Tubskull, and her mom owns some huge makeup company."

"Ripley Lansing received this letter yesterday," our contact went on, without emotion. A piece of deep red paper filled the game player's screen. Letters from different newspapers and magazines had been glued on to form the message: "You win the $$$. You lose your life."

"Her parents have requested security at the highest level for Ms. Lansing, so the police have opted to bring in ATAC agents. Your mission is to go undercover as participants in the contest—details will not be available until you arrive at the villa—and find out who has threatened to kill Ms. Lansing. You will also need to determine if any of the other contestants are in danger."

The screen went blank and stayed blank. That was the only time we'd get our mission info. The cartridge erased itself after it was played once.

Joe picked up the book with the hollowed-out center and started flipping through the other stuff ATAC had sent us. "Tickets to L.A.," he said.

"Cash." He raised his eyebrows. "You're not going to believe the cover story they came up with for us. It's like something out of a soap!"

He took a few more moments to scan the material. "Here's the deal. You and I are brothers."

"That is hard to believe," I commented. I reached over and brushed what I thought were some doughnut sprinkles off the front of Joe's shirt.

Joe ignored me. I guess that was only fair. "We got adopted by different families when we were babies," he explained. "We didn't even know about each other until a few months ago. I have really rich parents. Your family's more blue-collar."

"It's pretty extreme. Why do you think ATAC came up with something so out there?" I asked.

"Because they needed to get us on a reality TV show," Joe answered. "Those shows love extreme. Brothers separated as wee infants. One rich. One poor. I bet the producers ate that up with a spoon. I bet they think they'll get tons of drama out of us. Maybe they even think you'll try to beat me up—because I grew up with all the luxuries you never had."

"Have you ever considered the possibility that you watch too much TV?" I asked.

"Have you ever considered the possibility that you don't watch enough?" Joe shot back. "You didn't even know who Ripley Lansing is—and she's at the center of our case."

He had a point. "You said you thought there were a lot of people who would want her dead. Why?"

"So many reasons," Joe answered. "She's stolen boyfriends. She's gotten tons of people fired—everyone from waiters, to a backup singer in her dad's band, to an airline pilot. She's always breaking cameras when people try and take pictures of her. If we googled 'I want Ripley Lansing dead' we'd get enough suspects to keep us working for years."

"At least the note narrowed it down a little. The person who wrote the death threat only wants Ripley dead if she wins the contest money," I reminded him.

"So I'm thinkin' that puts the other people in the contest at the top of the suspect list," said Joe.

"Whoever they are. And whatever the contest turns out to be." All missions start out with a lot of unknowns. But this one had more than usual.

Joe checked our plane tickets. "We'll find out tomorrow. We're flying out in the morning."

The first bell rang. "Right after school we need to strategize on what to tell Mom and Aunt Trudy," I said. Dad, of course, would already know the real deal, since he founded ATAC and everything.

I actually think Mom and Aunt Trudy would be cool with our missions.

They'd worry about the danger, yeah. But they would get how important what we do is. They'd get that sometimes there are situations where teenagers are the best undercover operatives possible. But ATAC rules require absolute secrecy, so we have to keep Mom and Aunt T out of the loop.

"No can do," Joe answered. "Right after school I have to do a little shopping." He showed me the envelope full of cash from ATAC.

"Is there some special gear we need?" I asked.

"I'm going undercover as a rich boy. I need to look the part." Joe grinned. "The first piece of equipment I need is a pair of Diesel sunglasses."

I stared at him. "The ones you were drooling over at the mall? The ones that were almost three hundred dollars?"

"Authentic cover can make or break a mission, you know that." Joe slapped me on the shoulder. "Dude, those sunglasses could save our lives!"

"I don't think going on the show is a good idea, boys," Mom told us at dinner. "You've already missed a number of school days this year, and we're not even halfway through."

Mom always has the facts. Maybe it's because she spends so much time in libraries. She works in one, in the reference section.

"I agree," Aunt Trudy said. "Those shows are death traps. People have gotten burned, bitten by snakes... I know someone lost a little toe, but I don't remember how. I'm sure that somebody is going to die on one of them soon, right in front of all the people watching at home."

"Aunt T, come on. All the contestants are teenagers. The producers are going to make extra sure everything we do is safe," Joe answered. "And it's me and Frank. You know we can take care of ourselves."

"Losers, losers, losers," Playback added from the kitchen. Our parrot seems to think he should have a part in every conversation. "Merry Christmas! Ho, ho, ho!"

Dad was the only one staying out of the discussion—for now. Joe and I are always telling him that we want to handle things ourselves, the way any other ATAC agents would have to. Agents whose father didn't start the agency. I think because we say that so much, sometimes he enjoys watching us sweat it out a little.

"Even if you don't die, they'll make you eat something horrible," Aunt Trudy went on. "Like worms. Then you'll come back with... with worms. Or parasites. Or some other nasty thing."

I looked over at Mom. "Can we go back to the school issue for a minute?"

She nodded.

"Joe and I have started designing an experiment around the experience of living in the house. We haven't worked out all the details, because we don't know what the specifics of the contest will be. We're definitely going to act as if we come from different socioeconomic backgrounds to see how that effects the judging. And we plan to come up with a few hypotheses on how the other people involved will behave under pressure." That last part was actually entirely true. "Our science and social studies teachers have given us the go-ahead to use the project to get class credit."

"And our English teachers are on board if we keep a journal every day and keep up on the reading. Plus we'll definitely get the assignments for everything else," Joe jumped in. "Even the principal thinks it's cool that the two of us could be on TV representing Bayport. Although we aren't exactly going to be ourselves. We're doing that socio-eco thing."

"I wish we knew more details," said Dad.

I couldn't decide if he was trying to make us sweat some more, or just trying to keep up his own cover of reasonable, concerned father who has no idea ATAC even exists.

"A million dollars could pay for lots o' college," Joe wheedled.

"True," Mom answered. She looked over at Dad. One of those looks that has a whole conversation in it. He gave a small nod. She gave in. "As long as you don't fall behind in school," she added.

"Great!" Joe was on his feet, gathering up dishes—even though no one had quite finished eating. "We're going to bring home the college money for sure," he said over his shoulder as he headed into the kitchen.

I picked up some empty plates and followed him. "You know we can't keep the money even if we win. We're not actually contestants. We're undercover," I reminded Joe, keeping my voice soft.

"Doesn't matter. It's only fair that if we win, we really get the money," Joe insisted.

"How do you figure?" I asked.

"Because if we get killed while we're undercover, we're really going to be dead."

He had a point.

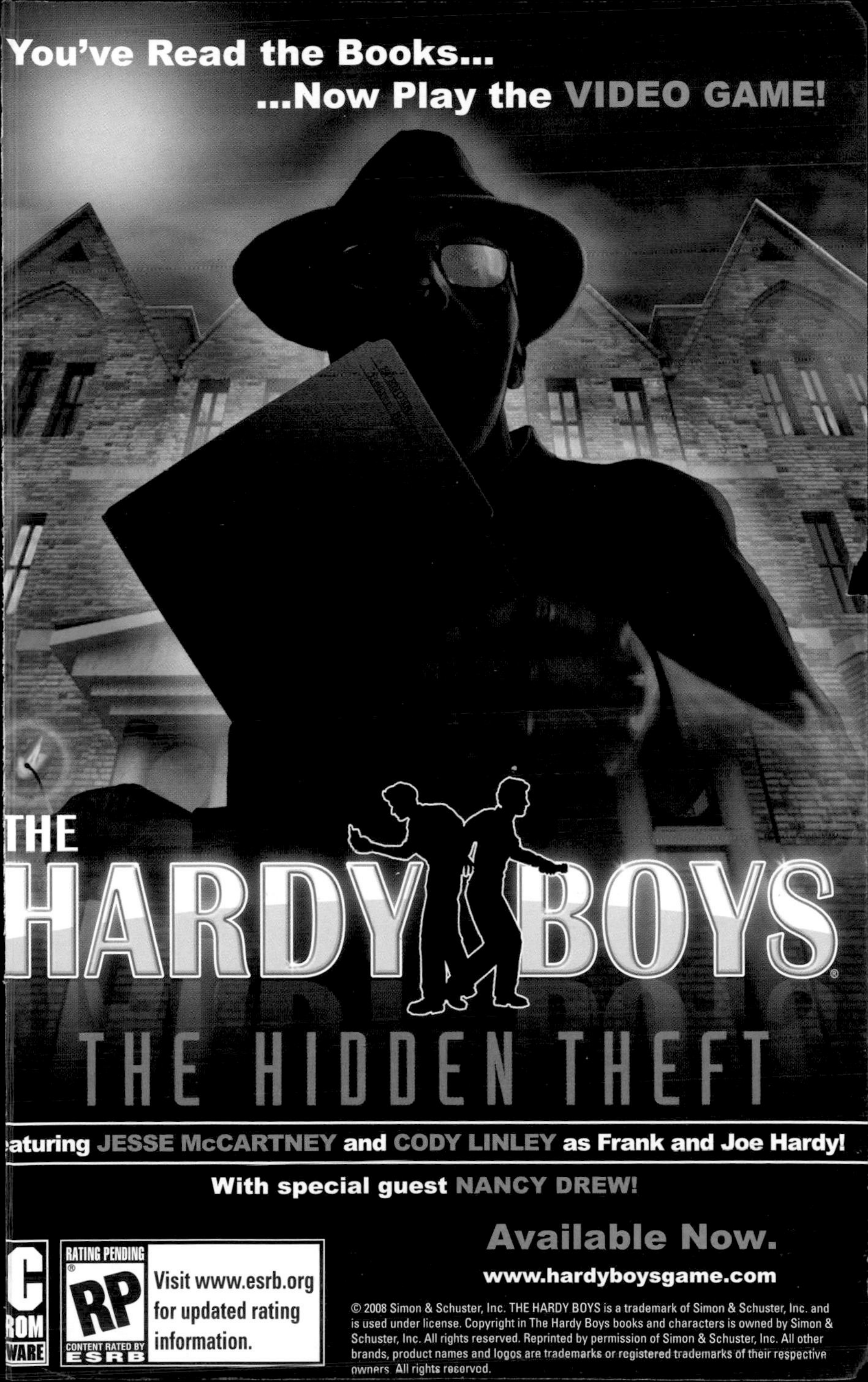
You've Read the Books...
...Now Play the VIDEO GAME!
THE HARDY BOYS®
THE HIDDEN THEFT
eaturing JESSE McCARTNEY and CODY LINLEY as Frank and Joe Hardy!
With special guest NANCY DREW!
RATING PENDING
RP
CONTENT RATED BY ESRB
Visit www.esrb.org for updated rating information.
Available Now.
www.hardyboysgame.com
© 2008 Simon & Schuster, Inc. THE HARDY BOYS is a trademark of Simon & Schuster, Inc. and is used under license. Copyright in The Hardy Boys books and characters is owned by Simon & Schuster, Inc. All rights reserved. Reprinted by permission of Simon & Schuster, Inc. All other brands, product names and logos are trademarks or registered trademarks of their respective owners. All rights reserved.

THE HARDY BOYS

Undercover Brothers®

New re... to show
how lon... luxuries.
Trouble... g at all.
C... dy

BOOK ONE IN THE MURDER HOUSE TRILOGY
HARDY BOYS
Undercover Brothers
Deprivation House
FRANKLIN W. DIXON

Deprivation House

BOOK TWO IN THE MURDER HOUSE TRILOGY
HARDY BOYS
Undercover Brothers
House Arrest
FRANKLIN W. DIXON

House Arrest

BOOK THREE IN THE MURDER HOUSE TRILOGY
THE HARDY BOYS
Undercover Brothers
Murder House
FRANKLIN W. DIXON

Murder House

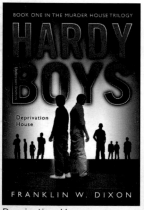

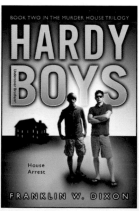

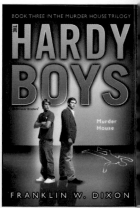